NO GOING BACK

NO GOING BACK

Lyndon Stacey

This first world edition published 2010
in Great Britain and in the USA by
SEVERN HOUSE PUBLISHERS LTD of
9–15 High Street, Sutton, Surrey, England, SM1 1DF.
Trade paperback edition published
in Great Britain and the USA 2010 by
SEVERN HOUSE PUBLISHERS LTD

British Library Cataloguing in Publication Data

Stacey, Lyndon.
  No Going Back.
  1. Ex-police officers – England – Fiction. 2. Runaway
  children – England – Dartmoor – Fiction. 3. Detective and
  mystery stories.
  I. Title
  823.9'2-dc22

ISBN-13: 978-0-7278-6883-1   (cased)
ISBN-13: 978-1-84751-219-2   (trade paper)

All Severn House titles are printed on acid-free paper.

Severn House Publishers support The Forest Stewardship Council [FSC],
the leading international forest certification organisation. All our titles that
are printed on Greenpeace-approved FSC-certified paper carry the FSC logo.

Mixed Sources
Product group from well-managed
forests and other controlled sources
www.fsc.org Cert no. SA-COC-1565
© 1996 Forest Stewardship Council

Typeset by Palimpsest Book Production Ltd.,
Grangemouth, Stirlingshire, Scotland.
Printed and bound in Great Britain by
MPG Books Ltd., Bodmin, Cornwall.

This one's for my agent, Dorothy Lumley,
for all her hard work on my behalf
over the past few years. Thanks.

ACKNOWLEDGEMENTS

A big thank you to the real Hilary McEwen-Smith, who generously bid in a charity auction for the chance to appear in this book. I hope I've done you justice!

Also to Dave McIver, Glyn Jones and police dog, Jerry, of the Avon and Somerset Police Dog Unit for their invaluable help and for the joy of a day spent watching them work.

For finding the time to answer my questions, thanks to my vet, Sophie Darling, and, as always, thanks to Mark Randle of the Wiltshire force for always being on hand to answer queries.

PROLOGUE

Somewhere a dog was barking, fretfully, without hope. In the distance, a siren sounded, the mournful rise and fall signalling misery for someone.

On the Jubilee Park estate in Bristol, the hard edges of the flat roofs were black against a night sky streaked with scudding clouds. Few of the windows along the balconied walkways were lit. At twelve fifteen a.m. in this neighbourhood, most people chose to stay inside, their doors double-locked and barred, and makeshift grilles on many of the windows.

On the third-floor walkway nothing moved except the wind-blown detritus of estate life: a couple of empty cigarette boxes, a condom wrapper and several empty crisp packets. Against one graffiti-covered door the pages of a newspaper fanned open and flopped shut unread, over and over, as if turned in boredom by some unseen hand. The disembodied head of a cheap doll lay close to the spent carcase of a red plastic lighter, and a few feet away, a curl of charred tinfoil skittered over the filthy concrete against the wall of number 231.

Moments later, the door opened, light spilling through the aperture to frame the tall figure of the man who stepped out. It seemed as though he would have walked away without pausing, but a slim, brown hand caught at the sleeve of his leather coat.

'When will I see you?' The thin face with its large, heavily made-up blue eyes was pathetically eager. Bottle-blonde and petite, the woman was wrapped in a red satin housecoat, its crossover front revealing a deeply tanned cleavage and a neck that had seen better days.

'In a day or two, maybe.' The reply was casual, his accent Eastern European. Strong, olive-skinned fingers unhooked the woman's clutching hand, the light catching the pale, puckered skin of an old scar. His dark eyes flickered dispassionately over her upturned face. 'I have to go.'

'But what about the smack? Did you bring it? You said you would . . .'

The man shook his head and clicked his tongue. 'Shelley, Shelley, you know it's bad for you,' he said, mocking.

'Just one more fix. You promised, Anghel! Please. I won't ask again.' Her eyes pleaded with him.

'And how are you going to pay for it? You don't work any more. Why should Yousef support your habit?'

'But I *could* work if he'd let me! I don't understand why I have to be here. What am I going to do? There's no one to talk to. I miss the girls. I miss Molly.' Tears filled her eyes and she clutched at the doorpost as if she needed its support. 'Please, Anghel – I just want to see my little girl.'

'You'll see her soon. You just be a good girl and everything will be taken care of. OK?' He put a finger under her chin and turned her face towards him. 'OK?'

Reluctantly Shelley nodded. She pulled the housecoat closer about her and shivered.

After a moment, Anghel took something from an inside pocket and dropped it in her palm. 'Here. Don't tell Yousef.'

Shelley's eyes lit up. Her fingers clamped shut on the sachet of greyish powder he'd given her, and she took a swift step backwards into the bedsit as if fearing he'd change his mind.

The door clicked shut, and with a shake of his head, the man turned up his collar against the chill wind and walked away, his footsteps echoing grittily and his broad shoulders throwing a moon-shadow on the wall. He descended to ground level, passing a group of drunken teenagers in the stairwell, his nose wrinkling as it was assailed by the stench of stale urine around the overflowing bins.

Leaving the building behind, he took a mobile phone from his pocket and flipped it open. Seconds later, he had a connection.

'Yes, it's me. It's all taken care of . . . No, no problems. See you later.'

Shelley leaned back against the black vinyl cushions of the sofa, her indrawn breath hissing through her teeth as the rush hit her. She hated that first shocking sensation, but yearned for the comforting glow that would follow. Soon everything would be all right; even the desperate longing for her daughter would fade into the golden haze. Anghel would look after her. Hadn't he promised he would? Anghel had always been kind to her – well, as kind as anyone . . .

She sighed deeply as her body and mind began to float, euphoria lifting her out of the squalid bedsit to a halcyon world where depression couldn't follow.

Briefly her eyes flickered open in alarm as her muscles were gripped by a powerful spasm; then it passed and her head lolled back, pupils narrowing to pinpoints as her heartbeat slowed and her breathing became shallow. Darkness crowded in.

As the first grey light of the winter dawn seeped along the concrete walkways of the estate, the city began to stir. Lights came on, cars started to fill the streets, and the pavements swarmed with jostling, chattering kids on their way to school.

At number 231 Jubilee Park, the only sound was the TV; the efforts of the cheerful breakfast presenters went unheard by the woman in the red satin housecoat, their images reflecting in her half-open eyes.

She lay sprawled across the faux-leather sofa surrounded by the tools of her addiction, one sleeve pushed back, the arm bruised and speckled with a lifetime of needle scars.

Only one man knew she was there and he wouldn't be telling. It could be weeks before her body was found.

ONE

'Trucker's Dog Saves Toddler,' the headline halfway down the front page of the *Western Post* declared.

The paper was nearly a week old, saved for Daniel by the owner of the roadside burger van where he'd bought his breakfast. He was parked not 20 yards from it now, in a lorry park on the side of the A386 between Tavistock and Okehampton. It was a designated picnic spot, but at this hour of the morning, there were more trucks than cars.

Pulling a wry face and shaking his head, Daniel Whelan took a sip of his latte-to-go and read on, his booted feet propped up on the dashboard of the lorry.

When farmer Peter Daley (58) and his wife, Sally (56), discovered that granddaughter Emily had been missing on their 135-acre farm near Launceston for over an hour last Saturday morning, they feared the worst. Peter and Sally aren't normally overanxious grandparents, but in this case they could be forgiven, because four-year-old Emily, who was staying with them for the weekend, is profoundly deaf.

'I thought she was with Peter and he thought she was with me,' Sally explained. 'We were especially worried because there were tractors working in the fields and the men might not have noticed such a small child. We were at our wits' end, not knowing where to look first, and of course it was no good shouting, because she couldn't hear us.'

Things might have looked very black indeed for little Emily if fate hadn't intervened in the shape of delivery driver Daniel Whelan and his ex-police dog, Taz.

When truck driver Daniel (28), who was delivering animal feed to the farm, heard what had happened, he offered the services of his German shepherd dog to locate the little girl. Taz had served 18 months with Bristol Police Dog Unit before being injured in the line of duty and retired last year. As a police dog, tracking was part of his work, although in those days it would have been runaway criminals that he trailed rather than lost children.

Shown a cardigan belonging to little Emily to give him the scent, Taz soon demonstrated that he had forgotten none of his skills, finding the lost child within ten minutes, playing in a hay barn just feet away from a herd of cows.

'Thank goodness the dog found her when it did,' Sally Daley said, still clearly shaken by the memory. 'Cows are generally placid, but they can be unpredictable – I dread to think what might have happened if she had wandered in among them.'

Daniel, who works as a driver for Tavistock Farm Supplies, preferred not to be interviewed, saying that all the credit belonged to three-year-old Taz, who travels everywhere with him in the lorry.

All's well that ends well on the Daleys' farm. Thanks to Taz, Emily is none the worse for her adventure – in fact, she has gained a new friend, 42-kilo Taz, proving that while he might have been tough on criminals, he is just a gentle giant at heart with a soft spot for little girls.

Daniel had to smile at the last line. The article was illustrated by a picture of Taz sitting dutifully with the child's arms wrapped round the thick fur of his neck, but to Daniel, who knew him better than anyone, the expression on the dog's face was one of slightly pained resignation rather than pleasure.

He held up the paper, turning to where Taz sat at the other end of the bench seat.

'Look, Taz, you're famous.'

The German shepherd thumped his tail on the seat a time or two and edged nearer, but his attention was firmly fixed on the dashboard, where a paper bag sat, containing a bacon and egg roll.

'If you're gonna start drooling, you can sit outside!' Daniel warned severely, but the dog wasn't fooled. He moved even closer, his gaze never wavering, knowing from experience that the last bite of bread and bacon would be his.

Moments later, the butty was forgotten as Taz threw himself at the passenger window of the cab, barking furiously. A sharp word from Daniel calmed him a little, but he remained on edge, growling ominously and hackles up, while he watched a small black Staffordshire bull terrier trot jauntily in front of the lorry and away at the heels of his cab driver owner.

'What? That scutty little thing?' Daniel teased. 'You'd make mincemeat of him. Here, have a bit of bacon.'

The German shepherd accepted the morsel, licked his lips and grumbled some more. He'd had a bad experience with a Staffie when he was just a pup and it would require more than a tasty bribe to take his mind off this one.

It was a cold, wet day and it was with a sigh of relief that Daniel climbed back into his cab after the last delivery that afternoon and prepared to head for home. He had finished early and with any luck would miss the worst of the Friday traffic.

Not that thoughts of home were particularly enticing just at that moment in his life: with a limited budget and the necessity of finding somewhere that he could park the lorry from time to time, the only accommodation he'd been able to find had been a one-bedroom flat above an empty shop in a lane off the Tavistock to Launceston road. The unoccupied downstairs space had most recently been a lawnmower showroom and still had the oil stains and stink of petrol to prove it. However, the property had scored on three important points: the rent was cheap; it had a good-sized car park at the back; and it was sufficiently removed from the nearest village to avoid upsetting anyone when he started the lorry's V12 engine at the crack of dawn.

The light was poor under an overcast sky, and the windscreen wipers swished monotonously to and fro, barely clearing the fine drizzle before it obscured the glass once again, making the headlights of oncoming vehicles star and spread.

All in all it was a dreary afternoon and there was nothing to stop Daniel's mind dwelling on the depressing turn his life had taken. Just three short months ago, he had had what he thought was a stable home life with a wife and eight-year-old son, a career in the police force and a circle of friends. Now, entirely as a result of his own actions, he had none of these and the realization was still raw every time it hit him.

The fact that it could be regarded as questionable whether friends and colleagues who had shown themselves to be so fickle were worth mourning gave him no comfort at all. There had been many times lately when he'd wondered if, given that period of his life over again, he would make the same choices, and he found he just didn't know.

Daniel rubbed his eyes tiredly. Such reflections were pointless.

The decisions had been made and he had to live with the consequences. End of story. He switched on the radio, reaching across
to ruffle Taz's soft coat. Lately the dog had become the only
constant in his life.

Taz rewarded his caress with a flattening of his ears. Daniel
suspected that *he*, at least, was very content with their altered
circumstances. Amanda hadn't allowed the dog in the house,
complaining that his constantly shedding coat made work for
her, so for the first part of his life Taz had mostly lived in a
kennel and run in the back garden. It wasn't so bad when the
dog was working, but after he'd been forced to retire, Daniel
had hated leaving him shut in while he was on shift. Now, the
dog had his company twenty-four hours a day and a daily walk
on the moor.

A sudden burst of the James Bond theme tune interrupted his
thoughts, bringing with it a sharp pang of regret: his son, Drew,
had downloaded the ringtone to his mobile one day without him
knowing, and now he couldn't bring himself to change it. The
display showed that the caller was Fred Bowden, his boss at
TFS. Hoping it wasn't extra work for the evening, Daniel thumbed
the 'call answer' button.

'Hi, Fred. I'll ring you back in five – I'm driving.' In his policing
days, Daniel had had to deal with the horrific consequences of
distracted drivers too often to take a chance, even if it hadn't been
illegal. Finding a place to pull in, he killed the engine and keyed
in the number.

'Hi. What's up?'

'Daniel, I've had a call from some bloke who wants to talk to
you. Apparently, his daughters went for a walk on the moor and
haven't come back, and he wants to know if you and Taz will
help look for them. Saw the bit in the paper, obviously . . .'

'But surely he should call Search and Rescue.'

'Well, that's what I said. Anyway, will you talk to him? Can
I give him your number?'

'Er . . . yeah, OK, I guess so,' Daniel said reluctantly. Even
though he'd been rueing the prospect of the evening ahead, the
idea of being sent out of his way to pander to a hysterical parent
whose kids would in all probability turn up without his help
wasn't one he particularly relished either.

He disconnected, and a minute or two later, his phone sounded
again.

'Is that Mr Whelan?'

'That's right,' Daniel agreed. 'Who am I speaking to?'

'John. John Reynolds.' The man sounded a little out of breath, as if he were walking.

'How can I help you, Mr Reynolds?'

'It's my daughters – they went walking on the moor and they haven't come back. I've looked for them, but it's hopeless. I've no idea which way they went. I read about your dog in the paper the other day – please, you must help me!' Reynolds spoke English very precisely, but as he became more agitated, Daniel could hear just the hint of a foreign lilt.

'Look, obviously I'd be very willing to help you, but I really think you should contact the police. They'll get on to Dartmoor Search and Rescue – it's their job, after all.'

'Yes, I tried them, but they say it's too soon and we should wait and see if they come back. But I'm really worried, Mr Whelan. It'll be getting dark soon, and it's cold and wet, and Elena's not very strong . . .'

'How long *have* they been gone?' Daniel was surprised at the attitude of the police. He'd not lived in the area for long but was already well aware of the respect the locals rightly accorded the moor, especially in winter.

'About forty minutes. But we're here on holiday, so they don't know the area at all, and they're not dressed for the weather. Look . . .' Reynolds hesitated '. . . the truth is, Mr Whelan, we had a bit of a row. Katya, the older one, is a moody girl – you know, typical teenager – and I'm afraid she might have run away to teach me a lesson. Her sister would follow her anywhere.'

Now they were indeed getting to the truth of it, Daniel thought.

'How old are they?'

'Katya's fifteen and her sister's twelve. Please, Mr Whelan, you've got to help me. They're all I've got.'

They're all I've got. The words stabbed through the defensive layers he'd so carefully gathered around him, bringing the past back with a jolt that made him physically wince. *Please. She's all I've got . . .* A plea uttered by a woman at breaking point. Daniel could still clearly see the sad shake of the doctor's head as he murmured, 'I'm sorry – there was nothing we could do.'

'Mr Whelan? Are you there?'

Daniel dragged his thoughts back to the present.

'Yes, I'm here.'

'Do you have any children?'

'Yes, a son.' He looked out of the window at the blowing mist of rain and imagined Drew wandering on the moor, lost and afraid. He sighed, reluctantly coming to a decision. 'OK, Mr Reynolds. Tell me exactly where you are and I'll get there as soon as I can. I'll need something belonging to the girls for the dog to scent.'

'Yes, yes, of course. I have a glove of Elena's. Thank you so much.'

'Well, I can't make any promises. What the dog can do depends on a lot of things – including the conditions, and if this rain gets any heavier, they are going to be far from ideal. I strongly advise you to try the police again.'

'I will, I will. But you will come, yes? It's a car park on the Princetown road.' Reynolds gave Daniel detailed directions and thanked him again profusely.

It was nearly twenty minutes later when Daniel drove into the moorland car park of Stack Bridge, and the visibility had deteriorated further. The parking area was situated in a hollow with high rocky sides, a stunted hawthorn the only tree in sight. The delivery truck took up nearly a third of the available space.

'Mr Reynolds? Any luck with Search and Rescue?' Daniel asked as he jumped down from the cab and was met by a slim, dark-haired man in jeans and a tailored black leather coat. Another, taller man stood by a massive black 4×4 that was parked a few feet away.

'I think they've got another emergency, over Bovey way.' Reynolds's accent was more pronounced in person and Daniel placed it somewhere in Eastern Europe. He was talking about Bovey Tracey, on the other side of the moor, and pronounced the word 'Buvvy', as the locals did. 'They say they'll come when they've finished, if we haven't found her, but who knows when that will be?'

'But . . . surely there's more than one team?'

Reynolds shrugged. 'I don't know. I'm just telling you what they said.'

'OK. Well, we'll give it a go with the dog.'

Daniel reached back into the cab for his coat and a fluorescent tabard. After the warmth of the lorry, the drizzle-laden wind felt bitter and he wasn't dressed for hiking. Any added protection would be welcome. Pity the youngsters out on the moor with no waterproofs.

From a compartment under the dashboard he took a small

LED torch and a large-scale walker's map of the area, both of which he stuffed in an inside pocket. He would have liked a couple of blankets, a flask of hot tea and a backpack to stow them in, but it couldn't be helped.

'Come on, Taz. Work, boy,' he told the German shepherd, who responded by jumping out of the cab with a whining bark of pure delight.

Reynolds took a step backwards, eyeing the dog a little warily. Daniel took no notice – Taz was a particularly big shepherd and he was used to that kind of reaction.

'It said in the paper that he's an ex-police dog.'

'Yeah, a friend of mine's a copper,' Daniel replied. 'The dog was injured and had to retire. I took him on.' Both statements were true, even if the whole was a little misleading. His years with the police had left him habitually close with information, and his reasons for leaving the service were something he certainly had no intention of sharing with a total stranger.

'Your wife isn't here?' he asked in his turn as he took a long tracking lead and a padded black webbing harness from a holdall behind the seat. The harness was trimmed with fluorescent strips, which shone brightly in the light of the cab. Since the episode with the deaf child, Daniel had taken to carrying it with him, just in case.

'No. The girls' mother and I have separated, but my brother is here.' Reynolds waved a hand to indicate the other man and continued, 'I'm afraid he won't come any closer. He was badly bitten by an Alsatian once.'

'Fair enough.' Daniel gave the man a brief nod before turning back to Reynolds. 'So, whereabouts are you from?'

'Bristol.'

'Do the girls normally live with you?'

'No. With their mother.'

Reynolds's reply was terse and Daniel reined in his curiosity; after all, he was no longer a policeman and it was no business of his.

Eager to work, Taz pushed his head through the harness when Daniel held it out, and it only took a moment to clip it on.

As he straightened up, he glanced around. 'It's quite a remote spot. What brought you out here?' He directed his question at the second man, but it was Reynolds who answered.

'We came for a walk and a picnic. There was a bit of a

disagreement, something quite trivial – you know what kids are – but Katya stormed off, taking Elena with her. I thought they'd be back when they'd cooled down, but when they didn't come, I started to get worried . . .'

'What about a mobile phone?'

Reynolds shook his head. 'They haven't got one.'

Daniel was surprised. A teenager without a phone was a rarity these days, especially as the 4x4 signified that money probably wasn't an issue.

'Oh well, it can't be helped. Mobile coverage on the moor can be a bit hit and miss, anyway. In a steep-sided gully or on the wrong side of a tor, there's no signal at all. Look, could they possibly have found their way home – to where you're staying, I mean? Where is that?'

'A caravan park. Er . . . The Pines.' Reynolds waved his hand vaguely. 'No, it's miles away, and anyway, they set off in the wrong direction.'

'You said on the phone that one of them isn't strong? In what way? Is she ill?'

'Elena has asthma.'

'And you told the police that?' Daniel probed, still more mystified about their apparent indifference.

'No . . . Yes, I think so . . . I can't exactly remember. I got rather angry,' Reynolds admitted.

Daniel zipped his leather jacket up to the neck and fastened the Velcro tabs of the high-visibility waistcoat. 'Well, we'll make a start, but I suggest you get back on the phone and explain your daughter's condition. I'd be very surprised if it didn't make a difference. Besides, it must be over an hour now. OK, where's the glove you said you had?'

'My brother has it.' Reynolds turned and beckoned to the other man, who came forward cautiously, holding out a red mitten. He didn't take his eyes off Taz for a moment. Perhaps responding to his fear, the dog growled deep in his throat, but quieted when Daniel put a hand on his head.

'Thanks.' Daniel took the woollen mitten and paused, looking the two men up and down. They were dark-haired, olive-skinned and looked to be in their late thirties. Both wore jeans and designer trainers, but where Reynolds had a jumper and leather coat, his taller companion sported a red hooded sweatshirt and some sort of canvas baseball jacket.

They were both woefully unprepared for a trek into the

wilderness of Dartmoor, and Daniel viewed the whole rescue mission with growing misgivings.

'OK,' he said briskly. 'When we get started, I need you to stay directly behind me. Keep as quiet as you can, and whatever you do, don't crowd me or the dog. Now, show me where you last saw the girls.'

'This way.' Beckoning, Reynolds left the car park and walked 20 or 30 feet back down the road. Crossing the narrow stone bridge that gave the beauty spot its name, he stopped at the point where a narrow sheep path wound uphill through the heather on to the moor.

'I assumed they'd started from the car park,' Daniel commented, catching up.

'No, they came this way until they saw me coming after them, and then they took off up there,' Reynolds said.

Daniel regarded the steep, wet slope without joy. At the top of the rise, it almost looked as though the rain-laden clouds were touching the dark-brown tips of the heather. With an inner sigh he switched his mind to the matter in hand and, taking Taz to the edge of the narrow road, told him to sit. Then, straddling the dog, he bent down and held the red mitten over his long, black muzzle.

He gave no command. The dog knew exactly what he had to do and immediately began drawing in deep breaths through the fabric, familiarizing himself with the girl's unique smell. After four or five breaths, he started to fidget and Daniel waited just a few more seconds before slipping the glove into his pocket and telling the dog, 'Go seek!'

Instantly Taz's head went down and within moments he had the scent and was away, Daniel hurrying in his wake, paying out the line so as not to hinder him.

What ensued was a gruelling test of fitness for the three men following the dog. In the rapidly failing light the uneven ground was treacherous and Daniel thought grimly that it would be a miracle if one of them didn't suffer an ankle sprain or worse before they got anywhere near their quarry.

By the time they gained the top of the first rise, Daniel was breathing deeply and could hear the other two men labouring behind him. His trouser legs were saturated with water from the 18 inches or so of dank vegetation that crowded the path, and his face and hair were wet with the fine, misty drizzle. Of all of them, the dog alone was enjoying himself, powering forward at the end of the canvas line, unaffected by either anxiety or the unpleasant conditions.

Alternating between a jog and a fast walk, the three men made good progress for ten minutes or so before the path forked and the dog paused to cast around. The moor stretched away on all sides, a wilderness of rocks, grass, heather and the occasional stunted tree. Presumably the two girls had been unsure which way to go. Daniel waited, giving the shepherd plenty of line while he worked, and finally, after a false start up one trail, Taz set off with renewed confidence on the other.

The original track had been twisting and turning, gaining height almost imperceptibly, but this new, narrower track immediately began to climb quite sharply, heading deeper into the moor and, it seemed to Daniel, towards a rocky outcrop on the far horizon.

Did they hope to find shelter? he wondered. What manner of family argument sent two young girls into such desperate flight? He could only imagine that they had never meant to come this far but had lost all sense of direction in the bleak moorland land-scape. They certainly wouldn't be the first to do so.

The searchers had covered less than half a mile on the new track when conditions changed for the worse. It was Reynolds who noticed it first. Daniel was busy watching the dog work, while trying to keep his footing on the loose stones of the path, when he felt a hand tap his shoulder. Slowing his pace only fraction-ally, he turned his head.

'What is it?'

Reynolds nodded significantly to their right. 'Look!' he said urgently.

Daniel followed his gaze and had to blink and refocus. The world was shrinking. Somewhere between them and where the horizon had been just a few minutes ago, the brown carpet of wet heather now disappeared under a soft wall of greyish-white. Even as Daniel watched, the wall appeared to roll closer, swallowing up even more of the view.

'Shit!' He wasn't worried about the mist interfering with the dog. With a sense of smell forty times sharper than a human, Taz had no need of good visibility to find the lost girls, and the trail seemed to be a good one. His concern was that the dense fog would make the already difficult terrain downright treach-erous, not only for his group but also for the youngsters ahead.

'We will keep going, yes?' Reynolds looked anxious. He held out a small handheld device. 'We won't get lost – I have GPS.'

'Well, we might need that before this is over, but I'd be happier if it could tell us where the bogs are.'

A flicker of alarm crossed Reynolds's face. The chance of blundering into one of Dartmoor's infamous bogs clearly hadn't occurred to him.

'We should be all right as long as we're on the path, but you'd better tell your brother to stay close. We don't want to get separated when that lot hits us.'

Daniel picked up the pace once more, scrambling up the steep rocky path after the eager dog.

It seemed the girls had had the good sense to stay on the path, for Taz followed it unerringly, over the next rise, down a steep incline to a stream of bright tumbling water and up an equally steep slope to the base of the rocky outcrop. The water in the stream was icy, a fact to which Daniel could unhappily testify, as the only rocks that stood above the surface proved too slippery to use as stepping stones, depositing him knee-deep in the February torrent.

Daniel cursed as his boots filled with water and he attacked the slope with legs that were beginning to burn with fatigue. From the colourful language behind, he guessed his companions had fared no better.

Halfway up the hill, the fog caught them, enfolding them in a smothering white cloud, like some huge damp duvet, deadening sound. All at once visibility was a 3-foot circle round their feet and Daniel's contact with Taz became restricted to the tug of the lead as he leaned into his harness some 10 feet ahead.

Rocks and low clumps of gorse took on sinister shapes, looming out of the gloom and just as quickly disappearing once more.

After ten minutes or so, the dog paused, and feeling his way cautiously forward, Daniel found that they were at the foot of the rocky cliff they had seen from the other side of the valley. Taz cast around the base of the rock, apparently unsure, allowing his human followers a grateful moment or two to catch their breath.

Daniel looked at his watch. They had been on the moor for almost an hour, keeping up a steady pace. Surely the two girls couldn't be very far ahead.

As if reading Daniel's thoughts, Reynolds suddenly said from close behind, 'When we find them, you must move back with the dog, straight away. Elena will be terrified if it gets too close.'

'I'll do my best, but the dog will naturally reach them first.'
Reynolds's dictatorial tone grated on Daniel, but he didn't let
his annoyance show. The man was under severe emotional strain.
'When he does, he'll bark, but he won't touch them.'

Reynolds looked less than happy, but before he could reply,
Taz picked up a strong scent to the left of the rock and surged
forward.

'Steady, Taz. I can't see a bloody thing!' Daniel told him, slipping and stumbling over the smaller rocks at the base of the
outcrop, but the shepherd was excited now, his enthusiasm trans-
mitting clearly down the tracking line to Daniel's hand. All at
once the line went slack and a short, sharp bark carried back on
the swirling misty air.

'Good lad. Stay there!' Daniel began to gather up the looping
canvas and feel his way towards the dog. 'He's found them,' he
said over his shoulder.

As Taz uttered another bark and then another, Reynolds barged
roughly in front of Daniel and plunged ahead into the fog.

'No, wait!' Daniel's command went unheeded, and swearing
under his breath, he hurried after him, gathering in the line as
he went.

After a moment, he saw Taz through the milky whiteness and,
beyond him, a taller shape that was almost certainly Reynolds.
Daniel heard a scream, cutting off abruptly, and then Reynolds
shouted, 'It's Elena. Take that dog away!'

When Daniel reached Taz, he was growling in a low, grum-
bling fashion, no doubt unsettled by Reynolds's interference
– as he saw it – in the execution of his duty. Daniel calmed
the dog's ruffled feelings with a word and told him what
a clever boy he was, pulling a tug toy from his pocket as a
reward.

As he played with the dog, the second man passed him and
went to where Reynolds, just feet away, was cradling the slight
figure of a child. The girl's jumper now showed as a splash of
orange through the fog and Daniel caught a glimpse of a thin,
white face with enormous eyes and dark, straggly hair before
her father hugged her closer and snapped crossly, 'Take that
fucking dog away!'

Your daughter would still be lost if it wasn't for the 'fucking
dog', Daniel thought, keeping a lid on his temper with an effort.
Police work had taught him to accept that stress can adversely
affect the behaviour of the most genial of people, and he doubted

that Reynolds was ever particularly genial, even on a good day. He retreated a few paces.

'Is she all right? Are they both there?'

'No. Katya's gone on alone. We have to find her.'

'We can try, but it won't be easy,' Daniel warned. 'The dog's been working for an hour or more. He'll be tired, and as far as he's concerned, the job's done.'

'But he can do it, right?' Reynolds materialized out of the mist, empty-handed. He made a quick gesture behind. 'Elena's OK. Just a bit cold and frightened. My brother will stay with her. I'm sorry I shouted. We must go on.'

'Does Elena know which way her sister went?'

'She's not sure.'

Daniel sighed. 'I wish they'd stayed together. It's so important.'

Leading the dog on a little further, away from the confusing scent of his first quarry, he gave him the command to 'seek on'.

At first, Taz was unenthusiastic, casting about in a half-hearted way before coming back to Daniel with his ears flattened and his tail held low. He was clearly unsure of what was expected and Daniel repeated the command. Obediently the shepherd dropped his nose once more and began to quarter the area. In spite of the unpleasant conditions and the desperate urgency of the search, Daniel felt a warm glow of pride for his dog. He was fairly young and relatively inexperienced, but he was trying hard.

Just when it seemed that all his efforts were going to be in vain, Daniel saw Taz's tail come up and begin to wave, and with a renewed sense of purpose he set off once more, pulling into his harness as he moved away along a ridge.

'Good lad!' Daniel exclaimed low-voiced, paying out the lead and starting to jog.

For perhaps ten minutes Daniel could tell by the pull on the tracking line that the scent was strong. In the ever-thickening fog he and Reynolds hurried in the dog's wake, slipping and sliding down a patch of scree, across an open space of knee-high heather and dead bracken that threatened to trip them at every stride, and down to a rocky stream. Here, the dog faltered and the line went slack.

'Why have we stopped?' Reynolds wanted to know, catching up, breathing hard.

'He's lost the scent,' Daniel said quietly, watching Taz come and go in the whiteness as he tried, without luck, to recover the trail. 'It happens. It seemed quite strong, but she obviously didn't come straight out on the other side of the stream. We'll try following the bank.'

They walked upstream for some minutes without success, and when the dog drew a blank downstream as well, Daniel was forced to concede defeat.

'But we can't stop now,' Reynolds stated. 'We have to go on. Get the dog to try again.'

Daniel shook his head. 'I'm sorry – it's pointless. We don't know whether she's gone upstream or down. We could walk for hours in the wrong direction. We'd do better to shout for her. She may not be far ahead.'

They shouted as loudly as they could for several minutes, pausing every few moments to listen, but the all-encompassing fog seemed to swallow their voices and no answering call was heard.

Shaking his head sadly, Daniel put a hand on the other man's shoulder. 'We'd better go back. Elena needs to get into the warm. Call Search and Rescue again. At least you've got coordinates on the GPS. They can start from here.'

Reynolds protested, but Daniel was adamant and they turned to retrace their steps. As they rejoined the others and began the weary trek to Stack Ridge, Reynolds's phone picked up a signal and he dropped back to make the call for help.

Reynolds's brother carried Elena, who clung to him under cover of his baseball jacket, her dark eyes just visible through her fringe. She looked cold, miserable and frightened, and Daniel's heart went out to her, but when she realized he was watching her, she quickly hid her face against the big man's shoulder.

Daniel noticed that the hand that supported the girl was heavily scarred, and remembering the dog attack Reynolds had spoken of, he kept Taz at a distance.

Back at the car park, Daniel checked that Reynolds still had his mobile number and asked to be informed when the older girl was found. Then, with nothing more he or the dog could do to help, he elected to get the lorry back on the road before the rescue vehicles blocked it in.

Just under half an hour later, Daniel let himself into his flat, dried the German shepherd's thick coat as best he could, fed him and ran a bath for himself.

Sinking wearily into the steaming water and feeling the

circulation come tingling back into his toes, Daniel closed his eyes and prepared to enjoy a relaxing soak, but after a few moments, he knew it wasn't to be. Although his body was ready to call it a day, his mind was still buzzing and he found he couldn't banish the image of the child's pitiful face from his consciousness.

Sure, she'd been through the mill that afternoon, and she was almost certainly worried about her missing sister, but Daniel didn't feel that that completely accounted for the haunted expression in her eyes.

In the course of his career he had seen countless teenagers caught up in events beyond their control and he knew the face he had seen – that he was still seeing, in his mind's eye – was that of a child who had reached the end of her tether. Her expression had been compounded of fear, desperation and hopelessness, and to Daniel it begged the question just what *had* the girls been running from?

TWO

Daniel wasn't good with unsolved mysteries. He'd been the kind of copper who would think nothing of putting in hours of unpaid overtime just to follow up a lead or see an investigation through to its conclusion. At such times he'd been far more popular with his superiors than with his wife, but it was this same drive that saw him out of the bath after only a few minutes and reaching for his mobile phone.

A quick search through his call log brought up Reynolds's number, and a few seconds later, a man answered curtly.

'Patrescu.'

'Er, can I speak to John Reynolds?'

There was a pause and then the voice said, 'Who is calling?'

'Daniel Whelan.'

After another short interval, Reynolds spoke. 'Mr Whelan. I was going to ring you . . .'

He left the statement hanging, and after waiting a moment or two for him to elaborate, Daniel said, 'So, any news? Have you found her?'

'Yes, indeed. Katya is safe and well. She found her own way

off the moor and reached us just after you left. She was cold
and tired and very sorry for the trouble she'd caused, but we've
put it all behind us now and we're just glad to have them both
back.'

'That's excellent news!'

'Yes, well, I'm sorry I hadn't got round to ringing you. We
just wanted to get the girls home and into a hot bath.'

'That's all right. Just as long as they're both OK.'

'They're fine. No harm done. Thank you for your help,
Mr Whelan. And give your dog a big bone from me, will you?'

Daniel said he would and rang off, wondering why he didn't
feel more joy. By the time he'd sorted himself out some supper,
he'd decided it was because the instinctive antipathy he'd felt
towards Reynolds at the outset just wouldn't go away, and neither
would the memory of Elena's desperate face. Reynolds had said
all that was proper, but somehow his words lacked the ring of
sincerity.

And who was Patrescu? The brother? Another relative? How
many men were sharing this holiday with the girls? Daniel didn't
like the direction his thoughts were taking.

Waiting for the microwave, he found himself dwelling on
certain inconsistencies in the day's events and decided that, if
only for his own peace of mind, he needed to clear them up.

The Internet connection at Daniel's flat ran at a snail's pace
– due, he supposed, to its rather remote location. These days,
he generally only used it to exchange emails with Drew and
very infrequently with Amanda, so it didn't bother him unduly,
but on the odd occasion that he wanted to surf the net, it
invariably reduced him to swearing at the machine in sheer
frustration.

This was one of those occasions.

Hair curling damply from his bath, Daniel sat at the table that
did duty as a desk, with a bowl of yesterday's bolognese in his
lap, and tapped his fingers impatiently as the screen morphed,
bit by painfully slow bit, from one webpage to the next. He was
dressed in jeans and a thick sweatshirt to make up for the in-
adequacy of the two-bar electric fire that was the room's only heat
source at present. The boiler was on the blink, and although his
landlord had promised to get it seen to, as yet no technician had
materialized.

From the table beside the laptop he picked up a photograph of
Drew, taken last year on his eighth birthday. Daniel had taken him

to Longleat Safari Park for the day. A day to remember, one of the last really happy ones before Daniel's life began to disintegrate.

In the picture, Drew was smiling broadly, high on the excitement of seeing lions and wolves in the flesh. Opinion was pretty evenly divided on whether the boy took more after his mother or father. He had inherited Daniel's wideish mouth, hazel-brown eyes and wavy brown hair, but there were definite echoes of his mother's smaller, sharper features about him too. Luckily, he'd shown no signs, so far, of having inherited Amanda's nasty temper, Daniel thought, replacing the photo.

The dog was asleep, lying flat on the rug close to Daniel's chair, blissfully untroubled by the doubts that were disturbing his master. As far as he was concerned, he'd done his job, received his due praise and was content.

Feeling the cold air on the back of his neck, Daniel pulled up the hood of his sweatshirt, recalling a handful of times when he'd worn it that way as a disguise, on duty on the streets of Bristol.

Young enough, when he'd joined the police, to get away with mingling with gangs of teenagers, he'd quickly got a name for himself as one who could keep his cool in sticky situations, a reputation that had made his subsequent career interesting and varied.

Memories of his previous life brought depression pushing like a dark cloud at the edges of his mind. He didn't dislike his job with TFS. With no references or work skills that were relevant outside the force, he'd expected to have to take manual work of some kind and indeed, after watching everything he'd lived and worked for swirling down the pan, he'd been grateful to find anything that would get him away, and the further the better.

In Devon, no one knew him; no one had heard the rumours or asked awkward questions. Tavistock Farm Supplies was a small company; Bowden asked few questions about his police career; and everyone else seemed to accept without curiosity his vague claim of having been a civil servant.

Fred Bowden had proved to be a very fair boss, content to leave his drivers to their own devices, as long as they got the job done, and Daniel had met some friendly and decent people at the farms and stables he delivered to. It wasn't all bad.

Google finished its search and the monitor flickered and triumphantly produced a list of results for the given keywords, 'Dartmoor' and 'Search and Rescue'.

Daniel scanned the list, his eyes narrowing. There were no

less than four subgroups in the area, all part of Dartmoor Search
and Rescue. Considering Reynolds's location at Stack Bridge, it
seemed to Daniel highly unlikely that either of the two nearest
groups would have been called out to a search near Bovey Tracey,
as he had claimed. According to the website, it was usual for
two groups to attend an emergency, with two remaining on
standby in case they were needed, but Bovey was on the other
side of the moor and it seemed logical that the Ashburton and
Okehampton branches would have dealt with any such call,
leaving Plymouth and Tavistock free to attend to the call to find
Reynolds's missing daughters.

It was interesting that Reynolds had used the local pronunci-
ation of the name Bovey. In Daniel's experience, that was fairly
unusual for a visitor, but then maybe he'd visited the moor before.

Taking a twisted forkful of the cooling pasta, Daniel tapped
in the name of the caravan park where Reynolds had claimed to
be staying. Once again the computer began the peculiar ticking
noise that meant it was cogitating and once again Daniel could
do nothing but tap his fingers and wait. He supposed it would
be less stressful to visit a library with Internet access after work
the next day, but patience had never been one of his strengths
when he was engaged on any kind of investigation. Unlike Taz,
he was unable to rest content in the knowledge of a job well
done and the more he went back over what had happened, the
more he found to disturb him.

Reynolds's insistence that Daniel should stay well back with
the dog when the girls were found was not in itself suspicious
– many people felt a little threatened by a dog of Taz's size –
but the forceful manner in which he had made his wishes known
had bordered on threatening. At the time, Daniel had put it down
to the natural stress of a worried father, but with hindsight he
wasn't so sure. Was it the dog he didn't want close to the child
or Daniel himself? Had Reynolds been afraid of what she might
say?

The cry he had heard when Reynolds had found Elena had
been bitten off short – perhaps by a hand being clamped over
the child's mouth to ensure her silence. What if it had been a
cry of fear?

The computer coughed up its results for his latest search and
Daniel turned his attention to these, pushing aside his empty
bowl. Listings for 'The Pines, Devon, caravan' were numerous,
but after half an hour or more trawling through them, Daniel

still hadn't found a caravan park of that name anywhere, let alone within a reasonable distance of Stack Bridge.

A search of the online phone directories didn't produce anything more helpful and Daniel gave up, deciding to ask at the local post offices the next day. He wished he'd thought to get the 4×4's number plate.

Sitting staring at the screen, his mind drifted again. Had the older girl really not heard their shouting when the dog had lost her scent, or had she been hiding somewhere, watching fearfully as they hunted for her? And why *had* Taz lost what had seemed to be such a strong trail? Katya might have waded up or down the stream with the intention of confusing the dog, but if that was the case, why had she then returned to her father of her own volition shortly after?

It brought him back to the original question: what was it that the girls feared? Had it really been a case of a family row that had gone too far, or was it something more sinister? Was their father abusive? Was he even their father? Daniel fervently wished that he'd asked more questions when he'd had the chance.

Reynolds had said that the authorities seemed uninterested, but Daniel was beginning to doubt that he'd ever called them. He turned cold as he realized that in helping the two men, it was just possible that he'd unwittingly delivered a young girl back into the hands of her abusers.

He toyed with the idea of calling the police himself, but several minutes passed and he made no move towards the phone. After all, what could he tell them? That two girls had been lost on the moor but had now been found? Case open, case closed, as far as they would be concerned. They were unlikely to be interested in a handful of unproven suspicions.

Quite apart from this, he had his own reasons for avoiding any contact with the police, being well aware that it would set off a chain of questions, starting with 'May I ask who's calling?' and quite possibly culminating in them running a search and turning up his record, and that was something he could well do without.

With a sigh he turned off the computer, picked up the day's paper and transferred to the sagging leather sofa, where the dog presently joined him.

That night, for the first time in several weeks, the nightmares returned.

*   *   *

With a busy schedule of deliveries the following morning, it was nearly two o'clock when Daniel slammed the door on the empty lorry for the last time and was able to concentrate fully on what had been in the back of his mind all morning. He wasn't going to know any peace of mind until he'd settled one thing: had Reynolds contacted the emergency services the day before or not?

If he had, then – like him or not – Daniel had no real reason to suspect the man of any wrongdoing. If he hadn't, then he'd blatantly lied, and if he'd lied about that, what else might he have lied about?

Just what he could do about it if he found out that Reynolds's story *was* made up, Daniel didn't know. His first problem was how to discover the truth without exposing himself to the curiosity of the local police.

'How did it go yesterday? Did you find those girls all right?' Fred Bowden came towards Daniel as he washed the lorry down with the pressure hose in the concreted-over farmyard that was the TFS head office and depot. At 5 feet 8, ex-army sergeant Bowden was 4 inches shorter than Daniel but probably a stone heavier, built like a nightclub bouncer. He looked tough, and was, with his receding grey hair cut razor-short and a small earring in his left ear, but the crow's feet around his eyes spoke of a ready humour.

Daniel turned off the water and wiped his hands on the front of his boiler suit. His employer had been at a farm sale that morning and it was the first time they'd spoken.

'Yeah, they both turned up, eventually,' he said, and explained what had happened.

'But you're still not happy about it,' Bowden observed, absent-mindedly rubbing at a patch of paintwork that had escaped Daniel's cleaning.

'I just don't trust the man. I'm not convinced he ever called the rescue people. I'd like to check, but I don't know whether the police will tell me.'

'No need for that,' Bowden said. 'Figgy's a Search and Rescue volunteer. He'd know if anything was called in last night, for sure.'

'Figgy? I didn't realize. Is he still here?'

Andy 'Figgy' Figgis was one of Daniel's fellow drivers at TFS, but such was the nature of the job that in the three months or so that he'd worked there, Daniel had exchanged no more than early-morning platitudes with him, or any of the others, come to that.

'No, he's gone on, but I can give you his mobile number. I'm sure he won't mind. He's a good lad is Figgy. Come over to the office when you've finished here.'

Ten minutes later, stripped of his overalls and with the lorry safely parked in its bay, Daniel rapped on the half-open door of Bowden's office.

'Come in, come in.'

Daniel did so, stepping a foot or two inside and waiting.

'Come right in and shut the door. It's brass monkeys out there! Where's Taz?'

'Outside.'

'Well, call him in, man. Have a seat. Coffee?'

'I'm fine, thanks,' Daniel said, but Bowden poured him one anyway, standing the slightly chipped mug on the corner of his desk.

Taz came eagerly in response to a low whistle, slinking in to sit at Daniel's feet as he sank reluctantly into the chair opposite his boss.

'He works well for you, considering,' Bowden commented, apparently absorbed in leafing through an address book.

'Considering . . . ?'

'Well, Alsatians are pretty much one-man dogs, aren't they? I know some of the army dogs would do anything for their handlers but might just as well've been deaf for all the notice they took of anyone else. Lucky for you he's adapted so well.' He looked up, fixing Daniel with a sharp eye, and Daniel suspected Bowden wasn't fooled by his story of having got the dog from a friend.

'Well, he's only young, and besides, one whiff of a bacon butty and he'd work for anyone,' he joked, electing to continue the bluff.

His interview for the job with TFS had been a casual affair. At the time, it had seemed that as long as Daniel had a current HGV licence, Bowden was happy and not too bothered about his employment history. Now Daniel was uneasy. If he probed, Bowden would find that while Daniel had told no lies, he had been economical – if not to say miserly – with the truth.

Bowden shook his head. 'No, I've seen the way he looks at me. He's happy to leave me alone as long as I behave myself, but if I put a foot wrong . . .'

'It's nothing personal.'

'Oh, I know that.' Bowden tossed a TFS business card across

the desk to Daniel. 'There you are. Figgy's number. Use my phone. What'll you do if Reynolds *was* lying?'

Daniel shrugged. 'I don't know, really. If I can't track him down, there's not much I can do. Let's hope he wasn't.'

'Then you'll be happy?'

'Well, maybe happy is pitching it a bit strong, but *happier*, definitely.'

Figgis answered his phone promptly and seemed incurious as to why Daniel wanted the information.

'Last night? Nah. Quiet night, last night. Been a quiet few days. No call-outs, just training.'

'What about over Bovey way?'

'Not that I know of. I'll likely see Brian in the pub later. He'd know, but I haven't heard anything, and usually I do. All right, mate?'

'Yeah. Thanks for that.' Daniel replaced the receiver and sighed.

'Reynolds was lying,' Bowden said, watching his face.

'Yes, he was. Damn him.'

'So he *has* got something to hide.'

'Looks that way, doesn't it?'

'So what now?'

'Well, right now I'm going to take Taz for a walk. As for Reynolds – or whatever his name really is – I'll have to give it some thought.' He finished his coffee, put the mug back on the desk and got up to go. Taz stood instantly, waving his bushy tail in anticipation. Walk was one word he thoroughly approved of.

'You should come to supper one night,' Bowden suggested. 'Meet my wife. She's gagging to see Taz. She loves dogs.'

'Thank you.' Daniel responded automatically but without any intention of taking Bowden up on the offer. It was a shame. He liked the man, but in his experience social occasions nearly always led to awkward questions sooner or later. It was only natural.

Over the next few days, with nothing he could usefully do about it, Daniel tried to relegate the Reynolds affair to the back of his mind. Further attempts to track down The Pines had proven unsuccessful and led him to conclude that there was no such place.

He had toyed with the idea of contacting one of his ex-colleagues to see if anything could be gleaned from Reynolds's mobile number, but he shied away from actually doing it, unsure of his welcome. His departure from the force had been attended

by much unpleasantness, and he had no doubt that in the intervening months his reputation would have been further blackened
by those he had crossed.

If those last days and weeks had taught him anything, it was
that when push comes to shove, most people ultimately look
after number one. Even, it seemed, those who professed to be
friends.

He might still have chanced it if he'd been a bit more certain
as to what he could do with any information he might obtain.
Even if he had an address for Reynolds, he could hardly ring
the doorbell and demand to see the girls: he had no authority or
grounds to do so.

Reluctantly he let the idea go and life settled back into its
unexciting routine, until the Friday a week after the search, when
Daniel was making an early delivery to Quarry Farm Racing
Stables, southeast of Tavistock, a regular drop on his round.

It was a smallish yard, nestling in a steep-sided valley, where
owner Tamzin Ellis trained around a dozen point-to-point and
National Hunt horses. The stables were old but serviceable, and
beyond them, a number of paddocks sloped up on either side of
a small stream.

As he parked the lorry close to the feed store, Tamzin herself
appeared.

'So, where were you last week?'

Large, expressive grey eyes, long fair hair caught up in a loose
knot and a pencil-slim figure made her a sight to gladden the
heart of any red-blooded male, and Daniel was no exception.

He made a rueful face. 'Figgy did this area instead. Luck of
the draw.'

'I missed you,' Tamzin said. 'Figgy's OK, but he doesn't do
this . . .' She leaned forward to give him a lingering kiss in the
privacy of the open cab door.

'Oh, I don't know . . .' Daniel responded straight-faced. 'I'm
sure he would have done. Did you ask him?'

Tamzin dug him in the ribs with a stiff forefinger. 'Cheeky
bugger! You'd better get on with your work or I'll report you to
Fred!'

She moved away, laughing, and after an appreciative look at
her departing rear, Daniel went round to the back of the lorry. The
attraction between them had been instantaneous, and although he'd
fought it at first, he had eventually given in to loneliness and her
blatant encouragement and asked her out.

To begin with, it had all been very casual and Tamzin seemed to accept his reluctance to talk about himself, but of late she'd started to tease him about his 'secrets'. Because of this, the relationship had begun to be a stress Daniel could well do without and he'd almost subconsciously started to back away from it.

He sighed, wondering if he would ever feel able to trust anyone with the mess of his past.

With the tailgate lowered, he began the laborious job of unloading. In the past, he had used the gym when he felt in need of a workout, but he had no such need these days. Some of the bigger farms had their own forklift trucks, but the smaller clients outnumbered those by far, and shifting heavy bags and bales of fodder and bedding all day long was keeping Daniel leaner and fitter than he'd been for a long time.

As he worked, he watched the lads and lasses leading their charges out preparatory to mounting, the thoroughbreds' thin skins protected from the cold wind by striped blankets over their loins. Daniel loved the horses. He'd grown up in the country-side, and he and his brothers and sisters had cadged rides on friends' ponies from an early age. Since moving to Bristol and joining the police at the age of eighteen, he'd barely given riding a thought, until his transfer to the Dog Unit had brought him into contact with the mounted division at HQ and he had once more felt the pull of equine contact.

Minutes later, the Quarry Farm string was mounted and filing out of the yard on to the road that led to the gallops, their many hooves beating a tattoo on the concrete and tarmac.

Tamzin stood by the gate, scrutinizing her charges as they went past, occasionally speaking to one of the riders.

'Watch Shiner when you go past Tyler's Farm, Maggie. He'll throw a hissy fit if that bloody dog runs out – I don't want him slipping and coming down on the road. Steve, take Romany quietly today – I don't want a repeat of yesterday's fiasco!'

Daniel glanced up, wondering what form 'yesterday's fiasco' had taken, and saw a rather sullen youngster slouched in the saddle of a lean grey horse. He knew the turnover of staff in the yard was very high – in common with many racing stables – and guessed that the unhappy Steve would soon join the ranks of ex-employees: he didn't look the persevering sort. Turning back to his work, Daniel's eye was caught by the rider of a chestnut mare, immediately behind the grey.

With cropped dark hair and a boyishly slim figure, Daniel's first impression was that it *was* a boy, but the size of the eyes and the fine bones of the face suggested a girl. It was something about that heart-shaped face that had arrested his gaze. Why did she look familiar?

He left the lorry and walked across to join Tamzin.

'Who's the girl on the chestnut?' Daniel asked quietly.

'Which chestnut?'

There were three chestnuts in the string of eight horses.

'The one that's just gone out.'

'That's Kat. She's new.'

'How new?' Kat – Katya. Could it be?

Tamzin turned towards him as the last horse filed away up the lane.

'Very. Just a couple of days. Why?'

'Do you know where she comes from? What's her surname?'

'I have to say I can't remember. She just wandered in while we were doing evening stables and asked if there were any jobs.'

'And you don't even know her surname? That's a bit casual, isn't it?'

'Yeah, I know. She may have said – I'm not sure. I was just so bloody glad to see her. We lost two last week – went home for the weekend and didn't come back – so we were a bit short-staffed. I can't tell you more than that because I haven't done any paperwork yet. To be honest, I don't bother until I'm sure they're going to stay more than a week or two. Otherwise I spend all my time filling out forms and then they bugger off! She's a very competent little rider, though. The horses go well for her.'

'And Kat is short for?'

'How would *I* know? Kathryn, Kathleen, Katrina . . . ? She didn't say. Your guess is as good as mine. Why the interest?'

'It's a long story.' Daniel was still watching the last of the horses' rumps disappearing up the lane, his mind racing. 'Does she live in?' Several of the stable hands that weren't local lived in a couple of purpose-built log cabins adjacent to the yard.

'Yes, she does. Look, I've got to go now, if I'm going to get to the gallops before they do, but why don't you come over tomorrow night – say sevenish. I'll rustle up a stir-fry and we can crack open a bottle of wine and you can tell me this long story of yours. Unless, of course, it's another of your secrets?'

'No. That sounds good. And maybe I could have a word with Kat too.'

Tamzin shrugged. 'I don't see why not. Now I *must* go.' She leaned towards him and they kissed lightly. 'Until tomorrow.'

Daniel returned thoughtfully to his unloading as the Land Rover left the yard. It seemed incredible, but was it just possible that Tamzin's new stable lass was Elena's sister?

Reynolds had claimed she'd turned up safe and well, but *had* she? Daniel only had his word for it, and that had so far proven to be worth very little. He thought back over his telephone conversation with the man, remembering the pause when Reynolds had waited for him to state his business. 'I was going to ring you . . .' he'd said, but instead of immediately sharing the good news about Katya's return, he'd waited for Daniel to ask.

Was that because he thought Daniel might himself have some news of the girl and therefore catch him out in his lie?

Daniel turned up at Quarry Farm with a bottle of wine in hand, just after half past seven the next evening.

Taking the path behind the stables and down the stone steps that led to the cottage, he was met at the door by Tamzin, who leaned forward for a kiss before standing back to let him into the low-ceilinged interior.

'Sorry I'm late. I took Taz for a walk and went further than I intended.'

'So where is he now?'

'In the car. He's a bit wet,' Daniel said, handing her the bottle and bending down to greet her menagerie of dogs. 'Besides, I didn't want to scare Kat. He can be a bit daunting at first.'

'Ah. About Kat . . .' Tamzin shut the front door and followed him into the kitchen, her Labrador, spaniel and Yorkshire terrier bustling through the doorway with her. 'There's a bit of a problem.'

'Oh?'

'Well, I asked her to come down here at about a quarter to seven – get some of her details sorted out and stuff – but she didn't turn up. So I went over to the cabins and they said she'd gone.'

'Gone? Where?'

'*Gone* gone. Taken all her things and cleared out – not that she had much. I must say, I was surprised. She seemed to be settling in quite well, but there you go.'

'Did you, by any chance, tell her that I was coming?'

Tamzin frowned. 'Yes. Wasn't I meant to? I'm sorry. You didn't say.'

'I didn't think of it. It's not your fault.'

'So what did you want her for? Do you know her?'

'I know *of* her – if she's who I think she is, and that's beginning to look increasingly likely. You say she didn't come with much gear?'

Tamzin shook her head. 'Hardly any. Just the clothes she was wearing – jeans, jumper and a jacket – and she had a tiny rucksack bag, you know, like the kids carry to school. I had to lend her some jodhs – she didn't even have those. To be honest, I wondered if she was a runaway, but she swore she was sixteen.' She took two wine glasses from the kitchen cupboard and, from a drawer, a corkscrew, which she handed to Daniel. 'Here, make yourself useful. So, *was* she a runaway?'

'In a way, yes.'

Tamzin paused in the act of taking stir-fry ingredients from the fridge and turned to face him. 'Are you going to tell me any more, or do I have to prise it out of you? Because – I don't mind telling you – I'm getting just the teensiest bit fed up with all these bloody guessing games!'

'I'm sorry.' Daniel couldn't blame her for losing patience with him. He handed her a large glass of ruby-coloured wine and, settling his rump against the edge of the granite worktop, proceeded to tell her the tale, including his subsequent doubts.

'And you think Kat is the missing girl?'

'I think it's possible, don't you?'

'But you don't know for sure she's still missing. I mean, why would this Reynolds guy lie about finding her?'

'Because he quite plainly doesn't want the police involved and I think he guessed that if he admitted she was still missing, I'd call them myself.'

Tamzin put a pepper on her chopping board and began to slice it. 'So why all the secrecy? What's he trying to hide?'

'I think he's scared of what they might say – I mean, he made damn sure I didn't get close enough to Elena to speak to her.'

'Oh my God! You don't think they're being abused?' Tamzin turned round with a pepper in one hand and a knife in the other, her face twisted with disgust.

'I don't know. It's one possibility, but there are others. Tell me, would you have said that Kat was English?'

'No, she wasn't, but that's the norm for this industry. Almost all the lads who come through the yard are Eastern European or Irish. I'm becoming multilingual. I can say, "Get a move on with that stable!" and, "Stop mucking around!" in six different languages. Kat speaks pretty good English, but Rafa – that's Rafail – says she's Romanian. I asked him.'

'I thought she might be. I'm pretty sure Reynolds and his so-called brother are too. I'm wondering if the authorities know they're here. That might explain the nervousness about getting involved with the police.' There were other possible explanations too, but he decided to keep them to himself for now.

'Will you go to the police now you've seen her?'

'And tell them what, exactly?'

'Well . . .' Tamzin hesitated. 'Yeah, I see what you mean. So what now?'

Daniel shrugged. 'Think again, I suppose.'

'I wish I hadn't told Kat you were coming. I'm sorry. It was stupid.'

'Don't be daft – you weren't to know. I expect she was afraid Reynolds had sent me after her. She might even have seen me with him on the moor the other day.'

'I wonder where she'll go, poor kid. She won't know anyone.'

'You say she seemed competent with the horses?'

'Oh, yes. She's been around them before, without a doubt.'

'Well, she might get out of the area altogether, but if Elena *is* her sister and she's close by, I have a hunch she'll stick around. I might try leaving word at all the local stables. If it's what she knows, it's just possible she'll try again. After all, she's got to eat.'

'I can have a word with the one in the village,' Tamzin offered. 'And also the trekking centre over at Goats Tor. I know Hilary quite well, and she's usually looking for staff with Easter coming up.'

'Thanks, that'd be great.'

Tamzin turned back to her chopping board but made no attempt to continue with her preparation.

'Why are you doing this?' she asked after a moment.

'Doing what?'

She swung back to face him. 'Going to all this trouble to find the girl? I mean, most people would have given up and forgotten about it after this Reynolds guy said she was back home. Why not you?'

Daniel shrugged. 'I told you. It just didn't feel right. The more I thought about it, the less I liked it. I couldn't just do nothing.'

'Some people would.'

'Yeah, well . . .' Daniel didn't know what to say.

'OK. You don't have to answer this, but what did you really do before you started working for Fred? You said you were a civil servant. Policemen are civil servants, right? Were you a policeman?'

Slowly Daniel nodded. 'For ten years.'

'So why all the secrecy? You're not undercover, are you?'

'No, nothing like that. I'm not in the force any more.'

'Am I allowed to ask why? I mean, I thought it was normally a lifelong career thing – a calling.'

'It is.' The horror, tragedy and humiliation of his last weeks on the force flashed uninvited into Daniel's mind, and with an effort he closed the memories down, saying tersely, 'I left. Stress basically.'

Again a half-truth. He was getting too good at those.

'Well, that's nothing to be ashamed of. It must be a terribly stressful job,' Tamzin said with a note of relief. 'I know I couldn't do it. But I wish you'd told me sooner. I was imagining all sorts of things! I mean, I even wondered if you'd been in prison or something.'

Her easy acceptance of his white lie made Daniel feel uncomfortable, but if the alternative were unpalatable to him, how much more so would it be to her?

When Tamzin and Daniel had finished their meal, they retired to what Tamzin called the snug, but which was in fact the cottage's only sitting room. There they sat on a blanket-covered leather sofa, wedged between two of Tamzin's three dogs, drinking wine in front of the small wood-burning stove that heated the whole building. Taz had been brought in from the car and now lay in the doorway, one eye sleepily fixed on his master.

Daniel sighed with rare contentment, and Tamzin slanted a look at him.

'I think that's the first time I've known you be really relaxed,' she commented. 'When we're out anywhere, you're constantly on the watch. You probably don't know you're doing it, but your eyes are everywhere. If someone moves, you see it. If someone new comes in, you watch them. It puts me on edge too.'

'God, I didn't realize I was such bad company,' Daniel said. 'Sorry. Old habits, I guess.'

'It's OK now I know. But all the same, it's good to see you kicking back.'

There was silence for a moment, punctuated by the sound of a log collapsing in the burner.

'What'll you do if you find Kat?' Tamzin said then, pulling her feet up on to the sofa and leaning against him.

'I don't know. I'll have to play it by ear, I guess. If she does turn up, we must be careful not to scare her off again. Best tell people to say nothing and just ring me.'

'OK. But before you give your phone number to half the females in Devon, how about putting another log on the fire and then giving me a cuddle?'

'We-ell.' Daniel made a show of looking at his watch, pursing his lips and shaking his head – 'I should really be going . . .'

'You ain't going anywhere with half a bottle of wine inside you, mister!' Tamzin told him. 'You're gonna have to stay right here, like it or not!'

'Well, I suppose I could be a gentleman and pretend to like it,' he said generously.

THREE

'**D**aniel! Wake up! Dan!' Tamzin's urgent tones penetrated the stark horror of Daniel's dream and finally achieved their aim.

'What? What is it?' He scrambled to a sitting position, images from his nightmare mixing confusingly with the unfamiliar reality of Tamzin's under-the-eaves bedroom. She had put the light on, and in the room below, the dogs were barking, Taz's deep voice among them.

Blinking sleep away, Daniel focused on the worried face beside him.

'What's the matter?'

'You tell me,' Tamzin suggested. 'You're the one who woke me up, yelling blue murder. You've even upset the dogs.'

Daniel frowned. 'Sorry, I must have been dreaming.'

'Well, I'm glad I don't have dreams like that. Are you OK?' she asked. 'That was pretty full on.'

'I'm fine. Did I say anything? I mean, anything that made any sense?'

'Not really. You kept saying "Put it down," over and over, and then you shouted out.'

Daniel grimaced. 'You should have woken me sooner.'

'I tried, believe me!' Tamzin reached out a hand and stroked his arm. 'Do you want to talk?'

'Not really.' He wanted to forget it not drag it all out again.

There was silence for a long moment. Then Tamzin said, 'Well, the offer's there. Look, come here and give me a hug and let's try to get back to sleep, shall we? I've got to get up in an hour or two.'

She switched off the bedside light and obediently Daniel slid over and wrapped his arms round her, laying his cheek against her silky hair and breathing in the warm smell of her. Her closeness was comforting, and after a minute or two of staring into the grainy darkness, he closed his eyes and hoped for peaceful oblivion.

Tamzin murmured something unintelligible and within moments her deep and steady breathing showed that she had gone back to sleep, but Daniel could only lie awake and envy her. Every time he let his mind relax, fragments of the drama that had been playing in his head rushed back to haunt him. Whirling from the darkness came the wild-eyed teenager with the knife held in his shaking hand and the terrified girl gazing at Daniel – begging, pleading, imploring him to *do* something . . .

The minutes dragged by, measured out by the faintly ticking second hand of the alarm clock on Tamzin's bedside cabinet. Gradually the darkness gave way to pre-dawn grey and Daniel was able to make out the contours of her sleeping face. Her long, blonde hair was tumbled across the pillow and with his free hand he smoothed aside a lock that lay across her eyes.

Stirring at his touch, she rolled away from him, and unable to bear the inactivity any longer, Daniel slid out of bed, pulled on his clothes and trod quietly down the spiral staircase to the snug.

He was met by four sleepy dogs, who nevertheless happily followed him out into the lightly frosted garden when given the option, showing no surprise at the oddness of the hour. Locking the door behind him, Daniel crossed the yard, where one or two of the horses whickered in anticipation of an early breakfast, and set off for a walk across the fields, the sharp air clearing his mind and raising his spirits.

When he returned, he found Tamzin in the kitchen, freshly showered and making coffee, face bare of make-up and hair twisted into an untidy knot.

'Thought you'd done a runner and stolen my dogs,' she

commented, and she was so totally different from Amanda that he wrapped her in a hug and then kissed her soundly.

'Sorry about last night,' he said awkwardly.

She looked up at him, her skin golden against the white towelling robe. 'Don't be daft! As long as you're OK.'

'I'm fine.'

'Why don't you ride out with us this morning?' she suggested, handing him a mug. 'On exercise, I mean.'

'Because I haven't ridden since I was a kid,' Daniel responded. 'And I hardly think exercising a racehorse is the best way to ease back into it.'

'Nonsense – it's like riding a bike. It'll come back to you. You could ride Rex – he's as good as gold.'

'He'd need to be,' Daniel said with feeling. 'Look, thanks for the offer, but I'd better get on.'

'Oh, OK. Didn't realize you were busy.' Her disappointment showed.

'I'm seeing Drew this afternoon – picking him up for lunch.'

Daniel saw his son once a fortnight, and on the one weekend in six that he didn't work on Saturday, Drew sometimes joined him at the flat, staying Friday and Saturday nights.

'Oh, I see. Well, why don't you bring him over? He might like to see the horses.'

'Thanks, he'd love it, but he's in Taunton and we've booked a bowling lane for the afternoon.'

After an early breakfast, Daniel remained long enough to see Tamzin ride out on exercise with her string: seven blanketed horses, muzzles snorting steam, eager to be on the move. Tamzin rode at the back, sitting easily on a brown gelding that jiggled sideways and tossed its head impatiently. She raised a hand in farewell as she passed Daniel, and he thought he detected a certain wistfulness in her smile. He had an uneasy feeling that their 'no strings' relationship was assuming a more serious nature, and half regretted his weakness in staying the night.

Leaving the yard, with a couple of hours to spare before he needed to set out for Taunton, Daniel turned the wheels of his red Mercedes estate towards Stack Bridge. He was sure Taz wouldn't turn down the chance of a second walk, and he wanted to take another look at the place in broad daylight.

The car was a scruffy, high-mileage example of the marque, bought when he was in the Dog Unit, primarily for the purpose of transporting his dogs to and from his base, where he would pick up his van. When they broke up, Amanda had claimed the smart sports saloon they'd jointly owned, but he wasn't precious about what he drove. At least there was no need to worry about dirt or the odd scratch on this one, and very little chance of it being targeted by thieves. His colleagues at work had joked that a full tank of petrol doubled its value.

Stack Bridge car park on a sunny Sunday morning was somewhat more populated than it had been on the Friday evening Daniel met Reynolds there. Parking the Mercedes next to a gleaming new sports car whose owners looked as if they feared that such decrepitude might be contagious, he let the dog out, calling him immediately to heel. Leaving the car park, he retraced the route he'd taken with Reynolds.

Moments later, a black 4×4 approached at high speed, barely slowing to take the rise of the bridge so that its seconds scraped the tarmac briefly on the other side. Within seconds it had rounded the bend and disappeared from view.

In his haste to pull Taz to safety, Daniel had missed getting the number plate, but as the car flashed by, he'd caught a glimpse of the driver, and unless he was very much mistaken, it was none other than Reynolds's surly 'brother'.

Well, well. So they were still around, were they?

Daniel moved on down the road to where, the week before, the dog had picked up the girls' trail. The more he'd thought about it, the less he'd been convinced that the girls had ever been in the car park at all.

As he'd suspected, the track they'd followed was mirrored by another one on the opposite side of the road. Perhaps Reynolds or his brother had followed the girls on foot until they lost them and then driven to the car park before making the decision to call Daniel.

The trail on the lower side of the road appeared to follow a fairly straight path, as far as he could see, heading for a dark line of trees several hundred yards away.

According to his map, the wooded area was about half a mile from one side to the other, and beyond it were fields and then a road flanked by what looked like a scattering of large properties. If the girls had followed that path, could they have started out from one of those houses?

The sheep path was too small to be marked on the map, and the only way to find out if it did indeed lead to the wood

was to follow it. Glancing at his watch, Daniel decided he had
time to investigate and, with a word to the dog, set off at a
jog along the narrow path.

The apparent straightness of the sheep track was somewhat
misleading, as it meandered across the open space, circum-
navigating boggy areas, and it took Daniel a quarter of an hour
to reach the trees. After another ten minutes or so, he emerged
from the gloom of the woodland on to a stony track that ran
along the back of the fields he'd seen on the map. At this point
he was at a stand. There was no obvious point of access to the
property in front of him, and it was impossible to guess which
way the girls might have come: right or left. If indeed they had
come that way at all.

He began to retrace his steps. It was time to head for Taunton
to pick up Drew. Another day he would try and find the lane
from the other end, but realistically without Katya's help he had
little hope of tracking Reynolds down.

As was often the case, Daniel left Taunton that evening with a
mixture of relief and regret. In the short period he'd lived there,
both his working and home lives had been tense and unhappy,
his new colleagues wary of him and Amanda constantly blaming
him for taking her away from her friends, though the choice
hadn't been his.

Even in Bristol most of his socializing had been done within
the tight-knit community of the police service and there he knew
he had precious few supporters remaining. As for Amanda's
friends, he had no doubt that she'd have poisoned their minds
against him. As soon as it had become clear that his reputation
had suffered irreparable damage, she'd lost no time in distancing
herself from him, playing the victim and milking sympathy from
those around her.

Usually the enjoyment Daniel derived from his time with Drew
balanced out the unhappy associations the town held for him,
but this time the visit had only added to his stress. From the
start Drew had been quiet, and as the afternoon wore on,
he seemed increasingly withdrawn, even their trip to the bowling
alley failing to revive his spirits.

Over a luxurious hot chocolate in the restaurant of the
complex, Daniel attempted to discover the reason behind his
son's depression.

'Something on your mind, Drew? You seem a little quiet.'

Drew made a figure of eight with his straw in the cream on top of his drink and said nothing. He was wearing a navy hooded sweatshirt with some meaningless logo on the front, and a pair of expensive-looking trainers.

'Are you in trouble? Is it Mum? Or something at school? You're not being bullied?'

Drew shook his head mutely, but Daniel had enough experience of kids to know that whatever was on his mind, deep down he wanted to share it. If it were something he hadn't wanted to discuss, he would have made up some other excuse for his behaviour. If this was a cry for help, Daniel was going to do his damnedest to make sure he got it.

'Is it something *I've* said or done?'

Again the headshake.

'Well, can I help? You know I'll do anything I can.'

'Anything?' Drew looked up with hope in his eyes. His unruly brown fringe flopped across his forehead and he pushed it away with impatient fingers. 'Do you mean that?'

'Of course. If I can.'

'Then can I come and live with you? Please, Dad? Please?'

Oh God! *Anything*, he'd said. Yes, anything but that. He'd walked right into that one. But to be fair Drew hadn't mentioned it since the early days of their separation, and he'd assumed the boy had accepted the idea as impossible.

'Drew, listen . . .'

'You said anything! Dad, please!'

'You know I can't. It's not possible.'

'Why?'

'Because I haven't got a proper house, because I'm working six days a week, because you've got school, and not least because your mother wouldn't let you.'

'She couldn't stop me if I just went.'

'Don't you believe it! She'd take me to court to get you back, and I'm afraid she'd win.'

'But we could go away somewhere,' Drew persisted with the easy confidence of an eight-year-old.

'And live on what? Come on, Drew, you know it's not that simple.'

'You could join the police again, or drive lorries. Please, Dad. I hate living with Amanda.'

'*Amanda?*' Daniel was momentarily distracted. 'Who told you to call her that?'

'She did.'

'Since when?'

'A few weeks ago.'

'And do you like it?'

'It's a bit weird,' Drew admitted. 'But lots of the kids at school call their parents by their first names. It's quite cool, really.'

Daniel didn't agree, but it wasn't the issue at that moment.

'So if she's so cool, why don't you like living with her?'

'She's always going out or having friends round. She hasn't got time for me. She never does fun stuff like you and I do.'

'But you know if you lived with me, we wouldn't do this sort of thing all the time,' Daniel pointed out. 'It's just a treat because I don't see you very often.'

'It wouldn't matter,' Drew assured him earnestly. 'I wouldn't care.'

Daniel sighed. 'You would. You'd soon get bored, miles away from all your friends. But it can't happen, anyway. I'm sorry, Drew. It just can't.'

Drew had sat and stared at him, his dark-lashed brown eyes slowly filling up with tears until one spilled over and ran down his cheek to drop off his chin and into his half-full mug of chocolate.

'Drew, don't,' Daniel pleaded, the sight of those tears a far more compelling persuasion than any spoken word could be. 'I would if I could, I promise you, but I can't . . .'

Remembering the conversation now, as he accelerated on to the M5 and headed for home, he felt like a traitor. He had no worries that Amanda was neglecting the boy – for all her faults, she had always been a good mother – but to have to drop Drew off at the door with their issues unresolved felt like failing him. Daniel knew the memory of his son's drooping posture and unhappy eyes would stay with him for the whole of the next fortnight.

He was halfway home when his phone rang. A glance told him it was Amanda and he pulled over to answer it.

'What have you been saying to Drew?' she demanded without preamble.

Daniel groaned inwardly. He could do without an earful from his ex-wife.

'If this is about him wanting to come and live with me, I haven't said anything at all to encourage him, I promise you.'

'Then why's he suddenly started on about it again? Tell me that. He hasn't said a word for weeks until today.'

'Well, it's clearly been on his mind. He was very quiet all afternoon.'

'He's been fine until now,' she insisted, intent on fixing the blame.

'Well, Drew says you've been out quite a lot, so maybe you just haven't noticed,' Daniel countered, unwisely allowing himself to be drawn into the brewing row.

'How *dare* you criticize me? I'm young and I need a life of my own – my own friends. It was hard enough starting again after you dragged us all away from Bristol. Anyway, he's never left alone, if that's what you're suggesting.'

'No, that's not what I'm saying. I just meant that he's a quiet lad anyway, and it would be easy to miss the signs if you were busy.'

'I know him far better than you ever have, or ever will, come to that,' she said spitefully. 'You were always too busy working all hours of the day and night. And now you see him once a fortnight and think you can tell me what he's feeling! I don't think so!'

Daniel closed his eyes and took a deep breath. Letting this degenerate into a slanging match would benefit no one. Besides, there was a measure of truth in what she said: he *had* worked long hours, and shifts were never easy. Sometimes between Drew's school hours and his own work, he'd barely seen the boy for several days at a time.

'Are you seeing someone?' he asked then, wondering if that was why she'd gone on the attack.

There was a pause and then Amanda said with a note of uncertainty, 'Drew didn't tell you that. He doesn't know about it. Have you been spying on me?'

'Don't be ridiculous,' Daniel said witheringly. 'Do you think I haven't got anything better to do?'

'Well, so what if I am seeing someone? What's it got to do with you?'

'Nothing. But if you're serious about this guy, I think you should tell Drew. Make him part of it. Maybe he's feeling insecure.'

'My God! I don't need relationship advice from you – of all people!' she stated hotly. 'All I need from you is that you stop filling his head with ideas that aren't going to happen, ever! Do you understand me?'

'Loud and clear,' Daniel said wearily. There was only ever one winner in an argument with Amanda. Over the years he'd learned that you just had to plant the seed of an idea and hope that she thought it over when she calmed down. And to be fair, she usually did.

It was two days later, when he had finished a delivery near Launceston, that he first got possible news of Katya. He'd just climbed back into the cab and was checking the address of his next drop when he had a call on his mobile. A glance at the display told him nothing; the number was unknown to him.

'Hello?'

'Is that Daniel Whelan?' A woman's voice, clear and well modulated.

'Yes. Do I know you?'

'Not yet,' came the reply. 'I'm a friend of Tamzin Ellis. She might possibly have mentioned me. Hilary McEwen-Smith. I run a pony-trekking centre in Goats Tor.'

'Oh, yes. Yes, she did. Did she tell you about the girl I'm looking for?'

'Yes. That's why I'm ringing. I had a girl who fits that description turn up looking for work this very morning.'

'So what did you do?' Daniel held his breath. 'Is she there now?'

'She is. I wouldn't normally take someone on without a reference, but knowing you were looking for her, I told her I would give her a week's trial. She seems a nice enough girl. Foreign, would that be right?'

'It would.' Daniel could hardly believe his luck.

'And Tamzin says you'd like to speak to her . . .'

'I would. Very much.'

'Can I ask, is she in trouble?'

'No. At least, as far as I know, she hasn't done anything wrong,' Daniel said. 'But I think she needs help. The thing is, she doesn't realize I'm trying to help her and she's already run away from me once.'

'Tamzin says you're a delivery driver for Fred Bowden.'

'That's right.'

'That's interesting because the girl – she said her name was Katy, by the way – she asked me where I get my horse feed from,' Hilary told him. 'So if you're thinking of coming here, perhaps it might be a good idea to leave your lorry behind . . .'

In the end, they hatched a plan to allow Daniel to try and get close enough to win Katya's confidence before she had a chance to run again.

Making a lengthy detour from his scheduled delivery route, Daniel parked the lorry behind the White Buck Inn in the sprawling village of Goats Tor and left it with the windows half open and Taz lying across the front seat.

He had no qualms about leaving the three-quarter-full lorry: the trailer was protected by a coded locking system, and nobody in their right mind was going to try and get in the cab. Nevertheless, he was uncomfortably aware that he still had three drops to do and that he would almost certainly be very late indeed for the rest of his round.

He toyed with the idea of ringing Bowden and explaining the situation, but in spite of his earlier interest in Katya's story, Daniel wasn't sure he could rely on his boss being willing to relax his strict rule of punctuality. He decided that rather than be forced to disobey the man, he would do better not to ask at all.

A brisk ten-minute walk brought him to the cattle grid that marked the edge of the Dartmoor National Park, and shortly after this, following Hilary's instructions, he left the road for a gravel track marked with a bridleway sign.

The track ran along the edge of the moorland with a scattering of ancient oaks and silver birches on the right, while on its left a steep wooded slope dropped down to a stream in a rocky gully, some way below.

After a hundred yards or so, Daniel slowed his pace to a stroll, waiting to hear the sound of hooves catching him up. Rather than turning up at the yard, he and Hilary had agreed that this apparent 'chance' encounter was probably the least likely to alarm the girl.

Daniel was impressed with Katya's reasoning. It was smart thinking, questioning the stable owner about her feed supplier. She'd obviously remembered the TFS lorry in Tamzin's yard, connected it with Daniel and his request to speak to her and didn't want to run the risk of being seen by him again.

It wasn't surprising that she'd run; after all, she had no reason to expect anyone to want to help her and she may even have suspected him of being in league with Reynolds, especially if she'd caught sight of Taz in the lorry. She was showing herself to be both tough and resourceful, but then the way she'd managed to throw Taz off her scent had demonstrated that.

After a minute or two, Daniel heard the sound he'd been

waiting for and a glance over his shoulder revealed two ponies approaching at a trot. Resisting the temptation of watching them come, he kept his gaze steadfastly ahead until they were quite close. When they slowed to a walk, he stepped to one side and looked up at the two riders with a friendly smile.

'Hello, Daniel!' the older of the two ladies exclaimed on a convincing note of happy recognition. 'How are you?'

Both riders were mounted on the sturdy brown weight-carrying animals Daniel had come to recognize as the indigenous Dartmoor pony. They stopped and he went up to the closer of the two and stroked its neck, looking up at its rider.

'Hilary!' he responded. 'Haven't seen you for ages. I'm fine, thanks. No need to ask how you are – you always look in rude good health and I swear you never get any older.'

Hilary McEwen-Smith did indeed have an ageless quality, though he guessed she was possibly sixtyish. Underneath her riding hat her light-brown hair was shoulder length, and a rosy complexion told of a life spent outdoors. A little on the plump side, she wore brown corduroy jodhpurs and her waxed cotton jacket was unzipped to reveal a sweatshirt, somewhat surprisingly decorated with a large smiling frog.

Daniel flashed a brief friendly smile at her companion before turning back to Hilary, but it was enough to reinforce his previous impression of the powerful likeness between this girl and Elena. Way too great to be a coincidence, in the circumstances. She was wearing a sweatshirt and navy jodhpurs. Idly he wondered if they were the ones Tamzin had loaned her.

'Oh, by the way, this is Katy,' Hilary told him. 'All being well, she's going to be working for me. Katy, Daniel is an old friend of mine.'

'Hi, Katy.' Would she recognize him away from the lorry?

The girl nodded, her eyes distinctly wary. Seen at closer quarters, she was strikingly attractive in a dark-eyed, gamine sort of way.

'When he was a boy, Daniel used to help me out at weekends and after school,' Hilary told her, ruthlessly reinventing his past for him.

'You'll love working for Hilary,' Daniel put in. 'Have you been riding long?'

Now he had his chance, Daniel was struggling to find a way to gain her confidence. She was clearly suspicious and he felt that one false move would set her running again.

'I ride as a child,' she said, returning her attention to him. 'My uncle had a horse farm.' Her pony sidled a little and tossed its head, perhaps picking up on her anxiety, and Daniel moved to stand between the two, rubbing the animal's muzzle.

'Oh? Where was that?' He tried to inject a note of casual interest into his voice, but even so he sensed the girl stiffen.

'Why do you ask me?'

'I was just curious. I have a friend from Romania and you sound a lot like her.'

Daniel had hoped to provoke some sort of reaction, but he was totally unprepared for the violence of it. With no hesitation the girl dug her heels hard into the pony's sides, driving it forward. Its shoulder caught Daniel a glancing blow, sending him spinning away to land sprawling under the nose of Hilary's mount.

'Bugger!'

He was on his feet in an instant, but Katya was already several lengths away and the pony was galloping hard. Without considering the futility of doing so, Daniel set off in pursuit, angry with himself for having handled the situation so badly.

'Daniel!' Hilary shouted.

He halted and turned. She had dismounted and was offering him her reins. 'Take Dusty. You'll never catch her on foot.'

Daniel wavered, looking after the fleeing girl, and as he did so, Katya reached a fork in the track ahead and swung left, immediately dipping out of sight.

'No – second thoughts, leave Dusty,' Hilary told him. 'That track doubles back down the valley. If you go down the hill, you might just get there before her, but be careful, it's horribly steep.'

Daniel looked to where she was pointing and, closing his mind to the risk, set off down the one-in-three slope at breakneck speed, leaping and sliding in equal measure. Once he'd started his descent, having a change of heart wasn't an option, for his momentum carried him downwards, faster and faster, until it was difficult to move his legs quickly enough to keep them underneath him.

Eventually the inevitable happened. When he was perhaps three-quarters of the way to the valley bottom, Daniel's foot skidded on a hidden tree root and he pitched sideways, rolling and bouncing through a kaleidoscope of tree trunks, brambles and leaf mould towards the stream, where it wound through the trees, some 40 feet below.

The track came as something of a surprise. Hidden from above by an overhang, Daniel didn't actually see it until he hit the gravel with his shoulder, rolled and landed on his back.

His timing couldn't have been better.

Katya was less than 20 feet away and Daniel's abrupt and unheralded arrival startled her pony into swerving violently. Competent rider though she might have been, Katya was thrown completely off-balance and ended up hanging precariously over one side of the animal's neck.

Within moments Daniel was on his feet and at the pony's head. He dragged the girl off it, clamping an arm round her waist to keep her close, and thoroughly alarmed, the pony backed away, head held high.

Katya fought like a wildcat and was tremendously strong. It was as much as Daniel could do to hang on to her, winded as he was. One small booted foot scraped painfully down his shin and stamped on his instep; her arms flailed – elbows trying to land blows to his ribs; and she even tried head-butting him, but he'd had too much experience to be caught that way.

'Katy! Katya! Stop it. I want to help you,' he gasped.

'No, no! Let me go! Let me go!' she yelled, kicking him again.

'For God's sake, listen! I know about Elena.'

'No! No! No! Please let me go! Please.' Suddenly Katya stopped struggling and began to sob.

Relieved but not wholly trusting the swift change, Daniel maintained his grip on her and was surprised by the appearance of a black and white collie, which jumped up, putting its front paws on his leg and barking.

The next moment something hit Daniel hard across the shoulders and a male voice thundered, 'Leave that girl alone! D'you hear me? Leave her alone, you pervert!'

The man punctuated each phrase with another blow, one of which caught Daniel across the side of the head, making his ears ring.

'For Christ's sake, man! Get off me!' Daniel exclaimed. 'It's not what you think . . .'

But at the prospect of help, Katya cried out again and the man with the stick stepped up his attack. When one of his blows caught Daniel on the elbow, the shock loosened his hold for a moment, sending paralysing pins and needles shooting along his forearm. A moment was all the girl needed. With a supreme effort she wrenched herself free and, without waiting to thank her saviour, ran off down the track.

Free, in turn, to defend himself, Daniel lost no time in twisting the knot-headed walking stick from the grasp of the military-looking gentleman who'd wielded it with such enthusiasm and throwing it as hard as he could up the track.

'You bloody interfering idiot!' he snarled through his teeth, before setting off in pursuit of the girl, who, seeing more walkers ahead, turned off the path, down towards the stream in the bottom of the valley.

Ignoring the blustering expostulations of the military man, Daniel followed.

The slope below the track was if anything even steeper than above, littered with fallen timber and slippery with moss. Forced to slow up, Daniel lost his footing again and again, whereas the girl seemed as sure-footed as a mountain goat.

Within moments she was at the overhanging edge of the deep rocky gully through which the stream flowed, some 20 feet below. She followed the bank until she arrived at a place where the gully was bridged by a fallen silver birch and then, glancing back at Daniel struggling in her wake, stepped on to the tree, paused to test its stability and ran lightly across.

Arriving at the same point, some moments later, Daniel knew the chase was over. The trunk of the birch was barely 6 inches in diameter, crooked and mossy in places, and spanned a good 15 feet with no handholds. Just looking at the drop to the rocky streambed below made a cold sweat break out on his body and he backed away, cursing, as Katya disappeared into the trees on the other side.

'I just want to help you!' he shouted after her.

There was no reply. She had gone.

FOUR

There was no sign of the man with the walking stick when Daniel climbed wearily back on to the track, but Hilary had arrived, having followed the track down, and she'd caught Katya's loose pony.

'No luck?' she asked, although the answer was rather self-evident.

'I'd have been OK if Colonel Blimp hadn't decided to wade in, waving his stick about,' Daniel said, and told her what had happened.

'Major Clapford,' she said, when he'd finished. 'War hero, pillar of the community and general pain in the backside. I saw him making off with his dog as I rode up. Not a good man to cross.'

'Bloody lethal with that stick of his,' Daniel agreed, rubbing a sore place on his elbow.

'Still, you can hardly blame him, I suppose. You'd probably have done the same if you saw someone apparently assaulting a young girl.'

Daniel sighed. 'Yeah, you're right.'

'So, what now?'

'I guess I'd better get back to work while I still have a job.' Daniel looked up the slope down which he had recently and in-elegantly travelled. 'I'm not sure I've got the energy to climb back up there. Is there another way back to the village apart from going all the way round?'

Hilary gestured to Katya's pony, which was standing calmly enough now, its thickish coat swirled and damp with sweat. 'Hop on and I'll take you the short way.'

Daniel regarded the pony doubtfully. 'I wouldn't be too heavy?'

She laughed. 'Tough as old boots, these Dartmoor ponies. He'd carry your weight all day without any problem. Come on, climb on board or I'll start to think you're chicken!'

When Daniel parted company with Hilary in the car park of the White Buck a quarter of an hour later, it was with the under-standing that if Kat should turn up at the stables again, she would lose no time in calling him, but neither of them held out much hope.

The lorry was just as he'd left it, Taz standing up on the front seat and waving his tail at Daniel's return.

'Are you going to move that bloody thing? This isn't a public car park, you know,' a voice informed him testily as he reached for the handle to the cab door.

Daniel turned to see a stocky, balding man standing in the back doorway of the pub. 'I know, I'm sorry. It was an emergency and there's not many places you can park something this size. What do I owe you?'

The man shook his head. 'Just shift it, OK? Next time I'll have it clamped.'

'OK, thanks.' Daniel waved a hand and made to climb into the cab. In his jacket pocket his phone was vibrating silently – no prizes for guessing who that would be. He must already be at least an hour late for his next drop and Bowden would be on his case in a big way.

'Move over, Taz!' He pulled himself into the lorry, fending off an enthusiastic welcome from the dog. Fishing out his mobile, he glanced at the display. It *was* Bowden, but before he could answer it, his attention was caught by a movement in his door mirror, and he bent to look more closely, hardly believing his eyes.

Katya was standing at the rear corner of the lorry, one hand on the bodywork, looking uncertainly towards the front.

Daniel froze, feeling a bit like a twitcher who's found a rare finch nesting in his window box. What on earth was she doing here, after fighting like a wildcat to get away from him less than half an hour before?

There was no doubt in his mind that she connected him with the lorry, Hilary had told him that, so it could only mean that she had decided to hear him out after all.

Very carefully he opened the cab door and leaned out, making his movements soft and slow, as if she were a flighty horse.

Katya held her ground, her dark eyes wide with apprehension, but she glanced behind her as if suspecting him of having an accomplice who might even now be creeping up to cut off her escape.

Daniel stayed in the cab, letting her make the first move, and eventually she did, edging forward alongside the lorry until she was only a matter of feet away. She was boyishly slim, and without her riding hat he could see that her dark hair had been very inexpertly cut. He imagined she had probably done it herself.

'I don't want to hurt you, Katya,' he said softly. 'I just want to help you.'

'Why?'

The question caught Daniel on the hop slightly. Why indeed? How to explain to someone with her likely background that his interest was purely philanthropic? He had an idea the concept would be entirely alien to her, but he had no other ready excuse.

'Elena is your sister, right?' he asked, hedging slightly.

Katya nodded slowly, and again glanced over her shoulder.

'I was there the day you ran away. The man – Reynolds, he said his name was – called me to help track you down. He said he was your father . . .'

'His name isn't Reynolds, it's Patrescu,' she said. 'I saw you on the moor with the dog. Why did you help him? Who are you?'

'I thought I was doing the right thing,' Daniel told her. 'He said you were lost. It wasn't until I saw how scared your sister was that I began to wonder why you'd really run away.'

'I had to leave Elena. I didn't want to, but she couldn't run any more. I thought if I got away, I could maybe go back for her, but . . .'

'But?' Daniel prompted.

'Now I don't know how I will do it. I don't even know where she is for sure.' Her eyes filled with tears, which she wiped away with an impatient hand. 'He – my father – will be looking for me. He won't give up.'

'If he's your father, why are you running from him?'

Katya's eyes dropped for a moment – the ridiculously long lashes sweeping her cheeks. 'He took us from our mother – stole us. He means to take us back to Romania, but we don't want to go.'

'And where is your mother?'

'She's in London.'

'Is that where you live?'

She nodded, her eyes dipping again briefly.

'And the other man, who is he?'

Her expression hardened. 'His name is Anghel. He works for my father. He is a brute.'

'What does your father do?'

Katya's eyes flickered up and away. She shrugged. 'I don't know. He left us when Elena was a baby. Will you really help me?'

'If I can, but you should really go to the police. They could do much more than me.'

'No!' Her reply was sharp and immediate, and she backed away a step or two, apparently afraid that Daniel was about to try and capture her and deliver her to the authorities himself. 'You can't tell them!'

'It's all right. Calm down. I won't do anything you don't want me to, but please believe me, it would be the best thing to do.'

'No. There would be trouble. You must promise you won't tell.'

'Trouble for your father, yes, but not for you,' Daniel assured her. 'You've done nothing wrong.'

She shook her head. 'You don't understand. We don't have our papers – he took them.'

'What papers?'

'Our passports.'

'But if you're not trying to leave the country, you don't need them,' Daniel pointed out.

'Please – you don't understand . . . He'll find out and I'll never see Elena again.'

She looked on the verge of bolting and he made a swift decision.

'All right. I'll do what I can and we won't tell the police unless you say so, OK?'

Before she could answer, a stentorian voice sounded from the doorway of the pub. 'Are you still here?'

'Just going.' Daniel raised a hand, seeing Katya shrink back against the side of the lorry, even though she hadn't been in the landlord's line of sight.

The man had the look of someone who was prepared to wait, so Daniel turned to the girl. 'I have to move the lorry. Will you get in?'

Apparently Katya wasn't yet ready to trust him that far, or maybe it was the dog she didn't trust, for again came the small shake of her head.

'OK. Go back to Hilary's. I'll let her know you're coming and I'll come there myself as soon as I can. This evening, maybe.'

'She won't be mad at me?'

'She'll be fine. Trust me.'

Under the publican's glare, Daniel started the lorry and, with a cheery wave of his hand, vacated the car park. Almost immediately his mobile began vibrating, and as soon as he was able, he pulled over to the side of the road and answered it.

It was Bowden, at first concerned that his driver had had an accident or a breakdown, and then rather less than happy when Daniel admitted that he had taken time out for non-TFS business.

'I've had Sedgefield Poultry Farm bending my bloody ear for the past hour, wanting to know where the hell you've got to, and I had to make up some story about a breakdown. Now I've just had a call from the kennels, worried that they won't have enough food for this evening, and you're off playing at being a bloody detective! I know you were worried about the girl, Daniel, but not on my time, OK?'

'Yeah, sorry, Boss. Won't happen again.'

Would Katya go to Hilary's? he wondered, lending half an ear to Bowden. Or would her distrust get the better of her again?

'So where are you now?' the TFS boss demanded.

'Just leaving Goats Tor,' Daniel said, seeing a man looking over his garden wall two or three houses along the road and recognizing the upright figure of Major Clapford. He was regarding the idling lorry with disfavour.

'Bloody miles away!' Bowden said disgustedly. 'Well, you'd better cut along to the kennels first, then. It's closer to where you are than the chicken farm. I'll ring them and let them know you're on your way. Be there in what? Half an hour?'

'Yeah, no problem.'

Daniel had cause to regret his easy confidence fifteen minutes later when he glanced in his door mirror and saw a police car hovering near the offside rear corner of the lorry, its lights flashing an unmistakable request for him to pull over.

'Oh bloody hell!' Daniel grumbled, seeking out a pull-in large enough to accommodate the HGV and hoping against hope that the patrol car had spotted a faulty light or something of the sort. He had no anxieties that there was anything seriously wrong with the lorry – Bowden was meticulous in the upkeep of his small fleet – but even an impromptu spot check would take time and would almost certainly include a check on his own details.

As he drew in to the side, the patrol car passed him and stopped, nose-in to the hedge, effectively blocking any attempt on his part to leave, unless he took the car with him. Daniel frowned. That was overkill, he felt. Sighing deeply, he climbed down from the cab and awaited developments.

There were two officers: one young, keen, eyes darting everywhere, the other overweight and fiftyish. The older one looked world-weary and was probably counting the days to retirement, Daniel guessed, watching him approach with a splay-footed, heel-scraping walk, shrugging himself into his fluorescent jacket as he did so.

'Thank you for stopping,' he said, coming to a halt in front of Daniel. 'Sergeant Naylor.'

'And?' Daniel asked, looking enquiringly after the younger officer, who'd gone on a tour of inspection around the lorry.

'Oh, Constable Innes. And you are?'

'Daniel Whelan. Is there a problem with the lorry?'

'Do you have your driver's licence with you, Mr Whelan?'

Daniel took his wallet from an inside pocket, found the plastic card and handed it over. The sergeant squinted at it and then took a pair of glasses from his pocket and put them on – a little self-consciously, Daniel thought, as though they were new to him. His eyes sorted he inspected the licence, looking at Daniel to check the likeness.

'Are you the owner of the vehicle?'

'No. It's owned by TFS. I'm employed as a driver. Is there a problem with the lorry?' he repeated.

'Er, no, that's just routine.' Naylor handed his licence back and then took off his cap to scratch his balding head. 'Actually, we're investigating a complaint by a member of the public concerning an alleged assault on a young woman. This person has identified you as the alleged attacker, Mr Whelan.'

'By name?'

'Er, no, but he observed you getting into this lorry.'

Major Clapford. Damn the man!

'Is that your dog?' Naylor asked, gesturing up at the cab window.

Taz was staring down at them, quite plainly excited by the uniforms and the association with his past working life.

'Yes, it is. Look, your informant misunderstood what he was seeing. The girl is a friend of mine. We'd had a bit of a tiff – you know how it is – and I was trying to calm her down. I've spoken to her since and we've sorted it all out. Everything's fine.'

'I'm afraid that's not quite the story that we were told, Mr

Whelan. The gentleman says you pulled her from her horse and she was screaming for help. When he tried to lend assistance, however, you turned on him with some violence. It's a very serious allegation, and I'm afraid I shall have to ask you to accompany us to the station while we look into it.'

Daniel rolled his eyes heavenwards. 'Please, Sergeant. There's truly nothing to look into. Major Clapford – I assume he's your informant – has blown it all way out of proportion. The girl is fine. I told you, we've talked it over.'

'So I assume you'd be happy for us to talk to her as well. And her name is . . . ?' He waited, pen poised.

From the start of the conversation Daniel had been anticipating that very question, and knew that with his refusal to answer it, his fate would be sealed.

'I'm sorry, I can't tell you. I'm not going to drag her into all this.'

'I'm afraid you have little choice.'

Daniel shook his head. 'No, I'm sorry.'

'Then *I'm* sorry, but I shall have to insist that you come down to the station.' He looked up questioningly as PC Innes appeared, having circumnavigated the lorry.

The younger man shook his slightly gingery head. 'Everything appears to be in order.'

Daniel fancied he looked disappointed.

'Right. Well, Mr Whelan will be coming with us,' Naylor said.

Daniel didn't argue. If he kicked up, they'd formally arrest him. All he'd accomplish would be to put their backs up and make them sure he had something to hide. As indeed he did, he reflected soberly.

'I'll need to phone my boss first,' he told Naylor. 'He won't want the lorry sat here all afternoon.'

'You can phone him from the station.'

'I'll phone him now.' Daniel got his phone out. It was a call he didn't relish, following as closely as it did on the last one.

'No one's going to nick it with that dog in there,' the sergeant reasoned.

'I'm not leaving him here for hours, and anyway, he can't guard the trailer if he's in the cab,' Daniel pointed out. 'Besides, we've got customers waiting and I'm late already. I hope this isn't going to take long.'

He knew, even as he said it, that it was a forlorn hope. They would be in no hurry. His irate employer and customers meant nothing to them.

'No reason it should, if you cooperate.'

Daniel keyed in Bowden's number.

Yelverton Police Station was more of a police house than a station, and the interview room might well have started life as a broom cupboard, Daniel thought, as he squeezed into a seat at the small wooden table. Lit by a single strip light and one high barred window in the end wall, it had discoloured cream walls and quarry tiles on the floor. It was a world away from its counterpart at Bristol Met.

At the back of the station, adjacent to a tarmac parking area, was a small wooden tool shed that was currently doing duty as a kennel for Taz.

The interview progressed satisfactorily to begin with, Daniel repeating his story of tempers flaring between friends and pointing out that in the absence of the alleged victim bent on pressing charges, they really hadn't got a case.

Ah, but Major Clapford might yet decide to press charges in relation to the assault on himself, Daniel was told.

'Oh, I don't imagine he'll do that,' he replied confidently. 'I think any jury would consider that taking a walking stick away from a man who is repeatedly using it to hit you is totally justifiable self-defence, don't you?'

'You're saying *he* hit *you*?' Naylor sounded uncertain for the first time that afternoon.

'At least half a dozen times, and I'm sure I've got the bruises to prove it.' His right elbow was indeed quite tender.

'He didn't tell us that.'

'Well, there's a surprise.'

'Were there any witnesses who could back your story up?'

Briefly Daniel thought of Hilary, but he didn't want to drag her into the affair if he could help it.

'Not that I know of,' he said.

'Would you mind if we took a look at the alleged injuries?'

Daniel did mind, but if it meant he'd get away sooner, it was a sacrifice worth making.

'I suppose so,' he said reluctantly, beginning to push up the right sleeve of his jumper.

The bruise on his elbow didn't let him down. Clapford's stick had caught an especially sensitive spot and the joint sported an egg-like swelling of impressive and colourful dimensions. Even Daniel was impressed: he didn't normally bruise easily and it was better than he could have hoped for.

There was a lengthy delay while Naylor called the police surgeon, who inspected the bruise, pronounced it recent and took a photograph for good measure.

'Are there any others?'

Daniel shrugged. 'One or two maybe, but that's the worst.' After a decade of tough policing his torso bore many scars that he didn't want to have to explain.

'A bruise on the elbow can be caused in a number of ways,' the surgeon observed. 'Multiple contusions, however, are a lot more interesting.'

'But I don't want to take this any further,' Daniel told him.

Just then they were interrupted by a WPC.

'Can I have a word, sir?' Although she addressed her request to Naylor, her eyes lingered on Daniel, and he remembered her as being behind the desk when he had been brought in. She'd given him a long look then too, but although he didn't kid himself that her interest was of a flattering nature, he'd searched his memory and couldn't recall having met her before.

When Naylor returned, Daniel could tell at once, just by the look on his face, that he was big with news.

'Well, well, Mr Whelan. You are a man of surprises, aren't you?' he declared.

Daniel's heart sank. It looked as though, somehow, the sergeant had found out about his past.

By the time Daniel finally emerged from the police station it was gone six o'clock and dark. He turned the collar of his leather jacket against the brisk northeasterly that had sprung up during his stay and followed PC Innes round to the back of the building to collect Taz, using his phone's index to dial his boss as he did so.

Bowden answered immediately.

'Fred . . . Look, I'm afraid I'm still in Yelverton. They've only just finished with me.'

'Are you all right? Not in any trouble, I mean?' Bowden sounded a lot calmer than he had earlier, for which Daniel was relieved.

'No, we got it all sorted out. What happened about the lorry?'

'I called Figgy in and he's finished your round for you, but he hasn't washed the lorry, so there's that to do.'

'No problem.'

'Had to promise him time and a half, so you owe us both. He's left my old pick-up in the lay-by with the keys under the bonnet, so if you could cut along there and bring it back – unless you've got anything else planned, that is?'

'Yeah, sure,' Daniel said, ignoring the sarcastic postscript. 'OK. See you later.' He slipped the catch on the tool-shed door and caught Taz's collar as he pushed forward, tail waving wildly, ecstatic to see him after too many hours spent alone.

'Yeah, well, I'm up to my neck in bloody paperwork, so I shall probably still be here,' Bowden grumbled.

Daniel severed the connection thinking, not for the first time, that he could have done a lot worse in his employer, and prepared to call a taxi.

Daniel drove into the depot just as Bowden was locking his office door, and while Daniel washed the lorry down under the security floodlights, he requested a complete run-down of the day's events. With the exception of the final, uncomfortable part of his session at the police station, Daniel obliged and it was Fred Bowden's expressed opinion that he should have turned the whole matter over to the police, however much Katya protested.

'But I've given her my word,' Daniel pointed out. 'It was the only way I could get her to tell me anything at all.'

'So what *are* you going to do?'

'I suppose try and find the house where they were being held. I've got a rough idea where it might be and I'm hoping Katya will recognize it, if I can get her somewhere near.'

'You're certain she's gone back to this Hilary what's-her-name?'

'She has. I spoke to Hilary on the phone. Kat turned up just before it got dark. I'm going over there in a minute to see if I can get her to open up any more.'

'You don't think she's told you everything, then?'

'I think most of what she's told me is lies,' Daniel said bluntly. 'But only because she's scared. I have to convince her to trust me, which isn't going to be easy.'

He coiled the pressure hose back on to its bracket and turned to find Bowden looking at him quizzically.

'If she's so scared, doesn't it occur to you that perhaps *you* should be a little wary too? Do you really know what you're getting yourself into?'

'I think I've got a pretty good idea,' Daniel told him. 'And believe me, I intend being very careful indeed.'

It was a little after eight when Daniel arrived at Briars Hill Farm, a rather forbidding stone house that stood adjacent to the stable yard of Hilary McEwen-Smith's trekking centre.

Austere it might appear from the outside, but the inside had the kind of lived-in, homely shabbiness that he had grown up with and which couldn't have been further from the pristine cream carpets and smoked-glass coffee tables of his marital home.

Hilary welcomed Daniel like the old friend he was supposed to be, and led the way to the kitchen, which seemed to be dominated by the sleeping arrangements of Hilary's three dogs and two tabby cats.

A big red Aga stood in a fireplace at one end of the room, its chrome rail hung with an assortment of towels, socks and a sheepskin saddle pad. On a shelf above, a number of ornamental frogs vied for room with books, magazines and photographs of ponies, people and dogs.

In the centre of the room stood a table covered with a thick, fringed maroon cloth, though part of it was invisible under a pile of folded sweatshirts and horse blankets.

A ceramic teapot stood on a mat, and Katya was standing behind the table, cradling a mug and regarding Daniel with anxious eyes. She was wearing a grey cotton sweatshirt that sported a colourful picture of a Native American chief, and a pair of faded hipster jeans that might have been painted on. The sweatshirt was a couple of sizes too big and almost certainly belonged to Hilary, Daniel thought; the jeans just as certainly didn't.

'Leo the lurcher, Heidi the greyhound and Daisy the whippet – from largest down,' Hilary said, introducing the dogs. 'And the cats are Eric and Ernie. Would you like a cup of tea? Why don't you bring your dog in? It's not very warm in the car for him.'

'Oh, he's got a good thick coat,' Daniel said.

'All the same, it seems a shame. Mine won't mind in the least – as long as he doesn't chase the cats.'

'No, he won't do that,' Daniel assured her, and true to his

word, the German shepherd totally ignored everyone, helping himself to a drink at the stone water bowl and then flopping down half under the table by his master's chair.

Hilary seemed to take it as read that Daniel would stay for a meal and presently served up a homemade chilli of huge proportions.

'I'm the Queen of Stews and Casseroles,' Hilary claimed, ladling meat and rice on to large plates. 'I like to chuck the ingredients into a pot and leave it to do its thing while I do mine. That way it's ready whenever I am.'

She had changed from jodhpurs into a pair of tracksuit bottoms, and Daniel found her down-to-earthness very easy company. So, too, it seemed, did Katya, who visibly relaxed as the evening progressed, although not to the extent of entering the conversation.

'So, how long have you lived in England, Katya?' Daniel asked casually, as they drank coffee after the meal. 'You still have a very strong accent.'

'Please to call me Kat,' she said, looking down at the mug between her cupped hands.

'But you were born in Romania, right?' Daniel tried again.

'Yes. My mother brings us here about four years ago.'

'Against your father's wishes?' Hilary asked.

'He didn't know at first. He didn't live with us. He's a bad man and we are all scared of him.'

Hilary put out a hand in swift sympathy to cover Kat's, and the girl's face was transformed by a shy smile of gratitude.

Daniel hadn't shared his reservations about Kat's story with the older woman. Time enough when he could prove the girl was lying. For now, she deserved the benefit of the doubt.

'And he snatched you in London, you said. What happened?'

'Elena and I were walking to the shop for milk and a car stops beside us. The driver asks us the way, but when we go closer, a man gets out of the back and grabs my sister. It is my father. He pulls her into the car and says if I don't go too, I'll never see her again.' Tears shone in her eyes. 'He had his hand over her mouth and she was very frightened. I got in the car. I had no choice. We are very close, Elena and me.'

'And you didn't think it might be better to get away. To call the police? To tell your mother?' Daniel tried to keep any disbelief out of his voice. 'Does she know where you are now? Have you called her since you escaped?'

Katya shook her head, her gaze dropping. 'She doesn't have a telephone.'

Hilary was horrified. 'But surely there's someone – a neighbour, perhaps? She must be out of her mind with worry.'

'It is a place with not many telephones, I think. People are poor.'

'But we must do something!' Hilary turned to Daniel. 'Someone must be told. The police, surely, could find Katya's mother . . .'

'No! No police!' Katya also looked to Daniel beseechingly. 'You promised!'

'But your mother, my dear!' Hilary was deeply concerned.

'She will guess who's taken us. She was always afraid he would come.'

'But they could help you find your sister.'

'Daniel is going to help me?' The statement lifted into a question at the end, and her eyes pleaded with him.

'I said I'd try,' Daniel agreed cautiously.

'But I don't understand . . .' Hilary looked at him, quite plainly bewildered, and he responded with a lowering of his brows and a slight shake of his head. Thankfully, she read his meaning and merely shrugged. 'Oh well. If you know what you're doing.'

'I hope so. But we need to decide what to do next, don't we, Kat? You say you've no idea where your sister is. Don't you remember anything at all about the place?'

Katya shook her head helplessly. 'No, not really. It is dark when we are taken there and we aren't allowed outside. When we escape, we run really fast into the trees at the back and then across the moor.'

'How *did* you escape?' Hilary asked.

'We climb out of a window on to the roof and then down a tree,' Kat replied, as if it were the most natural thing.

'Oh, of course,' Hilary murmured.

'So you wouldn't recognize the house at all?' Daniel persisted. 'What about the garden? What could you see from the windows? Do you think you would recognize it if we drove by?'

Katya thought hard. 'There are gates. Big ones with stone posts and . . .' she made an indeterminate movement with her hands as she struggled to find the word she wanted '. . . circles?'

'Spheres?' Hilary suggested. 'Like a ball?'

'Yes.' Katya nodded eagerly. 'A ball on top.'

'Well, that's something to look out for,' Daniel said. He told them about his attempt to retrace the girls' steps from Stack Bridge.

'Did you do that this afternoon?' Hilary asked. 'I thought you were working.'

'No, at the weekend. Actually, I spent this afternoon trying to convince the boys from the local nick that I wasn't attempting to ravish a young girl in the woods earlier. Your friend the major didn't waste any time.'

'Oh dear. What did you tell them?' It was Hilary who asked, but Daniel was aware that Katya was watching him like a hawk.

'I said that the young girl and I were friends and everything was fine. They were very keen to speak to Kat – to check out my story – but as they hadn't a clue who she was, they were on a hiding to nothing.'

'So they let you go?'

'Eventually. After we'd dealt with the major's allegation of assault.'

'But *he* hit *you*, didn't he?' Hilary frowned.

'Mm. That's what I told them. It's all right now, but it took a ridiculous amount of time to sort out. And speaking of time . . .' He looked at his watch. 'I've got an early start tomorrow, so I'd better be on my way. I don't think the boss would be too pleased if I turned up late after today's fiasco.'

'But when will we look for Elena?' Katya wanted to know.

'If I can wangle an early finish tomorrow, we'll try then, but I'm not making any promises.'

Daniel got to his feet and immediately Taz was by his side, looking up expectantly.

'I'll see you out,' Hilary offered, pushing her chair back and following him to the kitchen door and down the long, narrow hallway.

Moments later, they both stepped out into the night and Hilary closed the door behind them, saying quietly, 'Don't you believe her story?'

'Not completely.'

'But why would she lie?'

'She's terrified and she wants my help. She thinks the truth might scare me off.'

'And do you know what the truth is?'

'I've got a good idea.'

'Are you going to share it with me?'

'Not just yet.'

Hilary was looking at him a little oddly in the light from the porch. 'You haven't always been a delivery driver, have you, Daniel Whelan?'

'And what makes you say that, Mrs McEwen-Smith?'

'Oh, there's more about you than that. A certain something I can't put my finger on, but I'm pretty sure you'd be climbing the walls after a few months stuck in a cab.'

'Actually, you'd be surprised how exciting it can be. Only the other week the sat nav took me up a dead-end lane and I had to back the whole way out.'

'Keep taking the Valium,' she said wryly.

'I've got a repeat prescription,' he assured her. 'By the way, I don't think you need fret too much about Katya's anxious mother.'

'You don't think she's worried?'

'I think it's more than likely she's still in Romania and knows nothing about all this. Look, thanks for letting Kat stay here. I don't think you'll have any trouble as long as she keeps a low profile, but if you're worried about anything at all, just ring me. My phone's always on.'

'You think her father is still looking for her?'

'I'd be very surprised if he wasn't, but there's no reason for him to come here.' Daniel leaned forward and kissed her on the cheek. 'You're a trooper, you know? See you in a day or two.'

He turned towards the car, and with a shake of her head and a slight smile, Hilary went back into the house.

FIVE

D aniel and Kat found the house with the stone gateposts within a very few minutes of the start of their search.

Two impressive stone pillars of 8 feet or more, mottled with lichen and each topped with a 12-inch sphere, formed a gateway that was flanked by laurel hedges half as tall again. Between them, a pair of elaborate wrought-iron gates stood open, their black paint peeling slightly. A brass nameplate identified the property as Moorside House.

Daniel slowed the Mercedes just long enough for Kat to confirm that they were indeed the posts she'd seen from inside the house, and then drove on by.

'What are you doing?' she exclaimed. 'That *is* the house, I'm sure.'

'And what do you propose we do? Ring the doorbell and demand to see your sister?' Daniel kept driving.

'But we *must* do something!'

'We will. We'll find somewhere quiet to stop and sort out what we're going to do next. Charging in at this stage would be disastrous.'

Kat said no more, apparently accepting the sense in his words, and shortly afterwards, Daniel turned into a side lane, found a field gateway and stopped the Mercedes.

Reaching into the back of the car, he retrieved a holdall from which he took a baseball cap, a pair of shades and his grey hoodie. He held them out towards Kat. 'Here, put these on.'

She made no move to take them, merely glancing at them and then across at Daniel.

'Come on,' he said with a touch of impatience. 'If it is the right house, the last thing we want is for you to be recognized. You look pretty boyish already with your hair cut short like that, we might as well go the whole hog.'

She frowned. 'The whole . . . ?'

'Hog. Complete the look. Finish the job.'

Dipping into the bag once more, he produced a navy-blue boiler suit and a bag containing a number of embroidered patches. Getting out of the car, he stepped into the overalls, zipped them up and then slid back behind the wheel.

Katya had put the hoodie on, its size swamping her slim figure, and was sifting through the patches.

'What are all these?'

'These,' Daniel said, lifting them from her grasp, 'are my passports to all sorts of places.'

He could see that she still didn't understand and picked out one of the patches, fixing it with its Velcro pad to the breast pocket of the overalls. Then, putting on a cockney accent, he said cheerfully, 'Good afternoon, love. Come to look at your boiler. Doing a spot check on carbon-monoxide emissions. Won't take a minute and won't cost you anything. You don't get much for free these days, do you?'

Changing the patch for another and his accent for a Scouse one, he said, 'Afternoon, sir. Telephone engineer. Had reports of an intermittent fault on the line. Have you had any trouble? No? Well, I'll just take a quick look while I'm here, shall I?

'That's a good one because you can lift a few numbers from the caller display if they don't watch too closely,' he added. 'See who's been ringing them.'

Katya was frowning again. 'You've done this before.'

'Once or twice.'

'I don't understand. Who *are* you?'

'I'm probably your only hope of getting your sister back, if you really *won't* tell the police,' Daniel said, sidestepping the question. 'Why won't you? What are you so afraid of?'

Katya stared at her hands, and after looking at her troubled profile for a long moment, Daniel sighed.

'All right. Put the cap and shades on and let's get going. And when we get there, you stay in the car, d'you hear me? Whatever happens. This is just a fact-finding exercise, so don't get any ideas about launching a one-woman rescue mission, whatever or *who*ever you might see, OK?'

Katya nodded, her eyes still downcast, but Daniel wasn't satisfied. She had a habit of avoiding his gaze when she was lying.

'Katya, look at me and promise.'

Her head came up. 'All right! I promise,' she said, her manner so much that of a sulky teenager that he was reminded she *was* only fifteen.

Daniel made another sortie into the holdall and came up with a grey beanie and a small plastic case from which he took two golden-coloured rings. Moments later, with the aid of the rear-view mirror, he wore one ring in his ear and the other apparently through the left side of his upper lip.

Katya's eyes were growing rounder by the minute. 'Is that . . . ?'

'The earring is real; the other's fake, and bloody uncomfortable, too, but facial piercings are great. People can't take their eyes off them – it's all they tend to remember.'

He pushed his hair back off his face and pulled the beanie on low over his eyes, assuming a 'whatever' attitude. Putting a stick of chewing gum in his mouth, he turned to Kat.

'What are you staring at?' he demanded, and she shook her head in disbelief.

'I wouldn't know you!'

'Well, that's the general idea,' he said with a broad wink. 'Right, we're ready to go.'

*   *   *

Swinging the old Mercedes between the gates of Moorside House, Daniel felt a quickening of awareness that was familiar from his police days. The slight fizz of nervous excitement sharpened all his senses, and suddenly he realized how much he'd missed it.

The house was a large square structure built of red brick and stone, with a shallow, slate-tiled roof just visible above an ornamental stone parapet. Pillars framed the white-painted front door, which was approached via three steps up from the gravelled drive.

Daniel swung the car left-handed round an island bed of overgrown shrubs and parked facing back the way they'd come. With this between the front door and the car, hopefully no one would notice Katya, as long as she stayed put, and he liked to have a clear run to the gate. You could never be too careful.

'OK. Stay there,' he told her as he cut the engine. He reached behind the seat for a slim, black plastic case. 'Whatever happens, you don't leave the car, right?'

Katya nodded. She looked at the case. 'What are you going to do?'

'I don't know for sure. I'd like to get a look inside, but I'll have to play it by ear – er, see how it goes,' he amended quickly.

'What if you see Elena?'

'I very much doubt that I will,' Daniel said, getting out of the car. 'Won't be long.'

He slammed the door and headed across the gravel, swinging the black tool case and whistling jauntily, in case there were eyes behind one of the many windowpanes.

The front of the porch was overgrown with some kind of creeper and the inside had been a spider's larder for some time. Without looking directly at it, Daniel noticed the still, unblinking eye of a lens high up in a cobwebby corner, and there was a spyhole in the centre of the door.

Beside the button for the doorbell was a speaker unit, and next to that a brass plate announced that the premises were home to Hot Images Photographic Studio. Interesting.

Daniel prodded the button, and after a moment or two, a light came on in the porch and a voice asked what he wanted. Affecting not to hear, he turned his back on the door, put his tool case on the step and stuck his hands in his pockets, looking out over the drive and chewing his gum. It was gone five and the light was fading.

The question was repeated and Daniel began to whistle cheerfully. For the benefit of the CCTV, he then looked at his watch and turned to prod the button again.

The voice became decidedly testy and after a short interlude the door was opened by the morose individual whom Reynolds had claimed to be his brother, and whom Kat had subsequently identified as Anghel. Tall, olive-skinned, black hair and eyes, annoyance writ large.

'What do you want?' he demanded without preamble. His English was heavily accented and in the house doorway he seemed much larger than Daniel had remembered.

'Ah, you *are* there,' Daniel observed, adopting a Bristolian brogue. He took a notebook from his pocket and flipped a couple of pages. 'Mr Patrescu, would it be?'

'He's not here,' the Romanian said, half closing the door.

'Well, I don't want *him*, as such,' Daniel admitted. 'It's your telephone, actually. My name's Johnson – I'm an engineer. We've had reports of an intermittent fault on the line in the area and I wanted to check yours was OK. Is it all right for me to come in? It won't take a minute . . .' He pocketed the notebook, picked up the black case and waited expectantly.

The man looked beyond him to where the Merc was parked. 'Where's your van?'

'Garage. Bloody alternator's on the blink.'

'Who's in the car?'

'Work-experience kid,' Daniel said dismissively. 'And that's a bloody joke, that is! I've had 'em before and work's about the last thing they're interested in experiencing, if you ask me. This one's more interested in sending text messages to his mates. Left 'im to it. Quicker on my own. It's no skin off my nose if he wants to waste his life.'

The man was frowning, plainly finding it hard to follow this diatribe, and Daniel took advantage of his bewilderment by taking a step forward and saying, 'So, where's this phone, then?'

After a momentary hesitation, the man stepped back, allowing him to pass. Daniel seized the opportunity with alacrity, finding himself in a spacious cream-painted hallway with several doors leading off it and a gracious sweep of stairs to one side.

'Thanks, mate. And you are . . . ?' He put the case down and took his notebook out once more.

'I work for Mr Patrescu.'

'Yeah, look, mate, I need a name for the records. Have to say who let me in. Regulations, see? Got to dot the "i"s and cross the "t"s.'

The man hesitated, then said, reluctantly, 'Macek. Anghel Macek.'

Daniel scratched his head with the back end of the pen, then started to write. 'So that'll be M-A-T—'

'C,' Macek cut in, spelling it out for him.

'Right. So what kind of photography do you do?' Daniel enquired, chattily. 'Portraits? Glamour? Arty-farty?'

'Why do you ask?'

'Oh, just being nosy – saw the sign outside the door. So, where's your main phone?' He looked from side to side at the closed doors.

'It's in the office. Look, I'm not sure Mr Patrescu . . .'

'I'll be in and out in five – he'll never know,' Daniel said.

'The door is locked.'

'Well, don't you have a key?'

'I . . . It's not . . .'

Macek was clearly in an agony of indecision and Daniel kept up the pressure by saying off-handedly, 'Look, if you're not happy for me to go in there, that's fine. It's all the same to me. Ten-to-one I won't find anything wrong, anyway – they're buggers, these intermittent faults – but if you *have* got a problem, you could lose your Internet connection and then you'll have to call someone out to fix it. I just thought I might save you the hassle – not to mention the expense . . .'

He made as if to head back to the front door. He was talking absolute rubbish, but most people were easily blinded by IT science, and the threat of being offline – even for a short time – in this technologically dependent age, usually induced something approaching a panic attack.

Macek was no exception. 'Wait! No broadband?'

'It's possible. But I'm sure you'd get someone out to reconnect you in a day or two,' Daniel added cheerfully.

While the beleaguered Romanian was weighing up the two evils, an interruption occurred in the shape of a young girl in denim dungarees and a jumper, who appeared running down the green-carpeted stairs.

She was giggling and looking back over her shoulder as if she were being followed. For one disbelieving moment, Daniel thought his luck was in and it was Elena, but as she neared the bottom step and turned to face them, he could see that it wasn't.

Probably a year or two younger than Elena, her colouring was similar but she had a more rounded face and her waist-length dark hair was a riot of curls.

When she saw the two men standing in the hall, she stopped so abruptly that she had to clutch the banister rail to keep her balance, her mouth opening in an almost comical 'o', which was then covered by her hand. Her dark-lashed blue eyes, opening equally wide, were the most beautiful Daniel had ever seen.

Even as the child froze, a voice called, 'Molly, come back!' and a young woman appeared at the turn of the stairs. Taking in the scene with a swift glance, she also stopped.

The Romanian said something sharply in what Daniel assumed was his own tongue and the woman replied in kind, her expression sulky. More striking than beautiful, with olive skin and long, improbably red hair that fell forward, hiding half her face, she wore a long flouncy skirt and looked a little like a Spanish gypsy. With time to study her, Daniel estimated she was probably somewhere in her late twenties.

Macek spoke again and her eyes flashed defiance, but she merely held out her hand to the young girl, who had been eyeing Daniel with the candid interest of the young, her eyelids lowered almost sleepily.

'Molly! Come!'

After one last look at the Romanian, the child turned and went with the young woman, obediently taking the proffered hand.

'Kids, eh?' Daniel commented lightly as the two disappeared from view.

Whether it was because the interruption had unsettled him or whether it was the hovering threat of losing their Internet access, Daniel didn't know, but Macek beckoned him to follow and crossed to one of the closed doors, saying over his shoulder, 'You must be quick.'

'Only take a minute,' Daniel said, moving up quietly behind him. He was assailed by a strong smell of garlic and was near enough to see a scattering of dandruff on the shoulder of the man's black turtleneck. More importantly, he was near enough to see Macek enter a series of numbers into a keypad on the wall next to the door.

There was a faint click as the lock opened and the Romanian turned his head, his face registering surprise and some annoyance at finding Daniel so close.

Daniel smiled. 'After you,' he said politely.

The room they entered had been adapted for use as an office with total disregard for the aesthetics of its Regency past. Boxy black leather furniture sat on bare floorboards and grey metal shelving units stood against the sage-green walls. A bar carrying spotlights had been screwed to the ornately plastered ceiling and Venetian blinds hung in the elegant windows.

A computer desk stood against one wall and it was towards this that Daniel was directed. The surface of the desk was disappointingly uncluttered, carrying only the computer keyboard, a pot of pens, two cardboard files and a phone with speaker unit.

Daniel put down the black case, picked up the receiver and listened briefly. It emitted a low hum, as he'd expected it to, but he nodded slightly for the benefit of his companion and asked when the unit had last been used.

Macek shrugged. 'How would I know?'

'Never mind. It'll be on here,' Daniel said, indicating the phone's display. 'Do you mind?'

He was answered with another shrug, which was academic as Daniel was already bringing up the unit's recent dialling history. Taking his notepad out again, he first made a note of the memorized security code for the office door and then swiftly took down the last four numbers on the display, feeling that any more would be pushing it.

'It is all right, yes? How much longer will you be?' The Romanian's nerves were clearly on edge.

'Nearly done,' Daniel reassured him. 'Just need to check your Internet connection. Couple of minutes, that's all.'

Opening his case, he took out a pair of headphones, which had once belonged on a personal stereo. On one end of the wire he'd fitted a small suction cup, and this he now held against the computer modem. With the earpieces in place he pressed the first of five speed-dial buttons on the phone.

He was in luck. Patrescu had indeed stored his most frequently used numbers. Quickly Daniel scribbled them down, interspersing the figures with forward slashes to disguise them, aware that Macek was now practically hopping from foot to foot. He could sympathise: he wasn't overly keen on being there when Patrescu got back either – especially with the written evidence of his prying in the notebook. He had a feeling Patrescu wouldn't be so easily taken in as Macek had been.

Finally he took off the earphones.

'It is good, yes?' the Romanian asked eagerly.

'No problems at all,' Daniel said, coiling the wire and replacing it in his tool case. With a smile he straightened up. 'All done.'

Sliding thankfully into the car a few moments later, Daniel was relieved to find Kat waiting for him. Part of him had worried that, in spite of her promise, she might have been unable to resist the lure of the house and the possibility of finding her sister.

Tossing the black case on to the back seat, Daniel lost no time in getting underway.

'So did you see Elena?' Kat asked impatiently. 'Why were you so long?'

'No, I'm sorry, I didn't see her. Tell me, Katya, how many sisters do you have?'

'What do you mean?' All at once she was wary.

'I mean I saw two others and neither of them was Elena, so who were they?'

Katya didn't reply, and shooting her a look as he drove, Daniel saw that she was biting her lip.

'Well?' he prompted.

Her head tipped forward. She was still wearing the baseball cap and it shadowed her eyes.

'I don't know.'

'You're lying,' Daniel said, without heat. 'When are you going to start telling me the truth?'

'I . . .' She drew a big breath and sighed. 'It's complicated.'

'Were those girls being held there too? Who are they?'

'I don't know! How do I know who you saw?'

'So there *are* more. How many, Katya?'

Katya looked away out of the side window and didn't reply.

Daniel gave a groan of pure frustration. 'How can I help you if you won't tell me what's going on?' His visit to the house had reinforced his own suspicions about what line of business Patrescu was in, but he wanted to hear it from her.

It would appear today wasn't the day.

Katya remained stubbornly silent, apparently watching the scenery, as they travelled the twenty minutes or so back to Briars Hill. It wasn't until they turned into the driveway to the trekking centre that she spoke.

'When can we go back for Elena?'

'I don't know. I'm not even sure we can.'

'But you promised!'

Daniel parked the car in front of Hilary's forbidding stone

house and turned to look at Kat. With a shock, he saw that she'd been crying. Silently he offered her a handkerchief.

'Look, I said I'd help if I could, but that's before I saw the set-up there. There are cameras everywhere, to say nothing of Macek and Patrescu and quite possibly others that I don't know of.'

'It's only them. I never saw anyone else.'

'But we don't even know where in the house she might be, or even if she's still there.'

'That's why we have to go soon. Before they move her on.'

'On where, Kat?'

'I don't know,' she said helplessly. 'Anywhere. Please, Daniel, we have to go back for her.'

Daniel looked at her, moved – in spite of himself – by the utter desperation in her face.

'And just how do you propose we do it?'

Katya brightened, taking hope from his words. 'We can get in the way I got out.'

The window in the roof? Dear God!

'I don't think so,' Daniel said dryly.

'No, it's easy. You'll see. The tree hangs right over the roof,' she said, dismissing the objection as unimportant.

'Yeah, well, look, before we do anything else, there's a couple of things I need to sort out, so you're going to have to be patient.'

'If you won't help me, I'll go by myself.'

'Don't be stupid!' Daniel said, more sharply than he meant to. 'How would you even get there? And if by some miracle you did get your sister out, where would you go? Don't you think they'd hunt you down like they did last time?'

'I'll think of something,' she said stubbornly. 'If you won't help me . . .'

'That's not what I said. I said I needed time to think. Look, if you try and don't succeed, you'll never see your sister again – I can guarantee that.'

'But we've got to do something . . .'

'We will,' Daniel assured her. 'You just have to trust me.'

'You keep saying that, but I don't even know you!'

'And *I* don't know *you*,' he retorted. 'We're both of us taking a lot on trust. *I'm* telling the truth. Are you?'

Once again Katya's eyes betrayed the answer.

'I trusted Yousef,' she said bitterly.

'Yousef?'

'Patrescu. He said he'd take care of us and I trusted him. He lied.'

That was a departure from her original story. Daniel made no big deal about the inconsistency, saying instead, 'He's not your father, is he?'

Kat shook her head but volunteered no further information.

'Where is your father?'

She shrugged. 'I haven't seen him since I was very young.'

'Well, I'm not Yousef,' Daniel pointed out. 'Come on, this is getting us nowhere. I need to pick up Taz and you need to find Hilary. I'll ring later.'

'You promise?'

Daniel rolled his eyes heavenwards. 'Listen, Kat, if I say I'm going to do something, you can take it as a promise, OK?'

'OK.' Kat smiled shyly. 'Sorry.'

As they got out of the car, the door of the house opened, as if Hilary had been watching and waiting for them to make a move.

'How did you get on? Did you find the house?' she asked as they approached.

'We did. Tell you about it later,' Daniel said. 'Where's my hairy hound?'

'In the boot room. Exactly where you left him,' Hilary said. 'He hasn't moved a muscle. I took him some water and a few biscuits, but he hasn't touched them. He's amazing.'

'Well, I told him to guard my coat,' Daniel said, pleased. He'd never left him on duty for so long before and had half expected him to come bounding out when he heard the Mercedes. 'I'd better go and release him.'

'You'll stay to dinner?'

'I'd love to, but I've got a few things to take care of. A few phone calls to make . . .'

'I have a phone. You can use the one in my office if you want to be private.'

Daniel wavered. 'I'll pay you.'

'You bloody won't!' she exclaimed. 'Next thing I'd be charging you for coffee, or dinner. Don't be ridiculous!'

Ten minutes later, settled in Hilary's office with a mug of tea at hand, Daniel made a start on working through the list of numbers he'd lifted from the telephone at Moorside House. He had no clear idea of what he expected to find, but a major part of police work was gruelling enquiry, trawling through a suspect's every contact in the hope that just one of them – however unlikely – might throw up a vital clue.

On this occasion he struck lucky with the very first call.

He had decided to begin with the numbers listed under Patrescu's speed-dial facility.

The first was a mobile number and it was answered after four or five rings.

'Yeah. Naylor.' The two words were drawled so they became one. In the background, Daniel could hear a hum of voices and laughter that possibly denoted a pub.

'Would that be *Sergeant* Naylor?' It had been no part of his plan to ask questions, but this one burned in his brain. Could it be?

'Yes. Who is this?' Naylor had come sharply to attention now. Daniel said nothing.

'Where did you get this number?' Naylor demanded, but Daniel was not about to give him that information, and when there was no reply, Naylor cut the connection.

Daniel replaced the receiver and sat staring at the wall. It couldn't be by chance that Sergeant Naylor was on Patrescu's list of frequent contacts, and to Daniel, the fact reeked of corruption. Any lingering thoughts of enlisting the help of the local police on Elena's behalf vanished as if they had never been. It was disturbing, for although he personally had had no wish to involve them, and had promised Kat that he wouldn't without her permission, he was realistic enough to know that there might well come a time when their involvement was unavoidable. Now, it seemed even that failsafe was rife with complications.

Glad that he'd withheld the Briars Hill number, Daniel cracked on with the other numbers on his list.

'Tonight? You mean it?'

It was the first time Daniel had seen Katya look truly animated. They were sitting at Hilary's kitchen table waiting for her to dish up a lasagne.

He nodded. 'Well, early tomorrow morning, to be more precise, so you'd better get to bed early and try and get some sleep.'

'I'll never be able to sleep. What time do we leave?'

'About one o'clock, I should think. We don't want to get there while they're still up and about. But I don't want you to get your hopes up. It may be that we can't get in tonight – for whatever reason – and even if we do, it's possible we may not be able to find your sister.'

'No. We will find her,' Katya stated with certainty.

'Are you sure you're doing the right thing?' Hilary asked, scooping the lasagne on to plates. 'It seems awfully risky.'

'No,' Daniel said frankly. 'I have a horrible feeling it might be one of the stupidest things I've ever attempted, but just at the moment, I don't see any option. We will be careful, though.'

'Careful?' she exclaimed, pausing with the serving spoon suspended. 'You're planning on breaking into someone's house by climbing on to the roof from a tree – how is that being careful? At least leave Kat behind.'

'No!' Kat's protest was almost a squeal. 'I won't stay behind! Anyway, Daniel needs me to show him how to get in, don't you, Daniel?'

Daniel made a regretful face. 'I'm afraid she's right, but I promise you, we'll take no more risks than are absolutely necessary.'

'I know you don't want to, my dear,' Hilary told Kat, 'but I can't help thinking you *should* tell the police. I'm sure you wouldn't be in any trouble. You and your sister are the victims here, after all.'

'No. You don't understand . . .' Kat said desperately.

'Then why don't you help me to understand?' the older woman invited, but Katya just looked to Daniel for support.

'You promised . . .'

Daniel sighed. 'I did. And even if I hadn't, things have become a little bit complicated in that area.' He told them the result of his earlier phone call.

Hilary frowned. 'So what do you think's going on?'

'I don't know, but I can't imagine it's anything you'd find in the police codes of practice. I mean, it could be that Patrescu has been having a spot of bother with someone and needs a hotline to the authorities, but I'm struggling to believe that, and anyway, this was Naylor's personal number.' Daniel paused. 'I suppose you could either take this as proof of Patrescu's godliness or of Naylor's corruption, and having met them both, I know which I'd put money on.'

'Patrescu is evil!' Kat said suddenly, low-voiced and fervent.

Hilary glanced at her in surprise and then across at Daniel, eyebrows raised. With a minute shake of his head he tried to convey that she should leave it, and once again, to his relief, she did.

'But if you think this Sergeant Naylor is corrupt, shouldn't something be done about it?' Hilary said presently, when they were all eating.

Daniel grunted. 'Not without cast-iron proof, in triplicate and signed by two witnesses of impeccable character. And probably not even then. Before you know it they'll have closed ranks and suddenly you're the villain.'

Hilary looked at him thoughtfully but said no more on the subject.

Two o'clock the following morning found Daniel in the shadows at the foot of a towering beech tree in the grounds of Moorside House. The night was clear and bitterly cold, the moon three-quarters full and the sky a mass of stars. He'd left Taz with Hilary, once again, and the car was parked close against the hedge, in a turning some 50 yards back down the lane.

Daniel was feeling unsettled. Not only by the prospect of the task ahead, which seemed more foolhardy by the minute, but also because of a phone call that had come through just as he and Kat were preparing to leave the car.

'Dad?'

'Drew? What the hell? It's a quarter to two in the morning!'

'I know. I almost didn't ring in case you were asleep.'

'I should be, and so should you. Please tell me you're at least in bed.'

'I *am* in my room, but I couldn't sleep. Can I talk to you?'

Daniel made a face his son couldn't see. 'Well, no, not really. Not now.'

Drew continued as if he hadn't heard. 'Why don't you want me to come and live with you? I wouldn't be a nuisance, I promise.'

'Drew, we've been through this before. It's not that I don't want you – look, this really isn't a good time . . .'

'Amanda says you don't – want me, that is. She says you think I'd get in your way, but I promise I wouldn't.'

'Well, Mum's got it wrong. I never said that,' Daniel told him, inwardly seething at the below-the-belt tactics his ex-wife was employing. 'You know you're the most important person in the world to me, but the thing is, I'm working a lot of the time. I wouldn't be around to look after you.'

'But Amanda's often out and I don't mind. Anyway, I'd be at school, wouldn't I? They do have schools on Dartmoor, don't they?'

'Yes, of course. Not actually on the moor, naturally, but nearby.'

'And we could go walking together, with Taz. It would be fun.'

'It would,' Daniel admitted unwarily, as much beguiled by the idea as his son.

'Then why can't I come?' Drew's voice took on the pleading note that usually presaged tears.

'I've told you why.'

'But if we move back to Bristol, I'll hardly ever see you.'

Daniel caught his breath. 'To Bristol?' he asked. 'Is that what Mum wants to do?'

'Yes. She says all her friends are there. She's been looking at houses, but I don't want to go, Dad. My friends are here now.'

Daniel silently swore. This was a new development, but in all honesty he should have seen it coming considering the rows the move to Taunton had provoked.

'OK. Look, I'll have a word with her.'

'When?'

'Well, not now, obviously – it's way too late. Maybe tomorrow. Now I have to go, OK?'

'Where?' The boy was momentarily diverted.

'I'll tell you tomorrow,' Daniel promised. 'I'll ring you. Now get to bed, for Pete's sake! It's a school day tomorrow.'

As he'd switched the phone off and stowed it in a pocket, he was aware that Kat was regarding him with curiosity.

'I didn't know you have a son.'

'Well, now you do,' he'd replied.

'And you're married?'

'Not any more.' Technically he was, but not in essence. 'Look, are we going to do this, or do you want to spend the night making small talk?'

Kat had cast him a meaningful glance and got out of the car with no further comment.

Now, beside him, she shivered dramatically. 'I'm freezing. What are we waiting for? This *is* the right tree, I'm sure of it.'

Daniel didn't doubt it. The trunk, silver in the moonlight, rose 20 feet or so before splitting into three massive branches, one of which grew out towards the dark bulk of the house and over-hung the parapet that hid the roof from view.

He broke out in a cold sweat. What the hell was he doing here?

'Daniel?' Kat was watching him anxiously.

Anxious that he might change his mind, Daniel thought, not anxious about the climb. He remembered her escape route the day he had chased her through the woods. She'd crossed the fallen tree over the gorge as if it were a pavement, 4 feet wide.

'What did you do – in Romania, I mean?' he asked.

'I was a gymnast. I was very good,' she said matter of factly. 'I was training for the Olympics, but then I slip and hurt my foot and suddenly they are not interested any more.' She looked up at the tree. 'That is finished. But we should go now. I will show you how. Just follow me.'

Just follow – ye Gods! If only she knew.

Daniel waved a hand. 'Lead on,' he invited airily. 'But remember, I'm *not* a retired gymnast and nor am I Spiderman.'

A flash of teeth in the semi-darkness indicated a grin. Spiderman had obviously found his way into Romanian culture.

'You'll be fine,' Katya assured him, and started to climb.

The first 15 feet or so proved no problem, even for Daniel. The vertical trunk was reassuringly solid, the hand and footholds not too widely spaced and – above all – there was no need to look down.

However, when Katya reached the fork in the trunk and started to climb up and out along the branch closest to the building, Daniel felt the beginnings of a cold wash of panic rising like a tide through his body towards his head.

Pausing, he closed his eyes for a moment. Quitting wasn't an option. He was almost sure that, having come this far, he wouldn't be able to call Katya back. She would find a way into the house on her own if he didn't follow her, and he couldn't let her do that.

'Daniel!' she hissed. 'Come on!'

He opened his eyes and focused on her lithe figure, some 10 feet above him. He wouldn't let her down. He had enough baggage on his conscience already.

Doggedly, he resumed the climb.

At the point where the branch split again, Katya moved out along the lower of the two, using the sub-branches from the upper as handholds. She made it look easy, stepping over and around branches that got in her way, steadily climbing the sloping timber as if she were two feet from the ground, not twenty.

Reaching the same point, Daniel paused, his resolve wavering, his shaking limbs seeming to lack the strength that would allow him to stand upright.

Helplessly he looked at Kat, who, apparently unaware of his predicament, was now just a few short feet from the parapet, and another wave of panic swept over him. He closed his eyes and hung on, his fingernails striving to dig into the bark of the tree and combat the lure of the frozen earth below.

How he made it through the next couple of minutes and across the intervening 8 feet or so, he would never know, but finally he was standing next to Kat, with the roof of the house less than 6 feet away and perhaps 4 feet below. The branch underfoot was still fairly solid, but the one he was using to keep his balance was disconcertingly mobile.

'Just two or three steps and you can swing down,' Kat said encouragingly, and Daniel watched in horrified fascination as she proceeded to do so, landing soft-footed just beyond the stone parapet.

No way, Daniel's mind told him, as the branch, relieved of Katya's weight, rebounded under his feet, the leafless twigs rattling like dry bones. He closed his eyes once more, fighting the terror, until the movement slowed and ceased.

There was no way he could follow her, and yet returning the way he'd come was equally impossible. He had reached a mental and physical impasse.

An image of Drew flashed across his inner eye. Was his last memory of his father to be their recent telephone conversation in which, to the boy's eyes, he had been rejected once more?

There is nothing to fear except fear itself. The phrase rose unbidden from Daniel's subconscious. The words of wisdom had been the favourite maxim of Sergeant Sid Dyer, his unofficial mentor during his first years on the force. He could almost hear the sergeant's deep rumbling tones. *Fear is the enemy, but it can only win if you let it.*

Taking a deep breath and exhaling slowly, Daniel began to concentrate on the rhythm of his breathing, forcing his mind away from its paralysing obsession with falling.

'Come on! What's the matter?' Katya whispered loudly.

He opened his eyes and saw her, leaning on the parapet, peering up at him.

'Nothing,' he lied, shaking like a leaf.

Breathe in, breathe out. Move one foot and then the other. Focus on the mechanics of the task and forget the yawning emptiness below.

There was a moment, when he was over the roof of the house

and had to transfer his grip from the higher branch to the lower, when his careful concentration faltered, but the goal was in sight and the panic successfully quelled with a deep, steadying breath.

A rush of cold air whooshed past his ears as he bent, grasped the branch and swung smoothly down, his knees buckling as his feet met the stonework sooner than he expected. Landing sprawling against the slope of the roof behind the parapet, for several seconds all Daniel could do was splay his fingers against the frosty slates and thank a God he wasn't sure he believed in for deliverance.

He opened his eyes and found Katya staring at him.

'Why didn't you tell me you were afraid of heights?' she demanded accusingly.

'What difference would it have made?' Daniel pushed himself to his feet, carefully not looking over the low stone parapet.

Katya didn't answer, but after a moment observed, 'It's harder getting back.'

'Well, thanks for that. Now where's this bloody window?'

SIX

The attic window, Daniel was pleased to find, was low on the slope of the roof and its loose catch and rotting wooden frame weren't proof against the multi-function penknife he produced from his pocket. Within seconds he and Kat had dropped down inside.

By the narrow beam of his pencil torch Daniel could see that the attic room was clearly being used as storage for surplus furniture. A sofa and cot were draped in dustsheets, and a stack of dining-room chairs stood beside the window. Two armchairs, a bookcase, a pile of roughly folded curtains and an assortment of cushions and lampshades reduced the floor space to a 2-foot-wide walkway that led from the window to the door. The contents of the room reinforced Daniel's supposition that Patrescu was probably renting the house.

Treading carefully, Daniel crossed to the door and tried the handle. He was mildly surprised to find it unlocked, having expected security to be stepped up after the sisters had escaped.

On the other side of the door, a quick scan of the area revealed no obvious CCTV equipment and cautiously they stepped out into a dark, narrow passageway, which stretched away to right and left with doors on either side. A threadbare floral runner was laid on floorboards that creaked a little underfoot. Daniel knew from questioning Katya that the corridor formed a square route round the top floor of the house, a floor that would once have housed the servants in the building's distant past, he guessed.

'What else is up here?' he whispered.

Katya shrugged. 'More rooms like that one,' she said. 'And some with locked doors – maybe bedrooms? I don't know. We weren't allowed up here.'

They had started to move along the corridor towards the right-hand end, and as they turned the corner, Daniel saw one doorway with a keypad next to the frame. A small red LED flashed above it. He grabbed the sleeve of Katya's fleece-lined denim jacket, stopping her.

'What's in here?'

'I'm not sure. I think the studio.'

'*Is* it now?' Daniel paused, looking thoughtfully at the keypad.

'It's locked,' Kat said impatiently. 'It always is. Come on. We have to find Elena.'

'I just want to try something. It won't take a minute . . .'

'*Daniel!*'

'Sssh!'

Searching his memory, Daniel tapped in four numbers and mouthed a silent 'Yes!' as the flashing red light turned green and the lock clicked open.

Cautiously Daniel turned the knob. The room was in darkness, and when they were both inside, he switched on the light.

'How did you know the numbers?' Katya asked suspiciously.

'It's the same as the code for the office downstairs. I took a chance,' he told her. 'Well, well. Look at this little lot.'

The room *was* indeed a studio, and quite obviously not your average family portrait studio either. Centre-stage and surrounded by lighting equipment stood an enormous bed, opulently dressed in black and silver satin, with a handful of sheepskin throws scattered about. Four cameras stood around, set at varying heights. The filmmakers clearly weren't intending to miss any of the action.

'They are making films?' Katya was staring at the bed, her lip curling.

'Yeah, but not for general release,' Daniel said, taking a slim-line digital camera from his inside pocket and switching it on.

'What are you *doing*?' she hissed with growing impatience. 'What about Elena?'

'Just coming.'

Evidence-gathering was second nature to Daniel. You just never knew when it might be vital to a conviction. After taking a couple of shots, he glanced around the room, wishing he had time to investigate the cupboards and filing cabinets that were ranged against one wall, but a small sound from the direction of the door warned him that Katya's patience had expired. When he swung round, he saw that she'd left the room.

Cursing under his breath, he slipped the camera back in his pocket and followed. In the corridor, a flash of the torch showed her disappearing round the corner at the end. He hurried after her, not daring to call out or even run in the silence of the house.

Halfway along the next side of the square, he came upon a narrow flight of stairs illuminated dimly by a light on the floor below. Kat was already partway down and he risked hissing a furious 'Wait!'

Katya looked up and, to Daniel's relief, did as she was told.

'What the hell are you playing at?' he demanded as he caught up with her, stepping carefully near to the wall to minimize any creaking of the old treads.

'I have to find Elena. That's what we came for.'

'I know, but not like that. We must stay together. Now, let me go first.'

With a hint of sulkiness, Katya moved aside and Daniel went on down the stairs, pausing at the bottom to peer round the wall and check that the coast was clear.

'Which way?' he whispered over his shoulder.

Katya indicated right with a movement of her head, and the two of them set off once more.

In marked contrast to the top floor, this corridor was wider and by far more luxurious. The carpet, though by no means new, had obviously once been expensive, and lighting was in the form of pairs of bronze art deco wall lights with glass shades shaped like lilies.

As far as Daniel could see, there were no watching lenses. He supposed the ones in the hall below recorded all conventional visitors.

Kat tapped him on the shoulder, pointed and headed to the second door along.

'This was our room. They've put locks on now,' she whispered as Daniel caught up.

The lock in question was in fact no more than a crude hook and staple affair, and Kat lost no time in unfastening it and reaching for the handle. In an instant, Daniel's hand covered hers.

'Be careful!'

Kat shook him off and quietly opened the door, the borrowed light from the passageway faintly illuminating four beds, all occupied by girls or young women. None of the sleepers showed any sign of stirring as Kat tiptoed from one to another, trying to see their faces. Daniel held his breath. All it would take would be for one of the girls to wake and cry out and they could be in real trouble.

As he watched, Katya shook her head slightly and came back towards the door.

'She's not here.' She looked shattered by the realization.

'In one of the other rooms, maybe,' Daniel suggested, feeling sorry for her but not surprised. Katya had always believed that finding Elena would be easy, just as long as they could get inside the house, and his warnings to the contrary had consistently fallen on deaf ears.

Kat brushed past him and out the door, going immediately to the next one along.

'Katya, wait!' Daniel was closing the first door as quickly and quietly as he could. As he moved to join her, they were both shocked into stillness by the unmistakable sound of a door shutting somewhere below them, followed by voices, male and female.

Although at first they couldn't make out words, it was clear from the tone of the exchange that a heated row was in progress.

While Daniel hesitated, Kat pushed open the door to the second room and would have gone in if he hadn't caught her arm.

'Let me go!' she whispered angrily.

'There's no time. We've got to leave.'

'But she might be in here.'

'She might be in any one of these rooms,' Daniel pointed out. 'We haven't time to search them all.'

From the ground floor, a man's voice carried clearly but

incomprehensibly to Daniel. A glance at Katya's face, however, told him that it wasn't good news.

'What did he say?'

'It's Anghel! He says he is coming up to check.'

'To check what?'

'He didn't say.' Kat paused as the woman's voice was raised in reply. 'She says not to blame her, it wasn't her idea. And he says . . .'

'Never mind that! In here, quickly.' Daniel bundled her through the open door and pulled it close behind them, hoping against hope that the occupants hadn't been woken by the shouting and so cry out in fear.

'I can't see. Lend me your torch,' Kat whispered.

'Are you mad?' Daniel hissed back incredulously. 'Stand still and shut up!'

Katya did as he said, and although he could almost feel the indignation radiating from her person, at that moment he didn't care. Macek was on his way upstairs. Just what he was going to check up on, they couldn't know. Pray God it wasn't that all the doors were safely latched, because if it was, they were in big trouble. Even if it wasn't, they would be lucky if he passed without noticing the hook hanging down.

If Macek did see it, then the best they could hope for was that he might assume it had been left undone by accident and lock it again, leaving them some breathing space to consider a plan of action. The worst – and most likely – scenario was that he would check the room out. With the light on, there would be nowhere to hide.

This in mind, Daniel let go of Kat and risked a quick flash of the torch at the ceiling. One shaded light, hanging dead centre. Moving swiftly but quietly, he reached up and removed the bulb before returning to his position by the door hinges.

'He's coming,' Kat breathed. She reached for and held Daniel's arm and he could feel her trembling.

The creaking of the Georgian floorboards heralded Macek's approach and Daniel let out a long-held lungful of air as the heavy footsteps passed without stopping. Moments later, however, he froze again as the Romanian shouted out, just feet away.

'What did he say?' Daniel had to know.

'He says to check the windows downstairs,' Kat translated. 'Why would he do that?'

Daniel frowned. Why indeed? Had Macek seen and recognized

the Mercedes, parked back up the road? If so, he was more
on the ball than Daniel had given him credit for.

When they heard Macek continue along the corridor and turn
up the stairs, Daniel came to a rapid decision. Whether or not
he found the window they had forced, they couldn't stay where
they were, and as their escape route to the roof was cut off, they
had to take a chance on going down and getting past the woman
without being seen.

'Quickly!' He grabbed Katya's arm as he opened the door
and, after a brief look up and down the passageway, pulled her
after him as he set off towards the head of the main stairway.

'But Elena . . .'

'Not now!'

'What if Yousef's down there?'

'We'll deal with it somehow.'

Down the first flight of stairs, turn, three more and then down
the flight that led to the hall. Still holding Katya's hand, Daniel
made straight for the front door.

'Keep your head down,' he instructed. 'There's a camera in
the porch.'

But it seemed they were fated not to reach the porch, for as
well as being double-bolted, the heavy Georgian front door had
an old-fashioned lock and the key was missing.

Damn! They would have to escape via one of the windows.

'Come on.' Daniel turned Kat round and would have propelled
her across the hall but all at once their way was barred by the
flame-haired young woman Daniel had seen earlier that day. Her
mane of curls tumbled around her shoulders and across her face
as before, but now she wore a jade satin dress, which hugged
her curvy figure. Her eyes were wide with fear.

'Katya! Mamă de Dumnezeu! Are you mad?'

'Marika!' Katya took a step forward, speaking rapidly in her
native tongue, gesturing towards the locked door, her tone
pleading.

Marika looked from her to Daniel and back again, and her
response was equally incomprehensible to him, but she seemed
to have come to a decision. 'Wait!' she commanded and disappeared through an open doorway.

Katya turned to Daniel. 'Anghel has taken the key, but she
says there is another.'

'Can we trust her? He could be back any moment.'

'Yes, I think so.'

Seconds ticked by and Daniel glanced nervously at the stairs. 'This is crazy – we should go . . .'

Just as he was on the point of moving, Marika reappeared, holding a key, which she pressed into Kat's hand, speaking in English.

'Go! And don't ever come back. There's nothing you can do for Elena. Forget her.'

Katya's protest was cut short by a thunderous voice from upstairs.

'Marika!'

She answered him in her own tongue and then, turning to Daniel and Kat, said, 'Quickly. You must go!'

Katya rushed to the door, fitting the key into the lock with shaking hands, but Daniel hung back.

'Come with us,' he urged Marika.

'I can't.' She shook her head vigorously, and under the curtain of her hair, Daniel noticed for the first time the purple line of an old scar running from the corner of her mouth to her cheekbone.

Vivid memories of an almost identical injury flashed across his mind, and the shock made him put out a hand.

'Did he do that?' he demanded, a cold fury rising.

She evaded his hand, shaking her hair forward again. 'It was my fault.'

'It's never *your* fault,' Daniel told her. 'Come with us now – please.'

'I can't. Where would I go? I have nothing – no life but here.'

'But you can't stay here. I'll help you, I promise.'

'You don't understand. The girls need me. And besides . . .' She shrugged, her mouth trembling as a bittersweet smile flickered across her face. 'I love him.'

'Daniel! Come on! Hurry.' Katya had the door open now and they could hear Macek's heavy tread on the stairs.

With a sad shake of his head, Daniel started to turn away from Marika, then gritted his teeth, spun back and hit her.

The blow was hard enough to send her staggering back. She caught the bottom stair with her heel and sat down sharply, her hand flying to her face and her eyes swimming with tears.

Behind him, Katya cried out in shock, but Daniel ignored her. He paused long enough to see that Marika was all right, then turned and ran for the door, pushing a wide-eyed Katya ahead of him.

'Go, go, go!' he urged, as they burst out of the front door into the icy air.

Katya said little on the way back and Daniel was content to drive in silence, turning the events of the night over in his mind and trying to make sense of them.

Finding Hilary waiting with open arms and sympathy was enough to break Katya's precarious control, however, and she sobbed her disappointment into the front of the older woman's fleecy housecoat, while Hilary gently patted her back.

When the tears abated, Daniel gave Hilary a brief run-down of what had occurred, while she prepared milky cocoa on the Aga. She listened in silence, even though Daniel knew her mind must be buzzing with questions, but as he recounted the final part of the tale and Marika's part in their escape, she swung round to stare.

'Oh, bless her! What a brave girl.'

'Daniel hit her,' Katya cut in, her lip all but curling with contempt. 'He knocked her down after she'd helped us.'

Hilary cast a quick look at Daniel. 'Did he?' she said. 'Well, perhaps he knew she'd be in terrible trouble if this Macek character thought she'd helped you of her own free will.'

Daniel blessed her for her insight. 'I tried to get her to come with us, but she wouldn't,' he said. 'There wasn't time for her to lock the door again.'

'Do you think she'll be all right?' Hilary asked, handing the mugs round and sliding into a chair opposite Daniel and next to Kat.

He shrugged, remembering the scar. A man who could do that to a pretty face . . . He'd spared Hilary that detail.

'I hope so.'

He cupped his cold fingers around his mug, taking a sip of the rich chocolatey liquid. The mug had a smiley frog on it, but it barely registered; he had long since ceased to be surprised by their hostess's somewhat eclectic taste. In the warm haven of the kitchen, with the dog at his feet, he finally began to relax and felt, all at once, bone weary.

He turned to Katya. 'How many girls are there at the house?'

Kat's eyes dipped and for one exasperated moment, Daniel thought she was going to continue with the lies, but it seemed she realized the futility of it because after a moment she said dully, 'I don't know. Twenty – maybe thirty. They come and go.'

'Thirty?' Hilary exclaimed looking from one to the other. 'What on earth? Oh, no, not a . . . a brothel? Surely not here.'

'Why not here?' Daniel was amused. 'Are all Devon men celibate?'

'Of course not, but I mean . . .' Hilary stopped, confused.

Daniel rescued her. 'It's a common misconception that prostitution is confined to the big towns and cities. People are absolutely horrified to discover that the house just round the corner on their estate is actually a knocking shop. Half a dozen teenagers in a council house, an adult to take care of the business side of things and Bob's your uncle – or rather, your client.

'But, having said that, I should think Moorside is a bit too remote. I think we're looking at part of a big organization here. It's probably more of a holding house for the girls before they're shipped on to their final destinations, or perhaps taken for nights out to the cities – working, of course. Am I right?' he asked Katya. 'Were you brought here as soon as you arrived in the country?'

Kat nodded, not meeting his eyes.

'But your father . . . ?' Hilary was understandably bewildered.

'Yes, well, I'm afraid Patrescu is no more Katya's father than I am,' Daniel said dryly. 'Yousef Patrescu and his mate Macek are traffickers, bringing girls into the country from Eastern Europe for prostitution.'

'We didn't know!' Katya burst out. 'He said he could find work for me as a waitress or in a hotel. He said Elena was so pretty she could make lots of money modelling. He said we would be able to send money home to our family – more than we ever dreamed of . . .'

'Oh, Kat.' Hilary moved closer and put her arm round the girl's shoulders.

Katya looked up at her with tears in her eyes. 'You think we were stupid, but we all believed him, even my mother. We *had* to believe him. I come from a very big family. We are very poor.'

Daniel wondered how much the girls' mother had really known. Had she been taken in as Katya believed, or had she sacrificed two children for the benefit of the others? It was sadly far from uncommon for parents with large families to support. Had Patrescu in fact *bought* Katya and her sister from their mother? He thought it quite possible but kept it to himself.

'We don't think you're stupid,' Hilary reassured the girl, throwing a speaking glance Daniel's way.

'No, it's not your fault. They're pros,' he responded. 'They'll have done it hundreds of times before.'

'Patrescu got passports for us, but when we got here, he took them away. He said we owed him money for the journey. He said we had to work for him until we could pay him back. That's when he brought us to the house.'

'Was it just you and your sister?'

Katya shook her head. 'No, there were eight of us. They put us in a van. We were very frightened, except for one girl. She told us she used to work for Patrescu in Romania. She told us what she did . . .' She sniffed and Hilary handed her a handkerchief. 'It was like a bad dream. Elena didn't really understand, but she was scared and couldn't stop crying. Then her breathing got bad. She was . . .' Unable to find the words, Katya put her hand on her chest and went through the actions of someone struggling for air.

'Wheezing,' Hilary supplied. 'Poor girl. That must have been terrifying for both of you.'

'It was,' Kat agreed. 'And when we got to the house, they told us that if we tried to run away with no papers, the police would put us straight in jail. He told us things about women's jails. Horrible things . . .' She faltered to a stop, looking distressed.

'He lied,' Daniel said flatly. 'Girls like you and Elena are the victims in this, and you'd be treated as such if you went to the police. You wouldn't be sent to jail, I can promise you.'

'How can you be so sure?' Katya demanded.

'Just believe me. They were using your fear to control you. Sometimes they use drugs. Once the girls are hooked, they'll do anything to get their fix. They give up any thought of running and of course become deeper and deeper in debt.'

'Oh my God!' Hilary exclaimed, leaning away from Katya, the better to see her. 'They didn't . . . ?'

Kat shook her head. 'Some of the girls were talking about it, though. And Marika said if we caused trouble, that's what would happen. She also said Elena and I were going to be split up – that's why we had to get away when we did.'

'I still find it hard to believe,' Hilary said. 'I mean, with someone Katya's age it's bad enough, but a twelve-year-old girl.' Her face reflected her disgust.

Katya looked at Daniel. 'I heard Anghel and Yousef talking about Elena and another girl called Molly. She is only ten, but her mother is dead.'

'Yes, I met Molly this afternoon,' he murmured.

'Yousef called them cash cows. What did he mean?'

Daniel hesitated, but only for a moment. For all her tender years, Kat had been through a lot over the last couple of weeks. It was a bit late to start shielding her now.

'Some men will pay a lot – and I mean *a lot* – for a pretty, innocent young girl. A little girl that no one else has ever touched and never will. Wealthy businessmen – outwardly respectable – keeping a little plaything for their sick amusement. A little refugee from abroad – no one to know, no one to look for her . . .'

'You don't mean they *buy* them?' Hilary gasped. 'That's . . . that's inhuman!'

'Unfortunately, there's very little that isn't human,' Daniel said wearily. 'You only have to turn on the news.'

He stared into his half-empty mug, feeling depressed and thinking of starting work at eight o'clock the next morning. The hands of the clock above the dresser pointed to half past three. He supposed Hilary would have to be up early too, and said so.

She sighed, putting aside emotional issues for practical ones. 'Yes, we should all be getting to bed. Daniel, you'll sleep here, won't you? I made a bed up in one of the guest rooms earlier.'

'But what about Elena?' Katya exclaimed. 'Don't you care? You know what they'll do with her. We can't just leave her there. She's my sister! What are we going to do?'

'Of course I care, but we can't do anything tonight,' Daniel said reasonably. 'Right now I need some sleep, even if you don't. We'll talk about it in the morning.'

'Hi. Is that Yvonne? Could I speak to Jono, please?'

It was lunchtime. Daniel had parked up at a truck stop and had put a call through to one-time friend and partner Detective Constable Paul 'Jono' Johnson. Jono's wife had answered. Daniel pictured her plump, curvy figure, blonde highlights and oh-so-perfect nails.

'He's here,' she said, 'but he's down the garden. Hang on a moment and I'll take the phone out.' There was the sound of a door opening and the acoustics changed as Yvonne Johnson spoke again. 'He's messing about in his shed. You men and your bloody sheds! Er, sorry, who is it speaking?'

Daniel hesitated but could see no option other than the truth. 'It's Daniel Whelan.'

'Oh. Daniel.' The temperature dropped to cool. 'How are you?'

'I'm fine. Overworked and underpaid, of course.' He supposed pride had made him add that to show that he was standing on his own two feet and no object for pity. Immediately he was annoyed that he'd felt the need to.

'Amanda says you're driving a truck.'

Bugger Amanda!

'It's a bit more than that. Actually, I'm quite enjoying it.'

'Oh good,' Yvonne said vaguely, and Daniel had the strong impression that she was wishing she'd asked his identity before confirming that her husband was home. The days of their cosy dinner parties as a foursome with Daniel and Amanda were clearly well and truly consigned to history.

'I'll just pass you over,' she said then, and Daniel heard her say faintly, 'It's Daniel Whelan.'

'Daniel? What does he want?' Jono's voice was also quiet.

'Well, I don't know, do I? Just take it, will you?'

A short pause, then, jovially, 'Daniel. Hi! How are you?'

'I'm good. You?'

'Yes, fine, fine.' He paused. 'So, long time no hear. Where've you been?'

'I rang a couple of times, left a message,' Daniel reminded him mildly.

'Yeah, sorry. Things have been a bit manic – you know how it is. Anyway . . . ?'

'I wondered if you could do me a favour. Run a couple of checks for me.'

There was a pause, the silence resonating with reluctance.

'Look, Dan, I wish I could, but things are a bit difficult right now . . .'

'It's just a couple of PNC checks. Five minutes on the computer, no more – who's to know?'

'Dan, I can't risk it. I'm up for my sergeant's exam in a week or two.'

'Oh, congratulations.'

'Yeah, thanks. But you can see why I have to be careful. I mean, you know how Paxton feels about you. If he thought I'd been using the PNC on your behalf, well . . .'

'But he'd never know if you didn't tell him.'

'Oh, he'd find out somehow.'

'Please, Jono – this could be big. It could be to your advantage.'

'I don't know . . .'

For the first time Jono sounded less than obdurate, and Daniel pressed on.

'Does the name Yousef Patrescu mean anything to you?'

Another pause.

'Patrescu? I don't think so. Why?'

He was lying; Daniel was sure of it.

'How about Anghel Macek?'

'What do you want to know?'

It seemed Jono was finally wavering, but Daniel had reckoned without Yvonne.

'*Paul*, no!' she said quite clearly in the background and he did an immediate about-turn.

'I'm sorry, Dan. I really can't help you. We practically have to wash our mouths out with soap if we so much as mention your name. Look, why don't you try one of your old mates at the Dog Unit? What about old Joey Suzuki?' he asked, using a common and deliberate mispronunciation of the man's name. 'I heard he's working your spaniel now.'

'Is he?' Daniel was pleased. He didn't know the man particularly well, but he'd worked alongside Jo-Ji Matsuki a time or two and he had a nice way about him with his dogs. 'Thanks. Maybe I'll do that.'

'And look, Dan, if you're on to something, you really should report it, you know,' Johnson said.

'On to something, Officer?' Daniel repeated dryly. 'I have no idea what you mean.'

He rang off, and sat looking out of the cab window to where three men stood drinking hot beverages under the awning of the burger bar.

So, Joey had Bella, did he? Bella was a six-year-old black cocker spaniel, and one of the best drugs dogs in the area. Daniel had been gutted to lose her when he'd been taken off the Dog Unit. At the time he could only thank God that Taz had been forced to retire early and was therefore beyond his superiors' vindictive reach.

His thoughts slid back to Drew, as they had every few minutes throughout the day. In spite of his promise to speak to Amanda that morning, she had so far not answered or returned his calls. With little optimism, he keyed in her number once more, only to listen to the same bright, impersonal message. She was out, but if he left a message, she would call. Or not, he thought sourly as he cut the connection. Why wasn't she calling? Did she know what he wanted to talk about? Surely she knew they would have to discuss it sooner or later.

The alluring scent of sizzling beef found its way through the part-open window and he realized how hungry he was. Breakfast had been at seven o'clock, just three hours after he'd finally got to bed, and he'd shared the table with Hilary, who'd looked as heavy-eyed as he'd felt. Katya had been left to sleep on, for which Daniel was grateful. However much sympathy he felt for her – and that was a hell of a lot – he could well do without her persistent questions at that time in the morning.

As it turned out, Hilary had questions of her own.

'In my day, a comprehensive knowledge of sex-trafficking wasn't part of the HGV test,' she had observed, tipping creamy porridge into dishes from the saucepan. 'It seems Kat isn't the only one who's been keeping secrets. How long were you in the police force, or are you still?'

Daniel shook his head. 'I left three months ago.'

'Because?'

'I'd always wanted to be a lorry driver?' he suggested fatuously.

She sensibly ignored him. 'You don't strike me as a quitter, you're too young to have retired, and if it wasn't your vocation, then why would you have thrown yourself behind Katya's cause? Unless . . .' She froze in the act of sprinkling sugar liberally on her oats and fixed him with a suspicious gaze.

'What?' Daniel demanded. Then as the light dawned, 'Oh God, no! I'm not into cradle-snatching – teenagers have way too many moods and tantrums. Besides, there's Tamzin.'

'Is there?' Hilary asked mildly, apparently returning her attention to her breakfast. She blew on a steaming spoonful. 'I forgot to tell you she phoned yesterday, wanting to know if I'd seen you. She said you hadn't answered her texts.'

Daniel felt guilty. 'Yeah, I know. I just didn't get round to it, what with one thing and another. I'll see her this afternoon, anyway. I'm delivering to the stables.'

Hilary made a face. 'And that's going to make it all right?'

'OK. Point taken. I'll call her.'

Recalling the conversation later, as he sat in his cab, Daniel phoned Tamzin and left a voice message, apologizing for his silence, saying he'd missed her. Then, postponing the decision as to whether or not to ring Jo-Ji Matsuki, he climbed down from the lorry and went in search of a burger with all the trimmings, followed closely by Taz, who wasn't about to be left out if there was food on offer.

Driving home at the end of the day, Daniel could hardly keep his eyes open. Quarry Farm Racing Stables had been his last delivery, and he'd stayed to have a coffee with Tamzin before evening stables. She had been cheerful – maybe too cheerful, Daniel reflected – and hadn't made any reference to his lack of communication. When he brought the subject up, she'd dismissed it, saying they had probably both been busy. Daniel was grateful for her understanding.

It was half past eight when he turned the Mercedes into the weedy gravel drive that ran to one side of the former lawnmower shop and followed it round to the car park at the back. A light came on at his approach, illuminating the unlovely 1970s brick building with the paint peeling from its window frames, and the cracked concrete apron below.

He parked, nose in, and went to the back of the car, finding Taz in an apparent frenzy to get out.

'Steady on,' he told the dog as he lifted the tailgate. 'What's the matter? Desperate for a pee?'

Taz leaped out, almost knocking him aside in his eagerness, and tore across the concrete, his bark silenced now that action was on the cards. At the perimeter fence, he hardly paused before finding a place to squeeze under the wooden panels, his bushy tail the last thing Daniel saw of him as he disappeared.

Retrieving his torch from the car, Daniel followed, bending down to shine the beam through the gap Taz had found, but he could see nothing other than grass and brambles. Beyond the fence was a field of rough grazing, accessed by a gate into a narrow side road, so there was little point in trying to follow the dog, who would no doubt have put the fear of God into whoever or whatever he'd chased. Confirmation of this came seconds later, when Daniel heard a vehicle start up and move away in something of a hurry.

As the sound of the engine faded, Daniel whistled the dog and presently Taz returned and began padding up and down on the other side of the fence, snuffling excitedly.

'Come on, lad. Good boy!' Daniel said, and Taz obediently reappeared, panting heavily, a dead blackberry spray caught in his tail. As always, when the dog had been working, Daniel produced a tug toy from his pocket and played with him for a moment as his reward for a job well done, after which Taz trotted happily at his heels as he locked the car and made his way up to the flat.

The dog showed interest in the outside door and its handle, which suggested whoever had been there had tried it to see if it was locked. However, there was no sign that anyone had attempted to break in, and inside, the dog displayed none of the excitement Daniel would have associated with the scent of an intruder. It seemed most likely that the visitor or visitors had been disturbed by Daniel's arrival and, having had a taste of the dog, would be unlikely to return.

Daniel fed Taz and then unwrapped the fish and chips he'd bought on the way home. Taking a can of beer from the fridge, he took his meal and settled in front of the computer to check his email.

As the machine ticked and whirred into action, Daniel's heart sank as he saw no less than three emails from Drew among the dross the service provider failed to filter out. With a sigh, he started to read, sitting in the pool of light cast by the desk lamp, the earlier drama forgotten.

Two of them had been sent since their telephone conversation the previous night and they all followed a predictable theme, loaded with pleas backed up by childish reasoning, and Daniel was left saddened and frustrated by his inability to get Drew to understand the impossibility of his request.

Honouring his promise to ring after school, Daniel rang Drew's mobile, bracing himself for the expected familiar argument. He was surprised and relieved to hear a very upbeat young voice answer.

'Dad. Hi.' It sounded as though a Grand Prix was going on in the background.

'Hiya. I said I'd call. What are you up to?'

'We're go-karting and it's fab!'

'Who's we?'

'Me, Amanda and Ryan. And, Dad, Mum even had a go.'

'Did she?' Daniel said, impressed. She was clearly making an effort.

'Yeah, but she was *useless*.'

'So, is it Ryan's birthday or something?'

'No. Amanda just said it would be fun, and it is – it's awesome!'

The sound of engines rose to a crescendo as the karts revved up.

'Look, Dad, I've got to go. I'm in the race after this one. It's the semi-final,' he added proudly.

'Oh, well done! OK. I'll ring you tomorrow. Now go and win that race for me.'

Thoughtfully, Daniel rang off. Was this surprise outing an effort by Amanda to get Drew onside after upsetting him with talk of moving back to Bristol? Had she read his email's 'sent' folder and been alarmed by the content of his messages to Daniel? He couldn't imagine that go-karting had ever featured on Amanda's wish list. Whatever the case, it obviously hadn't been the moment to broach the subject of the proposed move with her.

Daniel brought up an online telephone directory and entered 'Matsuki' and 'Bristol'. Unsurprisingly, there was only one entry, and after taking a mental deep breath, Daniel phoned the listed number.

'Hello?' A female, young and unmistakably oriental.

'Hi. Um, could I speak to Joey, please?'

'I'm sorry, Jo-Ji is not here.'

'Oh. When would be a good time to call?'

'Who is it speaking?'

'Daniel Whelan. I used to work with Joey. I believe he's got my dog Bella now . . .'

'Yes, he has Bella, but Daniel, I'm sorry, Jo-Ji is in hospital. He was in a road accident three days ago and he has to stay for at least another week, they say.'

Daniel passed on his commiserations and, ringing off a minute or two later, sighed and shook his head.

'Buggered again, Taz,' he said. 'So what now, huh?'

Taz looked up under his brows without lifting his head. He was more interested in Daniel's meal than the conversation.

Had Jono known that Matsuki was out of commission when he made the suggestion? Daniel wondered, feeding Taz a chunk of fish. Probably not. It was probably just fate having a laugh again.

So what now? There were other people – ex-colleagues – he could call, but his conversation with Jono had left him wary.

Damn Naylor! If *he'd* been clean, the problem wouldn't exist, but the possibility of the sergeant's connection with Patrescu was one Daniel couldn't afford to disregard.

The idea of blowing the whistle on Naylor was dismissed without consideration. Even supposing Daniel – with the black marks already against his name – could get anyone at Yelverton to listen to him, it would be messy. Word would spread like wildfire in a provincial station like that and Naylor would just as swiftly warn Patrescu. By the time anything was done about Moorside House – *if* anything were done – the Romanians, the girls and the evidence would be long gone.

If that happened, Daniel knew, Katya could kiss goodbye to her little sister for good.

SEVEN

S till wrestling with the problem of what to do next, Daniel slept badly and awakened in a less than sunny frame of mind.

Mechanically, he went through the actions of making toast and coffee and feeding Taz before setting out for Tavistock through a windblown drizzle to collect the lorry and start work.

A dreary morning wasn't improved when he stopped for his morning break and was on the receiving end of a call from Amanda.

'Hello?'

'I just wanted to let you know that Drew won't be able to come to you next weekend. He's busy.' She flung the statement down the phone as if it were a challenge, which, in essence, Daniel recognized, it was. He kept his own voice even.

'Why, what's he doing?' Next weekend was *his* weekend – his and Drew's.

'We're taking him to Butlins for the weekend.'

'We?'

'Darren and I.'

Darren. The boyfriend, presumably. He *would* be called Darren, Daniel thought uncharitably.

'Does Drew know about this?' he asked. 'He didn't mention it when I spoke to him yesterday.'

'He's eight years old,' Amanda pointed out. 'He's not old enough to make his own arrangements. I do that.'

'He's old enough to know what he'd *like* to do, surely?'

'Oh God, I might have known you'd be awkward about it! He'll enjoy it – there's loads to do there for kids.'

Daniel sighed. 'All right. I'll see him the week after instead. Can I speak to him now?'

'What for?' she demanded suspiciously.

'He's my son – do I need a particular reason?' Daniel was struggling to keep his temper. 'I said I'd ring him, that's all.'

'You're not going to try and put him off?'

'Oh, for God's sake, Amanda!'

'Well, don't go upsetting him again. He was moody for days after he saw you last week.'

'That wasn't my fault.'

'It was because of you, though,' she retorted. 'I sometimes think it might be better if he didn't see you so often. It's very disruptive for him. I don't want his schoolwork to suffer.'

'Don't even go there!' Daniel warned. 'If he's upset because he thinks he wants to come and live with me full-time, how is seeing me less going to help? And while we're on the subject, what's this about moving back to Bristol?'

'Oh, he told you about that, did he? It's only an idea, nothing definite.'

'No? Drew says you've been viewing houses. Is this part of your plan to separate Drew and me? Because it won't bloody work, Amanda – I'll tell you that now!'

'Don't be ridiculous!' she protested. 'I wouldn't do that.'

'No?' At one time, he wouldn't have believed it of her either, but now he wasn't sure.

'No! I was just looking, but can you blame me? I get lonely sometimes and all my friends are back there.'

'But Drew doesn't want to go, does he?'

'He'd get used to it, and maybe it would take his mind off this stupid idea he's got. I mean, it's all right for you – you don't have to live with his moods. He's like a bear with a sore head.'

'All right for me? I'd love to live with him – moods or not. Leaving wasn't my choice, remember?'

'It was your choice to meddle in what didn't concern you and mess up a perfectly good career!' she snapped straight back. 'You didn't stop to think how it would affect me or Drew, did you? I mean, at least if you'd been invalided out like George Collis, you'd have got a pension and we'd still have our friends.'

'George has to walk with elbow crutches,' Daniel exclaimed incredulously. 'Is that what you'd have preferred for me? Anyway, you've still got *your* friends – you made sure of that when you cut me loose. Not one to let loyalty get in the way of your social life, were you?'

'Loyalty to what?' Amanda retorted. 'To a husband who was never at home? Who put work before his wife and kid? I lost count of the number of things we had to cancel because you were "needed at work". I swear you thought more of those bloody dogs than you did of me!'

'Well, at least they didn't desert me when the going got tough!' Daniel was stung to reply. 'I was a policeman when we met, Amanda. You knew what the job was.'

'But it wasn't *like* that to start with . . .'

He had to admit she had a point. In the last few years, general understaffing and an increase in officers on long-term sick leave had made the idea of regular hours a joke. His spell in the Dog Unit had been the best. Dogs don't do overtime, and his shifts had been as regular as clockwork, though he couldn't recall that it had made much difference to the atmosphere at home.

'Look, Amanda, I'm working. Let's leave it, shall we? We're never going to agree. I'll try Drew later on his mobile.'

Daniel tossed the phone down on the seat beside him, irritated that Amanda still had the power to rattle him, although realistically it was the power she had over his relationship with Drew that bothered him the most.

Aware of his mood, Taz sat up on his blanket in the footwell, flattening his ears sheepishly.

Daniel stroked the dog's head, pulling at one dark, velvety ear.

'It's all right, lad. Woman trouble, that's all.'

Daniel wasn't normally a big fan of parties, but when Tamzin rang to invite him to one that evening, he allowed himself to be persuaded with comparatively little protest. Whether this was due to his restless mood after Amanda's call or his reluctance to face Katya with no plan to offer, he didn't know. However, the thought of an evening spent in Tamzin's agreeable company, with good wine and food and no need to tax his brain with anything but the most banal conversation was suddenly quite tempting.

In the event, the idea that the party might be fun lasted all of ten minutes after their arrival, though the tedium of the prevailing conversation about Alexander somebody's new yacht, Abigail's new horse or the advantages of the Maldives over the Seychelles for one's holiday was balanced by the culinary splendour of the buffet.

Drifting to his side after a couple of hours, Tamzin extricated Daniel from the verbal clutches of a mildly flirtatious middle-aged lady and drawing him away, on the pretext of wanting to introduce him to someone, whispered, 'You're a fraud, Mr Whelan. Skiing in Aspen on a policeman's pay? I don't believe you've ever been there!'

'I didn't precisely say I'd *been* there – just said it was one of the best places to go. I've never skied anywhere more exciting than the dry slope at the leisure centre when I was a kid,' he confessed. 'But that wasn't what she wanted to hear.'

'Oh, and do you always tell people what you think they want to hear?' she enquired archly.

'Anything for an easy life – you know me.'

'Yeah, right!' Tamzin said dryly. 'Do you think we should make a move soon?'

'If you're ready . . . ?'

Ten minutes later, in the darkness of the Discovery, Tamzin glanced sideways at Daniel as she drove. 'You made quite a hit. Everyone thought you were lovely.'

'Well, I've been on my best behaviour.'

'My aunt particularly liked you,' Tamzin went on, ignoring his flippant reply. 'She said she was glad I'd found someone nice at last.'

Daniel had a vague recollection of a brisk, wiry, fiftyish lady who'd asked him if he had ever ridden.

'That doesn't say a lot for your previous boyfriends,' he joked, skipping lightly over the hint of permanency in her remark.

'Well, some of them *were* a bit alternative,' she admitted with a laugh in her voice. 'I think I was rebelling against the Oxbridge set I'd grown up with. Did you go to uni?'

'Nope. College and then straight to police training at eighteen.'

'You knew what you wanted, then?'

'My dad was a police officer. Still is, as far as I know.'

'You're not in touch with him?'

'No. He walked out when I was eight. Drew's age.'

'Oh, I see.' Tamzin hesitated, perhaps waiting for him to expand, but when he didn't, she said, 'I told Auntie Jane that you were only temporary, that you'd be moving on sooner or later. She was disappointed.'

Daniel's heart sank. He sensed an emotional storm brewing.

Why had he thought this would be an evening free of mental stress?

'You will, won't you?' Tamzin said as the silence lengthened.

'Eventually, I suppose. I haven't made any plans as yet,' Daniel hedged. 'Besides, my options are limited. Police skills aren't a lot of help in the job market.'

'Well, you could always come and train racehorses with me,' she suggested lightly. 'And on that subject, I'm one rider short in the morning, so I'm banking on you helping me out.'

'OK.'

'Really?' His placid agreement had clearly caught Tamzin by surprise.

'Yes. Why not?' he said.

'No reason. That's great,' Tamzin said. Then, on a different note, 'Oh, what's going on here?'

They had topped a rise and could see lights out on the moor to their right and, in a roadside car park, a gathering of emergency vehicles, fluorescent markings glowing and blue lights flashing.

'Someone lost or injured, perhaps,' Daniel said. 'There's a chopper circling too.'

Tamzin slowed the Land Rover as they drew close to the scene of the activity, but a yellow-jacketed police officer waved them on.

'Shall I ask him what's going on?' Tamzin said, continuing to brake, but Daniel shook his head.

'I shouldn't bother. He probably won't tell you.'

His thoughts flashed back to the night he'd searched for Katya and her sister. If only he'd taken matters in his own hands and called the rescue services then, he thought, he wouldn't be in the fix he was in now. But dwelling on if onlys was a destructive occupation – bitter experience had taught him that – and he'd had no real reason to distrust Patrescu at that first meeting; the doubts had come later.

Too late.

Sunday dawned bright and sparkling, the previous day's dampness turning to hoar frost, which rimed every branch, twig and blade of grass, and each ice crystal was lifted to diamond brilliance by the rays of the rising sun.

Warm breath from the horses' nostrils plumed and dissolved in the cold, dry air, and the rhythmic clatter of their hooves filled Daniel's ears, as they filed up the lane towards the gallops.

Immediately in front of him, the chestnut mane of his mount sloped up to a pair of long, honest ears. Behind the saddle, a striped blanket kept the fine-skinned thoroughbred loins warm and the top of a silky tail twitched from side to side with each hind footfall.

The thought of what was to come filled Daniel with a buzz of anticipation. Tamzin had assured him that the chestnut, known around the stables as Rex, might pull a bit but would do nothing untoward, so Daniel could only hope he didn't make a fool of himself by falling off in front of the other relaxed and capable-looking riders in the string.

Tamzin reined her bay in to drop back beside Rex. 'How's it going?'

'Great, but completely different from anything I've ever ridden before. I mean, compared with Hilary's trekking ponies, Rex could be a different species.'

'Well, you know what they say, "horses for courses". These guys would be pretty hopeless finding their way across Dartmoor. In fact, there was a thoroughbred had to be rescued from a bog last summer. Its rider was a visitor, staying with friends, and the horse had just blundered in. You'd never see a native pony making that mistake.'

'I suppose not. How deep are the bogs?'

'Oh, they vary. Some you could wade through; some are rumoured to be upwards of twenty feet deep. The bright-green ones are easy enough to spot, once you've been warned, though some of the others are more tricky, but the Dartmoor ponies know the signs, and Hilary knows the moors like the back of her hand. Now, here we are,' she said, as they swung off the road into a large field which sloped up to meet the deep blue sky. 'We'll go in twos. You and I first, along the bottom and then up the far side to the top. Don't worry, we'll take it steady. Take a handful of mane and get your weight well forward when we set off, then just follow me and do what I do.'

She fell back to pass on her instructions to the other six riders as they entered the field, and then caught up with Daniel, who was discovering that Rex had woken up quite a bit as he felt the turf beneath his hooves. They moved into a trot, keeping the horses on a tight rein as they loosened their muscles. Daniel's heart rate began to rise.

'Ready?' Tamzin asked and, at his nod, sent her mount into

a canter, heading along the lower edge of the field toward the far boundary.

Daniel had just enough time to wind his fingers into Rex's short mane before the chestnut shot away with a powerful thrust from behind the saddle that almost caught him napping. He threw his weight forward, standing in his stirrups, and tried to restrain Rex's urge to gallop flat out.

'Shall we move up a gear?' Tamzin called after a hundred yards or so.

In response to Daniel's nod, she eased her hands forward a few inches, giving her mount permission to accelerate. Mentally crossing himself, Daniel followed suit, gasping as the icy air began to whistle past his ears and sting his eyes to tears.

By the time they had reached the turn at the end of the field, Rex had caught Tamzin's bay and they were galloping stride for stride, nostrils flaring as they exhaled sharp snorts of steam in time to the drumming of their hooves. Daniel felt like yelling aloud with the exhilaration of it. Thirty miles an hour might seem a snail's pace in a car, but on the back of a horse, with the wind whipping past and the grass just a blur underfoot, it was real, raw speed.

For a moment or two, Rex headed the bay, but as they breasted the rise and began to gallop back along the ridge, Tamzin sent her horse forward again, and by the time they pulled up she had 20 or 30 yards on Daniel and Rex had slowed to a canter.

As Daniel brought the horse back to a trot and the euphoria began to ebb, a wave of tiredness washed over him and he became aware for the first time of an intense burning in the muscles of his legs and arms.

'That was incredible!' he exclaimed. 'What a buzz! But I'm absolutely knackered.'

Tamzin laughed. 'Well, we've got to wait for the others now, so you've got a chance to recover before we go on. I'm glad you enjoyed it.'

Standing up in her stirrups, she waved to the riders waiting below, and watching as the next two gathered their reins and set off along the lower hedge line, Daniel felt he could get to like the life of a racehorse trainer.

The phone call, just after lunch, jerked Daniel out of a haze of rare contentment. He had been making the fire up in Tamzin's tiny lounge while she made them both coffee. He pulled his jacket towards him and retrieved his mobile from the inside pocket.

It was Hilary.

'I'm sorry to bother you, Daniel, but it's Katya. She's in a bit of a state.'

'Why? What's happened?'

'Well, I had to pop out at lunchtime, so I took her with me because she seemed a bit down – I hope that was all right? I didn't think we were likely to run into anyone she knew.'

'But you did.'

'Well, in a way. Actually, we were on our way back when we got caught in a police roadblock. Apparently some poor girl has been found dead on the moor; we heard it on the news. A courting couple found her in one of the car parks late last night.'

That would explain the cluster of emergency vehicles he and Tamzin had seen, Daniel thought.

'So what upset Kat? Did they ask questions?'

'Only where we'd come from and where we were going, and had we used the road yesterday – which we hadn't. No, what upset her is that she's sure she recognized one of the policemen.'

'She did, did she? Where from?' Daniel's mind switched up a gear.

'She said he came to Moorside House to see Patrescu, though she didn't know he was a policeman then.'

'He didn't recognize her?'

'I don't think so. I don't think she's ever actually *met* him.'

'I don't suppose you got his name?' Daniel could hardly bear to hope.

'No, I'm sorry. I feel a bit useless, but I can't remember if he even told us his name and of course I didn't realize it could be important until we'd driven on and Kat told me.'

'That's OK. No problem. Can you remember what he looked like?'

'Well, quite stocky. Maybe late forties or early fifties. Going bald. Not much help, am I?'

'Don't worry.' It could have been Naylor, but equally Hilary's description probably covered half the officers in the Devon force.

'Hang on. I think he was a sergeant,' she said suddenly. 'Yes, he was. Another officer came over and he called him "Sarge".'

'And what did the other one look like?'

'Younger. He was pale and had gingery hair – you know, that gingery-blond colour – and really pale blue eyes.'

Bingo! Daniel thought. That sounded like Naylor's sidekick, PC Innes, so it was a fair bet Naylor was their man.

'Is Kat still upset? Do you want me to come over?'

'*Would* you? She keeps asking when you're coming again. When we first heard about the body, they were saying it was a girl and I think she immediately thought of Elena, but they're now saying it's a young woman, so she's calmed down a bit.'

'OK, I'll come over. See you soon.'

He put the phone down on Tamzin's coffee table just as she entered, carrying two mugs.

'You're honoured. This is real coffee, made with hot milk,' she informed him. 'Who was that? Did I hear you say you were going? Not before you drink this, I hope?'

'Absolutely not. It was Hilary. Kat's in a bit of a state about something. She wants me to go over, but there's no frantic rush. By the way, I've found out what that business was about on the moor last night. A young couple looking for a spot for a clandestine bonk found a body instead. Something of a passion-killer, I imagine.'

Sitting next to him, Tamzin frowned. 'Oh my God! How awful! Who was it?'

'A young woman, apparently.'

'But what happened? Do they know?'

'Hilary didn't know, but it's bound to be on the news later.'

'I guess so.' She snuggled close, cupping her hands round her coffee mug.

There was a long silence.

'You all right?' Daniel asked.

'Yeah, I was just thinking. I suppose you had to deal with stuff like that all the time. Dead people and such.'

'Mm. Part of the job.'

'So how do you cope? Doesn't it ever get to you?'

'Sometimes. Especially when it's kids. But you can't afford to go to pieces. The best thing you can do is focus on catching whoever's responsible – if anyone is.'

'You miss it, don't you?' Tamzin said, surprised. 'Being a policeman, I mean.'

Daniel shrugged. 'Sometimes.'

'But you said the stress did get to you in the end . . .'

'Yeah, it wasn't the actual work so much as the people.' He sat up, putting his half-empty mug down on the table. 'Look, I think I'd better be on my way. Hilary did sound rather worried.'

Tamzin touched his arm. 'I'm sorry. Have I gone somewhere I shouldn't?'

'No, you're fine,' he said. 'But I do have to go. Thanks for this morning – with the horses – it was incredible.'

'I'm glad you enjoyed it. Any time you want to do it again . . .'

'I'd like that, but I've got a feeling it's going to take me a day or two to get over this time,' Daniel said, standing and stretching stiff muscles. He bent to kiss her. 'I'll call you.'

'You do that.'

Hilary came out to meet Daniel as he parked the car.

'Thanks for coming. I'm sorry, perhaps I shouldn't have taken her out,' she said. 'But I had to go out myself, and she's been so restless since the other night I didn't like to leave her on her own.'

She looked so apologetic that Daniel was hit by a rush of guilt.

'Oh God, I'm sorry. I've been taking you completely for granted and none of this is even your problem.'

'It's as much my problem as it is yours, as far as I can see,' Hilary pointed out. 'No one forced *you* to assume responsibility for Kat either – you chose to do that and I'm making that choice too. The poor kid needs someone on her side.'

'You're a very special woman, Hilary McEwen-Smith, do you know that?'

'Yes, we're both the cream of humanity,' she returned dryly. 'And now we've finished patting one another on the back, shall we get down to business? Any luck with your contacts? I'm just assuming that's what you've been up to.'

'None at all, I'm afraid. As far as my ex-colleagues at the Bristol Met are concerned, I'm a career-advancement leper.'

They were walking towards the house by now and Hilary stopped and turned towards him.

'But why, Daniel? What happened?'

Daniel hesitated. 'It's a bit complicated.'

'Well, I like to think I'm reasonably intelligent. Try me.'

He shook his head. 'Please, Hilary. Just leave it, OK?'

She was clearly reluctant to do so, but, providentially, they were interrupted by the appearance of Katya in the doorway to the farmhouse.

'Daniel!'

As he turned towards her, she broke into a run and threw

herself at him, wrapping her arms round his back and resting her cheek against his chest.

Over her dark head, Daniel raised his eyebrows at Hilary, who shrugged. When he'd last spoken to Kat, he could hardly claim to have been flavour of the month with her. Perhaps his absence, be it only for a couple of days, had brought it home to her that with him lay her only real chance of getting her sister back, however unsuccessful his attempts thus far.

'Where have you been?' she demanded after a moment, stepping back to look at him. 'Have you been back to the house?'

'No. I've been trying to contact a friend who might be able to help.' He noticed that Kat's hair had been restyled from an untidy mop into a short and sassy bob. It suited her – made her look older and more sophisticated. She was also wearing some new clothes.

'And can he?' Hope sparkled for a moment in Katya's eyes.

'No. That is, I couldn't speak to him. He's in hospital.' Daniel cravenly avoided the issue.

'But that's no good! Elena is in danger now – you said so yourself.'

'I know. And that's why I think it's time we go to the authorities,' Daniel said gently, starting to walk towards the house.

'You mean the police.'

'They'd have to be involved, yes.'

'But you promised!' Kat stayed where she was, catching his arm and forcing him to turn and look at her.

'I promised I wouldn't do it behind your back – and I won't. I just have to make you see that it's our only option.'

'Look, I'll leave you to it. I have hungry horses to see to,' Hilary said. 'But listen to him, Kat, please. He knows what he's talking about. Trust him, OK?'

Katya followed Daniel into the house, where they drank tea – which he didn't really want – and Kat obediently listened as he did his best to make her realize that they could do nothing on their own.

Her expression remained obdurate.

'How can you tell me to trust your police when they are friends of that bastard Patrescu?'

How indeed? Daniel thought with sympathy. And who was he to urge trust in the authorities, with his bitter experience of betrayal at their hands?

'Tell me about the man you saw earlier,' Daniel said. 'You say he came to the house?'

'Yes.'

'In his uniform?'

'No. Just normal clothes.'

'Are you sure it was him?'

'Yes, I'm sure.' Her confirmation was totally convincing in its simplicity.

'Did you ever see him and Patrescu together? Did they seem to be friends?'

She shook her head. 'No, I never saw them together. We only saw him come and go. Our room looked over the driveway and we used to watch from the window, Elena and me. Twice we saw him, but I didn't know he was a policeman until this morning. He was on the television at lunchtime. On the news,' she added.

'Was he, indeed?' Daniel looked at his watch. 'There should be more news at six. I wouldn't mind seeing that, but just at the moment I think we should go and see if Hilary needs a hand. By the way,' he added, as they got to their feet, 'who did your hair? Hilary?'

Kat laughed. A rare occurrence.

'No. Hilary said if she cut it, I would end up looking like a horse! A lady came to the house to do Hilary's and she did mine too.' She tossed her head like an actress in a shampoo commercial. 'It looks nice, yes?'

'It looks very nice,' Daniel agreed.

The body on Dartmoor dominated the local news that night, with a great deal of time being devoted to moody shots of the moor under a lowering sky, which suggested a certain artistic licence, as the day had been bright and clear. An Inspector Mike Rutledge was interviewed at length by a young reporter who managed to extract little of importance from him.

The matter also had a slot on the national news, but their reporter had got one over on his local counterpart by discovering that the young woman was thought to be in her mid-to late twenties, and that unconfirmed reports suggested that she might have died of a drug overdose combined with exposure.

Naylor and Innes appeared on screen for no more than a couple of seconds, but it was plenty of time for Daniel to confirm their identities.

'I bet Inspector Rutledge would love to know what his sergeant gets up to when he's off duty,' Hilary commented.

'Well, he's not going to hear it from me,' Daniel responded. 'Been there, done that.'

'Got the T-shirt?' Hilary suggested.

'There wasn't one,' he said without humour.

Katya said little during the meal that evening and went up to bed straight afterwards, complaining of a headache, leaving Hilary and Daniel drinking coffee in front of the wood-burning stove in the sitting room, where the chairs were more comfortable.

'So, is now a good time to tell me about it?' Hilary asked, after a long silence punctuated only by the popping and crackling of the fire.

Daniel didn't answer, but neither did he pretend to misunderstand.

'What's the matter? Don't you trust me?'

'More than almost anyone I know,' he assured her. 'But it was all such a bloody mess . . .'

A log settled in the burner, sending a shower of sparks up the chimney, and Taz lifted his head enquiringly before settling back into his position at Daniel's feet.

Daniel took a deep breath and exhaled slowly. To revisit that time would be to touch a raw place, like lifting the dressing on a broken blister. Didn't he have nightmares enough without stirring up the memories afresh?

'Come on, Daniel,' she said gently, 'it obviously still bothers you. Won't you tell me? I'm a good listener and I want to understand. Why did you give up your career?'

'I didn't have a lot of choice,' he said finally. 'I went from being one of the lads to being the station pariah and it was compromising my work.'

Still watching the flames, Daniel began to tell his story for the very first time, and having started, the words flowed like pus from a lanced boil.

As Daniel eased himself out of the deep, saggy armchair shortly before eleven o'clock, it seemed as if there wasn't a fibre of his body that wasn't protesting. The physical effects of the morning's ride, combined with lack of sleep, had left him aching and drained of energy.

'Poor old man!' Hilary exclaimed, seeing his grimace.

'It's no joking matter,' Daniel said severely. 'I may never walk properly again.'

She put her hand on his arm as he turned towards the door. 'Daniel, you should tell Tamzin what you've told me, you know. She'd understand.'

'Yeah, maybe one day.'

His reply sounded unconvincing, even to himself, and Hilary gave him a long look before saying, 'Well, that's up to you, of course, but anyway, thanks for trusting me. I know it was hard, and I suspect you haven't told me everything, but that's OK.'

'Well . . . thanks for listening,' he said with a touch of awkwardness. 'And for not judging me.'

'That's ridiculous. What right do I have to judge you?'

Daniel gave her a half-smile. 'Tell that to the people I worked with for ten years.'

The night was clear and cold, and Daniel drove fast, thinking of his bed and wishing the flat above the empty showroom had central heating.

It had been a long day, and after a short distance, a combination of the warmth of the heater and the relaxing strains of a classical music station on the car stereo began to induce a dangerous state of drowsiness. Well aware of the danger and its possible consequences, Daniel gave himself a mental shake, opened a window to the icy night air for a spell and searched for something more stimulating on the radio.

Arriving back at his flat, some fifteen minutes later, Daniel swung the car thankfully into the drive and had to brake hard to avoid ploughing into a green plastic wheelie bin that lay prostrate across his path. Groaning at the necessity of stirring his tender muscles to action once more, Daniel opened the car door and went to shift the bin to one side. If it was his own, he didn't know what it was doing this far from the yard and could only imagine that bored kids must have dragged it round.

If Daniel's conscious mind was dulled by tiredness, at least his subconscious was still in good order. As he bent to lay his hands on the smooth plastic of the bin, some slight sound behind him – just the displacement of a pebble, maybe – brought his survival instincts surging to the fore.

Without stopping to consider, he dived forward over the bin

to hit the ground shoulder first and rolled, bringing the plastic container across his body as a shield.

A split second later, Daniel felt a heavy impact through the tough plastic as a knife, which had no doubt been intended to sink between his shoulder blades, hit the shiny surface and glanced sideways, its point lancing through the palm of his left hand.

EIGHT

D aniel's quick reaction not only saved his life, but had the added bonus of throwing his attacker off-balance, momentum carrying the man on to stumble over the top of his intended target and land sprawling on the gravel beside him.

Intensely aware that danger lay only the width of the wheelie bin away, Daniel heaved the thing with some force at the knifeman and scrambled to put distance between them as quickly as he could.

His plan – his only thought – was to get to the back of the Mercedes and let the dog out. Alone and unarmed, the advantage lay strongly with his attacker; with Taz in the equation, the balance would swing back overwhelmingly in Daniel's favour. Salvation was just a few short yards away, but it was clear that the knifeman knew that too, for as Daniel made it to all fours, his right foot was grasped and jerked backwards, dropping him abruptly on to his face.

With nothing to hold on to, Daniel found himself being dragged relentlessly back into perilous proximity of the knife. Expecting, at any moment, to feel the plunge of cold steel into the muscle of his thigh or buttock, Daniel tried to take the offensive by kicking out high and hard with his left foot.

A grunt indicated that it had made contact, but the hold on his right ankle remained firm, so he twisted on to his back and by the light of the car headlamps tried again, this time landing a vicious heel against his attacker's jaw.

Christ, the man was tough!

Even though his head snapped back at the impact, the knifeman's grip on Daniel's ankle seemed to tighten rather than relax.

Daniel lashed out a second time and twisted on to his stomach, desperate to cover up. The glimpse of the knifeman's face had confirmed his identity.

Anghel Macek.

He had the look of a man on a mission, and it didn't take a genius to guess what that mission was.

For an instant, Daniel thought his wild kick had achieved its purpose, for the vice-like grip on his ankle eased, but moments later the whole, and not inconsiderable, weight of Macek's body landed on his back, flattening him face-down on the gravel, and driving the air from his lungs.

Gasping for breath and unable to move, Daniel was powerless. In the car he could hear Taz going wild with a frustration that echoed his own, but just at the moment the dog might as well be the other side of Devon for all the help he could offer.

The Romanian took advantage of the moment to shift his weight further up Daniel's body, slipping his forearm under Daniel's chin and wrenching back his head.

Now completely immobilized, Daniel waited the space of several painful heartbeats for the cold edge of the blade to slice through his windpipe, severing the life-sustaining arteries and letting his blood drain away into the gravel.

He had seen bodies with such injuries in the course of his career, and wondered in an almost detached way who would find his. Would it be Naylor and his ginger partner, Innes? He imagined Innes taking one look and throwing up in the hedge. The image of Naylor gloating over his dead body brought a surge of anger and frustration.

Seconds passed and a glimmer of hope squeezed through. What was the man waiting for? Had he perhaps dropped his knife?

Even as he thought it, Macek shifted his weight forward a few more inches until Daniel could hear his coarse breathing next to his right ear. He was assailed by a strong smell of garlic.

'Where's the girl?' the Romanian growled.

'With the police.' Daniel's words came out in little more than a whisper.

Macek's arm tightened momentarily and darkness flashed behind Daniel's eyes.

'You lie!' he hissed. 'Where is she?'

Daniel knew his outlook was bleak, irrespective of whether he gave Macek what he wanted, and he was damned if he was going to hand the man a complete victory. With what was left of his breath he somewhat recklessly told the Romanian where he could go.

'No dog to save you this time,' Macek warned him as the darkness pressed in once more. 'This time you die!'

Daniel wasn't sure if Macek intended strangling him or breaking his neck – the end result would be the same – but in moving close to deliver his chilling promise, the Romanian had made a mistake, and as the pressure on his trachea increased, Daniel made one last, desperate bid for life. Throwing his head still further back and to the side, he felt a satisfying crunch as his skull connected with Macek's nose.

The Romanian cursed and for a split second the stranglehold eased just a fraction.

In that instant, Daniel reached up with his right hand, twisted his fingers in Macek's hair and yanked the man's head forward. Standard girly tactic – hair pulling – but he wasn't proud, and what's more it was surprisingly effective. With his head held next to Daniel's, the Romanian no longer had the leverage to complete the strangulation.

They had an impasse, which Macek broke by lifting his body to try and break Daniel's hold. That was his second mistake.

The instant he felt the weight lift, Daniel erupted into action, somehow drawing enough strength to push upwards and sideways, tipping the Romanian off-balance while his head remained anchored painfully by Daniel's unrelenting hold on his hair.

At this point, with his body no longer pinned to the ground, Daniel decided to cut his losses. He was under no illusions that his strength came anywhere near matching that of the bigger man. So, as the pressure on his windpipe eased, he brought his knees under him, gave the Romanian's hair one last vicious tug, which had the effect of bringing Macek's forehead into forcible contact with the ground, then heaved him sideways and scrambled away with as much speed as he could.

Macek was a big man, taller than Daniel, and quite possibly some 10 or 15 kilos heavier, but unfortunately for Daniel, the Romanian's bulk didn't seem to slow him down at all. Daniel made it to his feet and as far as the front of the car before he was tackled from behind and brought crashing down on the bonnet with a force that made the suspension bounce and the breath leave his lungs for the third time in as many minutes.

Afraid that Macek would attempt to repeat his stranglehold,

Daniel brought his arms up close on either side of his face, shielding his neck, and the Romanian responded by pulling him away from the car by the collar of his leather jacket and throwing him to the ground once more.

Daniel wasn't about to get caught in the same trap again. Even struggling for breath as he was, he had no sooner hit the gravel than he was rolling over and over to gain distance and confuse Macek's aim. After three revolutions, he came up against the fallen wheelie bin and looked up to see the Romanian's approaching form haloed in the headlamps.

Darkness – that's what he needed. If only he could reach the shadows by the wall of the building, he might conceivably be able to slip past the other man and get to the back of the car.

Remembering a tip from his Asian colleague Jo-Ji, Daniel pulled his knees up and went into a backward roll to confuse the Romanian. Macek was so close it didn't seem possible that Daniel would make it, but somehow he did, landing on his knees and getting quickly to his feet beyond the glare of the headlights.

Keeping close to the wall, Daniel moved swiftly towards the rear of the vehicle, the noise of his progress masked by the sound of the engine. For a moment he dared to hope that his tactics had worked, but he'd underestimated the Romanian. When he drew level with the tailgate of the car, he found Macek there before him, and to make matters worse, he'd been reunited with his knife. Six inches of razor-sharp steel reflected the moonlight, and as Daniel already knew to his cost, the Romanian wouldn't hesitate to use it.

Inside the Mercedes, Taz was beside himself with rage, the back of the car rocking wildly as he threw himself at the tough metal grille of the tailgate guard.

Macek ignored him. The driver's door was still open and in the faint glow from the car's courtesy light Daniel could see Macek's head moving from side to side, indicating that he wasn't sure exactly where his quarry was.

'Where are you, my friend? Come to Dada,' the Romanian invited, his teeth showing in an unpleasant smile as he held the knife up, twisting it to catch the light.

Was this the knife that had scarred Marika? Suddenly Daniel felt certain it was, and in the same instant feared that he knew who the girl on the moor was. If Patrescu suspected that Marika had helped Katya and Daniel escape that night at the house, they would no longer be able to trust her. Macek was doing Patrescu's housekeeping: cleaning up the loose ends that posed a danger to their operation. Marika had been one, and he – Daniel – was another.

It crossed Daniel's mind that he could just keep moving and leave Macek and the car behind. His mobile, frustratingly, was lying in the coin tray of the car, and it would be a longish walk to the nearest phone, but he might still have considered it if it hadn't been for Taz.

With his fear of dogs, there was no way Macek would risk opening the back of the car to tackle Taz face to face, but if Daniel slipped through his fingers, what was to stop him torching the car with the dog inside?

Moments later, as if the Romanian had read his mind, Daniel saw the flare of a lighter flame in his hand. Macek held it out towards the car and waved it gently to and fro.

'Say goodbye to the doggie,' he taunted, raising his voice above the furious barking from within.

It wasn't the goading that galvanized Daniel into action but the knowledge that in order to activate the lighter, Macek had passed the knife to his left hand. If Daniel was going to make a move – and at some point he *was* going to have to – there probably wouldn't be a better moment than now.

Bending to scoop up a handful of grit and pebbles, he lunged forward and threw it in the Romanian's face, following with a punch that held all the weight of payback.

He was aware of the big man staggering back, the expiring flame of the lighter describing a brief orange arc as it fell, but he saw it on the periphery of his vision, all his attention fixed on opening the back of the Merc and releasing the dog. As soon as the catch on the inner guard slid free, Taz barged out, knocking Daniel aside in his haste to get at the Romanian.

As Daniel recovered his balance, he heard the fence on the far side of the drive shake violently as the Romanian launched himself at it.

Taz was only inches behind him, his teeth snapping on empty air as Macek scrambled over. For a moment he continued to bark furiously, his claws raking at the wooden panels, and then yipped and whined a time or two before running off down the drive towards the back of the building.

Daniel hurried to the front of the car to kill the engine and retrieve his torch. By the time he turned round and switched it on, he was alone in the drive. Presumably Taz had wriggled under the fence where he had before and had taken off across the adjacent field in pursuit of his quarry.

His guess was borne out when he heard the shepherd start barking once again, a little way off, a sure sign that he was confronting his adversary.

Macek was shouting now, perhaps in an attempt to intimidate the dog, but Daniel knew Taz wouldn't be turned. As he prepared to tackle the fence and go to his partner's aid, there came some ferocious snarling, a muffled yelp and then a worrying silence.

Daniel's blood ran cold. He knew of only one thing that would silence his dog when he was tackling a suspect.

'Taz!' he shouted, then stood listening hard for some sound that would tell him the dog was OK. As he waited, his heart thudding with fear, he heard a car door slam, followed by the revving of an engine and the screech of tortured rubber as a vehicle pulled away along the lane beyond the field.

It seemed Macek had gone, but what should have been a huge relief was cancelled out by Daniel's fear for Taz. It wasn't the first time the dog had faced a knifeman, but there was always a risk, and the Romanian was, undeniably, a very powerful man.

Putting two fingers to his lips, Daniel whistled, pausing afterwards to listen.

Silence.

Panic rose sharply. Taz was just about the only constant in his life at the moment and the thought of losing him was bleak indeed.

He tucked the torch into his waistband and, gauging the height of the fence, took a step back, then two quick strides forward and leaped at the panelling.

Dropping to the ground on the other side, the first thing Daniel saw was a tiny gleam of reflected moonlight down at his feet. He bent to look more closely, parting the rough grass. Macek's knife. In his hasty scramble over the fence it must have slipped from his grip and he'd been too afraid of the dog to risk stopping to search for it.

A quick examination revealed that the weapon was a single-action flick knife. Straightening up, Daniel slid the blade back into its haft and slipped it into his pocket. Switching the torch on, he swept the beam across the field. The grass was long – the untidy remains of an uncut hay crop from last year – and the torchlight yellow and fading with the need of a new battery. There was no sign of the dog.

Daniel shouted again with no success and then tried to calm himself and apply logic.

There was a gate in the hedge on the far side of the field and if Macek had parked in the lane beyond, he would surely have been heading for that when Taz had caught up with him, so the sensible plan of action would be to search along that line. Walking at a brisk pace and sweeping the torch beam from side to side ahead of him, Daniel set off across the field, desperate to find the dog, yet conversely afraid to.

He was nearly at the gate when he spotted a dark mound in the grass to one side. The torchlight picked out dark fur, and with an incoherent moan, Daniel dropped to his knees beside the dog, his heart contracting with fear.

Taz was lying tumbled in a heap, partly on his belly, partly on his side. He looked lifeless, but placing a shaking hand on his ribcage, Daniel detected a slight movement and sent a quick word of thanks winging upwards. He put the torch between his teeth and carefully straightened the dog out, searching all the while for signs of injury.

It was when he put his hands gently under Taz's head that he found the root of the trouble. The dog was bleeding copiously from a gash between his left eye and ear, and the area was already badly swollen.

'It's all right. Good boy. It's OK,' Daniel said, even though the dog couldn't hear him.

He rubbed the warm fur of Taz's shoulder and looked back across the darkness of the field, his mind racing. First things first. He had to get the dog to the car – or rather, he amended, thinking of the impossibility of the panel fencing – the car to the dog. Thanks to the proximity of the lane, that was fairly easy, and with more words of reassurance to his unconscious partner, he stood up and started back over the rough grass at a run.

In less than five minutes, Daniel brought the Merc to a skidding halt in the lane outside the field gate. Killing the engine, he leaped out and threw open both tailgate and guard, ready to receive the injured dog.

Lying on the tarmac level with the gate was a length of wood, and pausing briefly to shine the torch on it, Daniel saw a broken fencing spar, some 3 feet long. A tuft of fur adhering to a bent nail on one edge labelled it as the weapon the Romanian had used on the dog, dropped as he made for his car.

When Daniel reached Taz, he hardly dared look, but the dog's condition seemed unchanged, which was both a blessing and a worry.

He was deeply concerned. Macek wouldn't have held back. What if the blow had fractured the dog's skull? He could, even now, be haemorrhaging into his brain; there was no way of knowing.

Daniel forced his mind away from the unthinkable and concentrated on carefully working his hands under the dog to lift him. Gathering him into his arms, he staggered upright with Taz's 40-odd kilos hanging limply in his grasp. *A dead weight*, Daniel's brain unhelpfully supplied as the dog's head lolled over his arm.

He carried him to the car and laid him gently on the blankets in the back, spreading one over his still body to keep him warm. In the dim light provided by the car, the dog's condition looked no more encouraging, and fishing for his mobile phone with fingers slippery with blood, Daniel searched his memory for a directory enquiries number. God, he heard the adverts on the radio all the time; they drove him mad! Why couldn't he remember the bloody numbers now, when he needed them?

Fred Bowden, he thought with a flash of inspiration. Fred's wife had a dog; they'd know where to find a vet and they lived closer than either Hilary or Tamzin.

Daniel's hands were shaking so much it took him two attempts to key in his boss's home number, and when the connection was made, it seemed to ring for ever.

'Come on, Fred. Pick it up,' Daniel begged. 'Please don't be out . . .'

He rubbed the dog's soft fur. 'Hang on, Taz, d'you hear me? You damn well hang on!'

'Hello?' Bowden sounded as though he might have been asleep.

'Fred, Taz has been hurt. I need a vet quickly.'

'Right. Hold on. I'll get the number. Are you at home?'

'Yes.'

Daniel waited, silently blessing Bowden's quick, quiet efficiency. His army training, he supposed. The last thing he'd needed just now was questions.

'OK.' Bowden was back. 'We go to a vet on the north side of Tavistock, but Meg says there's one closer to you. I'll hand her over while I ring ahead on my mobile and tell them you're coming.'

The next moment, Fred's wife came on, also blessedly brief and to the point, giving Daniel the name of the practice and the necessary directions before wishing him luck and ringing off.

Daniel leaned close to Taz and told him, once again, that he was a good boy and that everything would be fine, and then shut the back down, wiped his hands on his jeans and got into the driver's seat.

His left palm stung a little, still oozing blood, and for the first time since it happened, Daniel became aware of the knife wound. There was no time to stop and bind the injury properly. Irritated at the delay, Daniel grabbed a cloth from the pocket in the car door and hastily wrapped it round his hand, tucking in the loose end.

That taken care of, he reversed the car into the field gateway, pulled back on to the tarmac, changed gear and accelerated hard, wishing he could see the dog from where he sat.

'It's all right, lad,' he said over his shoulder. 'We'll soon have you sorted. You hang on, OK?'

Daniel drove as fast as he could without giving Taz too rough a ride in the back, desperately hoping he wouldn't have the bad luck to be stopped by a roving police patrol on the narrow back roads.

Thanks to Meg's efficient instructions, he reached the vet's surgery in just under ten minutes, drove right up to the building and ran the car to an untidy halt on the pavement outside the lighted glass door.

This was opened immediately by a slight, blonde female in a green uniform bearing the name of the practice.

'Daniel Whelan?' she asked.

'That's right.' Daniel went straight to the back of the car and lifted the tailgate, consumed by the fear that it would be already too late, but, incredibly, as the light came on, Taz's eyes were open and he lifted his head slightly.

Even though he knew Taz was by no means out of the woods, the relief brought tears to Daniel's eyes, and he buried his face in the dog's fur as he leaned forward to pick him up once more.

'Bring him straight in,' the blonde said, pulling the door wide. 'You were lucky. I had another emergency and was already here. So, what's been happening with this chap?'

'He tackled a burglar.' As he lifted the dog out of the car,

Daniel gave her the story he'd prepared on the journey. 'He gave chase, and when I found him, he was unconscious. He's got a nasty wound on his head. I think he was hit with a piece of wood.'

'In here,' the vet said, holding open an inner door as Daniel followed her across the reception area with the dog in his arms. 'Pop him on the table. When did this happen?'

'About fifteen or twenty minutes ago.' In the consulting room, Daniel carefully lowered Taz on to the rubber-topped table, wincing as the dog whimpered slightly. Although he was lying still, his eyes were open and black with fear. Daniel stroked the thick, soft fur.

'It's a good sign that he's coming round. I'm Emma, by the way.'

The vet got straight down to business, lifting one of the dog's eyelids to examine his pupils and his lip to assess the colour of his gums. 'That looks OK. You did the right thing in keeping him warm,' she added as she reached for a stethoscope. 'Let's have a little look at him.'

Daniel murmured reassurance to Taz, while Emma carried out a thorough examination and then gently cleaned the ugly wound on Taz's head with some moistened cotton wool.

'We'll get him X-rayed to rule out fracture and check for internal bleeding. You're a good lad,' she added, ruffling the dog's fur.

'Is he going to be all right?' Daniel had gone through such agonies of anxiety on the journey that he hardly dared to hope.

'I can't give you a positive until I've seen the X-rays. There's always a risk with head trauma, as I'm sure you're aware. I'd be happier if he was showing a little more willingness to move, but his vital signs are looking OK and his reflexes are normal, so that's all encouraging.' She broke off as the door opened and a round-faced girl with a shock of ginger curls came in, wearing a thick fleece over her uniform.

'Ah, Sarah. Good. Just in time,' Emma said. She introduced Daniel and explained the situation. 'Obviously he's going to need stitches and there's also a broken tooth that'll have to come out. I'll give him a painkiller and a shot of antibiotics for now, and then we'll keep an eye on him for half an hour or so before we anaesthetize, just to make sure there's nothing else going on.'

*   *   *

After forty tense minutes, Taz was taken in to surgery. Left alone in the waiting room, Daniel spent the time beating himself up over the events of the last hour or so.

How *could* he have been so stupid, he demanded over and over again, as to have been caught out like some rookie by what was practically the oldest trick in the book?

Yes, he'd been tired, but that was no excuse – especially when you took into account what had occurred just two nights before. If he'd been any kind of detective, he'd have considered the possibility that the prowler from Friday was one of the Romanians. Given his recent history, to have dismissed it carelessly as an opportunistic attempt at burglary was the action of a fool and it was Taz who had ultimately paid for it.

Daniel glanced down at his hand, wrapped hastily in a grubby green and white tea towel. It was throbbing heavily now that he had time to register the fact, but in some strange way he was glad of the pain – glad that he hadn't got off scot-free when the dog had taken such punishment. The cloth was soaked in blood where it crossed his palm and to a lesser degree on the back, but although he knew it should probably be stitched, his fingers and thumb were working normally, so he wasn't unduly worried.

He stared around the waiting room, trying to take an interest in posters depicting the life cycle of the flea, adverts for puppy parties – whatever they were – and reminders to vaccinate yearly, but he couldn't repress the voice in his head that repeated over and over that it was all his fault that Taz lay critically injured on the other side of the surgery door.

He jumped up as the door squeaked open to admit the vet, rubbing her face wearily.

'How is he?'

'Well, we've made him as comfortable as we can and you'll be pleased to hear the X-rays didn't show anything too worrying – no fractures, major internal bleeds or anything nasty like that.'

'So he'll be all right?'

'Yes, he should be, but I'd be lying if I said he was completely in the clear. You can never be a hundred per cent sure with head injuries. I'll be happier this time tomorrow.' She hesitated. 'He's been in the wars before, hasn't he? I noticed a couple of old scars. There's a nasty one on his front leg.'

'Yeah, he sliced it on a sheet of corrugated iron while he was searching a scrapyard last year.'

'Oh, he's a police dog?'

'Was,' Daniel confirmed. 'He's retired now. In fact, it was the leg injury that did it, but he made a full recovery in time.'

'And you? Are you . . . ? I mean . . .' She faltered. 'Sorry, I'm being nosy.'

'I left too.' Daniel didn't elaborate and she didn't pursue it. 'So, how long will it be before Taz comes round?'

'Technically, he already has, but I've given him an analgesic – a painkiller – that acts as a sedative, so he'll sleep for several hours yet. We can only wait and see. Now, I don't know about you, but I'm gasping for a cup of tea. I'd just put the kettle on when you arrived. Would you like one? You look as though you could do with something.'

Daniel said he would, and followed the vet through to a small room off the reception area, where white kitchen units, a sink and a fridge dominated the space.

Daniel watched as she filled the kettle and took three mugs and a packet of decaffeinated teabags from a small cupboard on the wall. She did everything with the sure economy of move-ment that had characterized her handling of Taz. Her hands were pale and lean, with the blue veins clearly visible, and she had blonde hair cut into a short bob, longer at the front than the back, and with a fringe that kept falling into her grey eyes and having to be pushed away.

The tea made, Emma pushed one mug towards Daniel, then found half a packet of digestive biscuits and offered the open top to him. As she did so, she appeared to notice the state of his left hand for the first time.

'What happened there? Did you get bitten?'

'No.' Daniel didn't take offence at the suggestion: even the friendliest dog can bite when stressed or in pain. 'It's a cut.'

'Let me see,' Emma said in a tone that brooked no argument. 'No, hang on. We'll have our tea first, then go through to the surgery. Here, pull up a stool before you keel over. You look shattered.'

After the tea and some uncomfortable questions about the fictional attempted burglary, Daniel followed the vet back to the room they'd first entered, where she put on surgical gloves before unwinding the bloodstained tea towel from his hand.

'This doesn't look the most sterile wound dressing I've ever seen,' she observed dryly.

'It's what I use to wipe the car windows with,' Daniel admitted sheepishly. 'It was all I could find in a hurry.'

Emma dropped the offending cloth in a pedal bin and turned back to examine his hand, the palm of which was slowly pooling with blood. Mopping it with a damp wad of cotton wool revealed a wound maybe an inch and a half long in the angle between his thumb and index finger, from which blood welled sluggishly. Pressing the wad firmly to the cut, she turned his hand over to reveal a similar wound on the other side.

'This needs stitching.'

Daniel didn't answer; he had known it did.

'If I didn't know better, I'd say this was a knife wound.'

'It does look a bit like it, doesn't it?' Daniel agreed.

Emma gave him a long, hard look, then asked, 'Can you still move your thumb?'

He could, and demonstrated it.

Emma shook her head in disbelief. 'Well, all I can say is you've been bloody lucky! It looks as though the blade slipped between the muscles, for the most part. Does it hurt very much?' She scrutinized his face as she asked the question.

'It throbs a bit,' Daniel told her. 'Will you stitch it for me?'

'Me?' Her grey eyes widened. 'No way! I'm a vet, not a doctor. I could get into a lot of trouble.'

'I won't tell if you don't.'

'I'm sorry, I can't. What if it became infected? They'd want to know who stitched it. Look, I'll run you to hospital, if you like. It needs to be properly checked out and you ought to have a tetanus jab.'

Daniel shook his head. 'You know what they're like. I'd be there for hours. I'm up to date with tetanus, and anyway, I'm not going anywhere while there's any doubt about Taz.'

'Sarah will be here. She's very capable.'

'Thanks but I'll wait. Perhaps you could let me have a cleaner bandage, though.'

'That wouldn't be difficult. Here, hold that in place. Press hard – we need to get the bleeding stopped,' she instructed, before fetching two cellophane-wrapped rolls, scissors, a dressing strip and some more cotton wool.

Halfway back to him, she paused, wavering. 'Look, if I did stitch it, you'd have to swear not to tell a soul . . .'

Daniel awoke with a start, his mind filled with the chaos of the familiar nightmare. He was sweating, his heart racing, and in those first waking moments had no idea where he was, but as the logical part of his brain started to function, memory seeped back by degrees.

Milky early-morning light shone through a gridded window on to shelves holding sacks of dog food, rolls of fleecy bedding and all the non-drug supplies needed by a busy veterinary surgery. He was on a camp bed in the storeroom next to the kennel area where Taz was recovering from his injuries.

There had been a short altercation about Daniel's stated intention of keeping watch over Taz.

'You're not really allowed in the kennel area,' Emma had told him. 'Health and safety, you know how it is.'

Daniel had raised his eyebrows. 'I think we've probably gone a bit beyond that,' he had observed, holding up his bandaged hand, and with a narrow look, she'd had to concede the point.

He had sat with Sarah for some time, battling increasingly heavy eyelids, before finally giving in to her suggestion that he should try and get a couple of hours' sleep while she watched over the dog. She had promised faithfully to wake him if there was any change.

Now there was a tentative knock on the door and a voice spoke his name. He sat up, the springs of the bed creaking and twanging as he moved. He was still deathly tired, and his body felt much like the camp bed sounded, letting him know in no uncertain terms that it had been abused.

The door opened a little further and Sarah's curly head peered round.

'Taz is waking up,' she told him.

'Thanks.' Daniel got stiffly to his feet. 'How does he look?' he asked, as he followed Sarah through to the kennel area.

'See for yourself,' she suggested with a smile.

Daniel approached the cage and was greeted by the sight of Taz sitting up, his eyes bright and cognizant. His face was still swollen, and the flesh around the sutures looked painfully inflamed, but he wagged the end of his bushy tail enthusiastically as Daniel came into view.

Mindful of the need to keep the dog calm, Daniel suppressed the surge of joy he felt, merely saying quietly, 'Hello, lad. How you doing?'

His partner had made it and suddenly anything seemed possible.

* * *

By eight o'clock, when the surgery was beginning to wake up for the day, with staff arriving and the telephones ringing almost continuously, Taz had eaten a little breakfast and drunk some water. Emma, who had arrived early to see her patient, pronounced herself cautiously pleased with his progress.

'I'm afraid I shall have to ask you to move your car,' she said then and Daniel remembered it was still parked on the pavement outside the door.

'Of course. I'll shift it straight away.'

'Look, Taz will be fine. There are loads of people here to keep an eye on him. Why don't you go home and get some proper sleep? I'm sure you didn't sleep much last night. I promise to call you if there's the slightest change in his condition.'

'OK, thanks,' Daniel said. He couldn't explain to Emma that going back to the flat now that it was on Macek's map could prove to be little short of suicidal, but neither could he hang around the surgery all day without being very much in the way. 'Thanks for everything. I'll pop back later.'

'Are you sure you'll be all right driving with that hand?' she asked doubtfully.

'Yeah, you've done a great job. It's as good as new,' Daniel lied, flexing his thumb and fingers. Under its swathe of crêpe bandage and bright-pink Vet Wrap, his hand was decidedly sore but serviceable. He had a sneaking suspicion the pinkness of the self-adhesive outer layer was Emma's way of getting her own back for the corner he'd forced her into.

In spite of a game effort by the sun, the air outside was still bitterly cold, and in the shade of the building, the Merc had a thick coating of frost. Daniel scraped away the worst of it with a credit card and slipped into the driver's seat, blowing on chilled fingers and wondering where to go.

Ahead of him, two doors down on the other side of the street, a bakery café was just opening its doors, the proprietor bringing out an A-frame board that promised a full English or Continental breakfast.

The decision took all of five seconds.

Reversing the car off the pavement, he located the nearest car park and paid for three hours before heading for the warmth of the café with its heady aroma of freshly baked bread.

As he took a seat by the window, Daniel's mobile began to vibrate in his jacket pocket and he fished it out.

Bowden. He'd rung earlier to enquire after Taz and to tell Daniel not to worry about getting in to work that day.

Daniel had been more grateful than he could say. He had intended taking the day off, anyway, but to be able to do it with his employer's blessing took a weight off his mind, and perhaps because of that he'd been a little more forthcoming with information about the previous night's attack than he would normally have been.

He hoped this second call didn't signal a change of mind.

'Hello?'

'Daniel, could you come to the house this evening? Say about eight?'

'As long as Taz goes on OK,' Daniel said cautiously. 'Is there a problem?'

'Can't talk now. Got to get on. See you later.'

Daniel sat staring out of the window with a slight frown. What did Bowden want? Was he to be given his marching orders, after all? The request had been brusque, to say the least.

He shrugged inwardly. If that was the case, then so be it. He could ill afford to lose the job, but there was no way he could abandon the two girls or, for that matter, Hilary, who was now almost as deeply involved as he was.

The waitress appeared and he put the matter to the back of his mind while he concentrated on more immediate concerns.

NINE

Fred and Meg Bowden's house was a white-painted Victorian building standing back from a tree-lined road on the outskirts of Tavistock. As Daniel parked the Merc on a tarmac drive bordered with ornamental brick edging, an outside light came on, illuminating flowerbeds stuffed with shrubs, drifts of snowdrops and clumps of early-flowering daffodils. Someone was a keen gardener, and somehow he couldn't imagine it being Fred, although appearances could be deceptive: he'd once known a tough duty sergeant who liked nothing better than a spot of knitting for relaxation.

The front door opened as Daniel approached and he was met by a slim, fiftyish lady in faded jeans, a beaded silk top and an

ankle-length purple mohair cardigan. She wore her long, salt and
pepper hair in a loose knot from which wisps had escaped to
hang around her face, and could have been no more than 5 feet
2 in her bare feet, which was how she was at that moment.

'Daniel? Hi, I'm Meg,' she said and leaned forward to kiss
him lightly on the cheek.

If Daniel was a little taken aback by this familiarity, at least
it boded well for his job security. It was hardly the welcome you
would expect from the boss's wife if you were on the point of
being sacked. Come to that, it was hardly the welcome you
expected from the boss's wife full stop – not on a first meeting,
anyway.

'Come on in. Fred's in the kitchen, cooking. We're eating late
tonight. You'll have some supper with us, won't you? Or have
you eaten?'

'No, I haven't. I'd like that. Thanks.' Things were definitely
looking up, but if he wasn't being dismissed, why was he here?

'Come in, then. How's Taz?'

'He's doing well, thank you. He's still at the vet's under obser-
vation because of his head injury, but he should be able to come
home tomorrow, all being well.' Daniel shut the door behind him
and followed Meg down the hallway towards the kitchen, where
an ageing black cocker spaniel lay across the doorway. It raised
its grey eyebrows enquiringly but made no move to vacate its
position. Meg stepped over it without breaking step, but Daniel
hesitated.

'Oh, I'm sorry about Mosely. It's his favourite place to sleep.
I think it's because he can see all the comings and goings from
there. He's a bit deaf, you see. Just step over him, he won't
mind.'

The kitchen wasn't particularly large but was fitted out with
cream-painted cupboards that stretched from the floor almost to
the lofty ceiling. Worktops were of stained timber, the sink an
old-style Belfast one, and a bottle-green Rayburn held pride of
place under a brick arch on one wall. Fred stood in front of this,
stirring the ingredients of a large stockpot with a wooden spoon;
the combination of a blue and white striped apron, earring and
razor-cut hair giving him a strangely Gallic look. An enticing
aroma of curry pervaded the air.

'Hi, Daniel. How's Taz?' Fred said, looking over his shoulder.

Daniel repeated his report.

'That's good news. But what about you? You look a bit rough

yourself.' He pointed the spoon at Daniel's bandaged hand. 'Was that from last night too?'

'Yeah, but it's nothing much. Listen, thanks for standing in for me today; that was a great relief.'

Fred slanted a look at him. 'I didn't think you'd turn up anyway with your partner at death's door, so to speak. I was just getting in first, keeping the illusion of authority.'

'Well, no, I wouldn't have,' Daniel admitted, noting Bowden's use of the word 'partner'. 'But thanks anyway.'

'Well, the rice is about ready,' Fred said, lifting the lid on another saucepan. 'Where's Tom got to, I wonder?'

'I'll lay the table. I'm sure he'll be here in a minute. He said he'd be finishing work at six when I spoke to him earlier, so unless something's come up . . .'

Daniel had no idea who the absent Tom was but supposed he would find out shortly. He wasn't left in the dark for long.

'Would you like a beer, Daniel?' Fred asked, going to the fridge as Meg disappeared with a handful of cutlery. 'Tom's our eldest son. We don't see him very often, but he pops in now and then for a spot of good home cooking.'

'Oh, then you'd probably rather I wasn't here. Thanks,' he added, accepting a bottle of real ale.

'No, you're all right. I budgeted for the both of you. Do you need a glass with that?'

'Of course he does!' Meg came back in. 'Don't be such a philistine. And take the top off for him too. He can't do it with a bad hand.'

Daniel's protests were interrupted by the sound of a key turning in the front door.

'Ah, there he is,' Meg announced.

Moments later there was a rush of cold air and a man's deep voice called out in greeting.

Daniel shifted his position so he could get a good look at the newcomer's approach, and saw a well-built man, perhaps a few years older than himself, with very short, greying brown hair. There would have been no doubting his relationship to Fred, even if Daniel hadn't been told. Apart from being slightly taller, he was a carbon copy of his father, with the same intrinsic tough-ness that needed no attitude to back it up. Here was a man you just knew you shouldn't mess with.

Before Tom even reached the kitchen, greeting the dog and then stepping over it as a matter of course, as his mother had,

Daniel had readjusted his mindset towards the rest of the evening. Unless he was very much mistaken, Fred Bowden's son was a police officer.

At least that explained the sudden and unheralded dinner invitation, Daniel thought as introductions were made. He was pleased to have solved that mystery. Even with the edited version of events that Daniel had given him, Fred had apparently decided that enough was enough.

On the face of it, Tom Bowden could be a godsend, especially if he was senior enough to have any clout in whichever station he hailed from, but one major hurdle remained: how would he react when he pulled Daniel's record at the Bristol Met?

'You go on in with your beers. I'm just going to put some veg on,' Meg said, shepherding them all towards the door. 'I can't work round you lot. This kitchen isn't big enough.'

Obediently the three men moved into the dining room, another high-ceilinged room, this time decorated with a theme of deep red and gold and dominated by a big, dark oak table with a gothic candelabra as its centrepiece. Daniel fancied he could see Meg's hand at work in the slightly Bohemian décor.

As he followed the others, Daniel allowed himself a secret smile, suspecting that this was to be the moment for the unveiling. Some perverse facet of his nature prompted him to take the initiative and let Tom know he was rumbled.

'So, which station are you from?' he asked casually, as if the subject had already been broached.

There was a noticeable pause and then Tom looked at his father. 'You've told him?'

'I haven't said a word,' Fred replied. 'He didn't even know you were coming until five minutes ago. It must've been your big flat feet that gave the game away.'

Tom held out his hand towards Daniel. 'DS Tom Bowden, Molton CID. How did you guess?'

Daniel shook the hand, shrugging. 'I don't know, really. Just knew.'

'Well, I can't say you've done wonders for my undercover confidence,' Tom remarked ruefully. 'And you are former PC Daniel Whelan of the Bristol Met and more recently of Taunton nick, but I can't claim any great intuition, just plain old-fashioned record-checking.'

It was Daniel's turn to look at Fred.

'I'm sensing a set-up, here. How long have you known?'

'Since the start, when you turned up for the job. You didn't really think I took your rather vague CV at face value, did you?'

'I did think you were a bit casual,' Daniel admitted.

'I asked Tom to check you out. I've had a couple of bad experiences with drivers in the past, so I don't take any chances these days. Can't afford to.'

'In that case – if Tom did his homework properly – I'm surprised you took me on.'

'Well, I don't pretend to know exactly what went on at the Met,' Tom said. 'In general, your ex-colleagues weren't over keen to talk. But I didn't find anything that made you a risk as a potential employee for Dad. Did I miss something?'

Daniel smiled faintly. 'Would I tell you if you had?'

Tom took a couple of swallows of his beer. 'I did speak to DCI Paxton,' he said then.

'And . . . ?' Daniel said warily.

'He said you and he hadn't always seen eye to eye but he had no complaints. Without giving details, he implied that you'd had something of a nervous breakdown and that your colleagues had lost confidence in you. He said that that was why he'd assigned you a temporary desk job. He seemed genuinely disappointed that you'd decided to call it a day.'

'Yeah, that'd be right!'

'I don't know of anything against Paxton and he's got a bloody good record for getting the job done,' Tom stated calmly, walking round the dining table and sitting in one of the chairs on the other side. 'But personally, I don't like the man and I don't trust him any further than I could spit him.'

Daniel glanced across, a glimmer of hope in his heart for the first time in a long while.

'So, do you want to tell us your side of the story?' Tom invited, waving a hand at the chair opposite.

Scanning the man's face, Daniel could see nothing except an apparent honest interest, and found that he did very much want to set the record straight, if only to this limited audience.

He stepped forward and pulled out a chair to sit on, standing his beer on a mat on the table.

'It started a couple of years ago, when I was still in the Dog Unit,' he said, staring at the beer glass, which he was turning with his fingers. 'There was a major drugs bust going down at a warehouse on the waterfront – it was the culmination of a big operation – and they wanted a couple of dogs on standby just in case anyone slipped the net.'

He glanced at Tom, who nodded. It was a normal precaution.

'So I was there with Taz, and as it happened, we *were* called in. It seems there was a tip-off at the last minute and before the lads could even take up their positions the suspects were legging it in all directions. It was chaos. Taz and I were in one of the squad cars tailing two of the main suspects who'd made off in a vehicle. Anyway, they crashed a couple of miles down the road, split up and made a run for it. The lads caught one of them pretty quickly, but the other one had it away on foot across country, carrying a rucksack. The chopper was tied up helping the boys on the ground locate a couple of runners back at the waterfront, so we were on. Taz picked up a good scent and set off at a hell of a lick – completely ran the legs off the sarge who was following me.' Daniel paused reflectively. 'Mind you, he was pretty soft – been sitting behind the wheel too long.'

'Anyway, we'd been tracking the suspect for a couple of miles when Taz suddenly stopped – bang – and did a ninety-degree left. Our runner had realized we were getting close and ditched the rucksack. He'd lobbed it into the bushes and that's what Taz had found. Once I realized what had happened, I put him back on the scent and we found matey up a tree, a hundred yards or so further on. I radioed my position, but he was so scared of the dog he refused to come down until back-up arrived, so I was able to leave the formalities to them. All in all, in spite of the tip-off, the waterfront operation had been a huge success and everyone was on a high. Much back-patting all round.' He paused and looked up to find Tom watching him closely.

'And?'

'Well, I took a quick look in that rucksack when I pulled it out of the undergrowth, and I'd say there was easily a couple of kilos of smack inside. The thing is, I found out later that when it was checked in at the station, there was only a fraction of that.'

Tom's brows drew down. 'You couldn't have been mistaken? Are you sure there wasn't anything else in the rucksack that could have made it feel heavier?'

'Nothing,' Daniel stated with absolute conviction. 'Somewhere between the collar and the evidence room, the major part of the haul went walkies.'

'And did you have any idea who might have taken it?' That was Fred.

Daniel shook his head. 'It could have been any one of a number of people. My shift was already over, and as I didn't actually make the arrest, I didn't go back to the station – just picked up my car and went home.'

'And you think it was one of your colleagues?' Fred again.

'It had to be, unless someone was criminally careless.'

'I'm afraid it's not unheard of,' Tom told his father. 'Officers supplementing their income with a bit of, shall we say, re-cycling?'

'You mean they sell it back to the dealers?'

'Yeah, or wherever,' he confirmed resignedly. 'They're not short of contacts.'

'They're no better than the dealers they're arresting,' Daniel said bitterly. 'Worse, really. Hiding behind their badges. One thing's for sure – someone made a pretty penny. The smack that did make it back was a hundred per cent pure. The jokers at the warehouse would have cut it and sold it on to the dealers.'

'Cut it?' Fred asked.

'Yeah, mixed it with something else to bulk it out.'

'What do they mix it with?' he wanted to know, and Tom answered.

'Powdered milk, sugar, baking soda, soap powder, talc, sink cleaners, detergent – you name it, basically. Any white powder; they aren't bothered. There was a case, years ago, where the Rolling Stones guitarist Keith Richards almost died when someone cut his dope with strychnine.'

'Strychnine?' Fred was horrified. 'But that's a poison!'

'So is heroin,' Tom said grimly. 'But you wouldn't really want to inject *any* of those fillers into your bloodstream. They'll prob-ably all kill you in the end if the heroin doesn't.'

Fred Bowden shook his head in disgust. 'And the cops are selling it back to the dealers,' he said. 'Christ! These are the people we pay to uphold the law.'

'So, what did you do about it?' Tom asked Daniel, coming back to the main thrust of the tale.

'I looked up my old sergeant, Sid Dyer, and had a word with him. He's not at the Met any more – he's community liaison officer for another nick – but I called him up and we went out for a drink. He was my mentor when I joined up. I was just eighteen then. He took me in hand and I thought the sun shone out of his arse.'

'And what did he say?'

'He basically advised me to look the other way. "Don't rock the boat. Nobody'll thank you for it," he said. "All you'll do is make trouble for yourself." I wasn't completely surprised, but I'll admit I was a bit disappointed. You see, when I'd worked with him, Sid had always been so straight, so principled. I hadn't seen him for a while and he'd changed. It was like life and the job had finally worn him down. He seemed tired, more cynical. He told me he was looking forward to his retirement.'

'I take it you didn't follow his advice,' Fred observed.

'I should've,' Daniel replied with feeling. 'I did think about it. Perhaps if I had, I'd still have a marriage, a career and a pension to look forward to. But I couldn't get away from the fact that keeping quiet would make me just as guilty as they were. I mean, it wasn't just a spot of petty pilfering. Heroin ruins lives – not just the users' but their families', and the lives of the people they mug and steal from in order to feed their habit. One of the rehab support workers I know calls it "powdered misery".' He looked at Tom, hoping he understood. 'I didn't *want* to get involved, but I felt I couldn't go on doing my job if I didn't. I just wished to God I'd never found out.'

'So who did you tell?'

Tom's face was impassive, and Daniel had a moment's fantasy that he was in fact Paxton's mole, that he would run to him and repeat everything. But that was ridiculous – he was no threat to Paxton now; the man had got what he wanted when he'd succeeded in forcing Daniel to throw in his career.

'Well, just before we parted, Sid said that if I did go ahead and blow the whistle, I should go high, so I did.' Daniel paused, taking a sip of his beer. 'But I still didn't go high enough. The DCI I chose to tell was full of praise for what he called my dedication to duty. He told me I'd definitely done the right thing in going to him and that I could safely leave it in his hands. It would be treated with the utmost urgency, he said. I left his office feeling satisfied that I'd made the right decision, and was prepared to go back to my unit and get on with my job. I didn't know I'd just thrown away any chance of a long and successful career.' He paused, his jaw tightening as he recalled the conse- quences of his action. The moral high ground had proven to be a cold and windswept place. 'Three days later, Taz injured himself and was put on indefinite convalescence. Two days after that, my drugs dog, Bella, was reassigned and I was pulled from the Dog Unit and put back on to regular duties.'

'And what reason were you given?' Tom wanted to know.

'Apparently, my work wasn't satisfactory,' Daniel said lightly. 'I was told there'd been several complaints, but unsurprisingly, nobody would give me any details.'

There was a moment's silence, during which the door to the kitchen opened and Meg appeared, carrying the large stockpot between two oven-gloved hands. Fred put down his beer glass and hurried to take it from her.

Daniel was grateful for the interruption. There was more to the story of his downfall, but some of it was still way too raw to let out of the safe padded cells of his mind.

Conversation during the meal was of an everyday nature and it wasn't until they settled down in the Bowdens' shabbily comfortable lounge with cups of fresh coffee and a bowl of broken mint chocolate that Tom returned to criminal matters, asking Daniel to tell him everything he knew about the runaway girl.

'Dad's told me what he knows, but it's a bit sketchy. I'm assuming there's a fair bit more to it,' he said, rubbing his foot up and down the belly of the spaniel, who had followed them in and now lay supine at his feet.

'There is.' Daniel hesitated. 'I promised not to tell, but I think it's got beyond that now. If nothing else, this little incident?' he held up his bandaged hand – 'proves that.'

Daniel gave the Bowdens the facts with as much detail as he felt was necessary. They listened in silence, apart from the odd question from Tom, who made copious notes in his pocketbook, and a small sound of disgust from Meg when she heard how Patrescu and Macek had tricked Katya and her sister into coming to the UK and of the methods they employed to force them to stay.

When Daniel came to the end of his tale, outlining his fight with Macek the previous night, she exclaimed in horror.

'My God! He was actually going to kill you?'

'Yeah, and he very nearly did. I can't believe I was so stupid as to fall for that old trick. I hadn't really considered that they'd come gunning for me – though why not I can't imagine. It's quite possible that I got caught on one of their CCTV cameras at the house, but even if I didn't, they were bound to put two and two together sooner or later. I mean, Katya doesn't know anyone in this country – who else would be trying to help her?'

'Pretty easy to follow you in that lorry of mine too,' Fred commented.

'Yeah, and the worst thing is, I think he might have been there a couple of nights before, but he got a taste of the dog that time, so he worked out a way to separate us, and I played along like a complete novice.'

'We all make mistakes from time to time,' Tom observed. 'Don't beat yourself up about it. But you're right – this has gone far enough. It may take a day or two, but I can confidently predict that Mr Yousef Patrescu will be getting a rather unpleasant surprise before he's very much older.'

'And it can be done without involving Yelverton?'

'I don't see why not. There'll no doubt be some friction about it when they find out, but we can live with that, especially if we can turn up some evidence of Naylor's involvement. Now the girl, Katya, do you think she's safe where she is, or should we bring her in?'

'I think so.' Daniel felt as though a huge weight were lifting from his shoulders. 'If they knew where to find her, they'd have picked her up by now. I'm the only one who knows where she is, so if she keeps her head down and I stay away until it's all over – so there's no possible chance of leading anyone there – I can't see any reason she should be in any danger. I'll phone Hilary and warn her.'

'Good.' Tom closed his pocketbook. 'I'll set the wheels in motion, but don't worry if you don't hear from me for a day or two. It all takes time, as you know.'

'Patrescu made a big mistake when he called you to help find the girl,' Meg said to Daniel, getting up to pour more coffee. 'From his point of view, he couldn't have picked a worse person. But it was Katya's lucky day, that's for sure.'

'It certainly was,' Tom agreed. 'Unfortunately, there are thousands like her who aren't so lucky.'

Fred cleared his throat. 'I think—'

They were never to find out what he thought, for at that moment Daniel's mobile started to ring.

The number wasn't familiar to him and – after apologizing to his hosts – he stepped out into the hall to take the call.

'Daniel?' A woman's voice, the accent vaguely familiar.

'Yes.'

'It's Sarah. At the vet's.'

Daniel glanced at the grandfather clock in the corner of the lounge. It was almost eleven, and his heart started to thump heavily as an icy foreboding drained all the strength from his body.

As if from a distance, he heard himself say, in a surprisingly normal tone, 'Hi, Sarah. Is anything wrong?'

'I'm afraid there is. I'm sorry to ring you so late, but there's a problem with Taz,' she said, and suddenly Daniel couldn't breathe.

TEN

For a long moment, time seemed to stand still for Daniel, his mind recognizing a kind of tragic inevitability about it all, while his heart rebelled against a reality it didn't want to face.

He should have been there. He should have stayed close. He had owed Taz that much – he owed him far more than that, for God's sake! He would never have left him if the dog hadn't seemed so much better, but then Emma had impressed on him, more than once, just how unpredictable head injuries could be.

Sarah spoke again. 'Daniel? Are you there? Look, I'm sorry to land this on you at this time of night, but I don't suppose you could come and collect him now?'

'Er . . . yes, OK.' It seemed an odd request, but Daniel was past logical thought.

'Oh, thank you. I wouldn't ask but it's completely manic here,' Sarah said apologetically. 'He was fine until the Staffie came in.'

'A Staffie?' Confusion began to permeate his ballooning grief. Had there been a fight, then?

'Yes, it just came in half an hour ago,' Sarah went on. 'Suspected poisoning, poor chap. He's too ill to make a nuisance of himself, but Taz is going crazy, barking and growling.'

The relief was almost as overwhelming as the sorrow had been. Daniel closed his eyes. His hand, holding the mobile phone, was visibly trembling.

'I wouldn't mind,' Sarah's voice came again, perhaps

misinterpreting his silence, 'but we've got a bit of a full house tonight and he's upsetting some of the others. I don't suppose it's doing him much good either, come to that.'

Daniel pulled himself together. 'No, you're probably right. I'll come and get him immediately.'

'Brilliant. Thanks.' Sarah sounded almost as relieved as he felt, but for a completely different reason.

The call over, Daniel leaned against the wall in the hall, closed his eyes and took several deep, steadying breaths before returning to the lounge.

'Everything OK?' Meg asked.

'That was the veterinary nurse – I'm afraid I've got to go.'

'Oh, no, not Taz?' she said softly.

'Yes, but it's all right – he's OK. Actually, he's causing havoc. They've had a Staffie brought in and Taz can't bear Staffies. He was badly bitten by one as a youngster and he's never forgotten. Anyway, I've got to go and pick him up so they can get some peace.'

'Where will you go then?' Fred wanted to know. 'You won't go back to your flat at this time of night?'

'It's a bit late to go anywhere else,' Daniel said, thinking briefly of Tamzin, but she kept early hours. The same applied to Hilary, and anyway, he could no longer go there without compromising Katya.

'Well, he'll come back here, of course,' Meg said, looking at Fred, who nodded. 'We've got a spare room. Would Taz be OK with Mosely?'

'Yes, it's only Staffies he has issues with,' Daniel assured her. 'But I can't do that. For one thing, it'll be past midnight before I get back.'

'So? It's not the end of the world if we lose an hour or two's sleep. I don't have to be up early and Fred can go to bed if he wants. Go on. Go and get him and bring him back here. We'd love to have you both. And don't rush. I'm going to do some beadwork while I wait, and I'd happily do that all night.'

'I can vouch for that,' Tom put in, getting to his feet. 'Anyway, I'm blocking you in, so I'll be on my way too.'

'Are you sure?' Daniel asked Meg, hugely grateful.

'Go.'

Outside, in the frosty air, he shook hands with Tom.

'Thanks, for . . . well, you know.'

'No problem. I'll be in touch. Meantime, try and stay out of trouble, if you can.'

Daniel nodded. 'Oh, I will, believe me. Look, there's just one more thing. Remember I told you about the girl Marika, who helped us when we went looking for Elena? Well, yesterday there was a woman's body found on Dartmoor and there was some talk of an overdose. I just wondered . . .'

'OK. I'll see what I can find out.'

With a wave of his hand, Tom Bowden headed for his car and, moments later, backed out of the drive and was gone.

Feeling more optimistic than he had for weeks, Daniel slid behind the wheel of the Mercedes and set off to pick up his partner.

Taz's recovery was swifter than Daniel could have hoped, and as his own hand was sore rather than incapacitated, they both returned to part-time work a couple of days later.

Climbing into the cab out of a steady downpour at eight thirty, with a full load in the back and Taz already settled on his blankets, Daniel was glad to be doing something useful again. Both he and the dog had started to chafe at their inactivity.

Apart from a text giving a description of the body found on the moor, he hadn't heard from Tom Bowden, and could only trust that the wheels were turning in whatever department had taken on the investigation into Patrescu. From Tom's description, Daniel confirmed that the dead woman was almost certainly Marika and, in the absence of any available relatives, was asked to informally identify the body.

As he expected, it was indeed Marika, the scar on her face showing livid against her sallow skin, and he was saddened to think that she'd paid so terrible a price for helping them escape. Mentally he added her death to the score he had to settle with Macek.

Pushing aside the memory, Daniel started the lorry, gave a wave to Fred Bowden in the office and headed for the gateway. The cab lifted slightly as he turned out of the yard on to the road and the powerful engine tackled the climb of a mile or so to the top of the hill. Once over the brow of the hill, it was downhill all the way to the main road, but as Daniel's lorry neared the crest of the rise, his phone began to ring and a glance at the display told him it was Amanda. Groaning inwardly, he accepted the call, hoping that she hadn't just rung to have another go at him.

'Amanda, I'm driving—' he began, but she interrupted him, her voice sharp, urgent.

'Daniel, is Drew with you?'

Daniel's heart missed a beat. 'No. Why would he be? It's a school day, isn't it?'

As he spoke, Daniel indicated left and pulled into a shallow lay-by. There was already a minibus parked there and it was a tight fit, but it couldn't be helped.

'It's half-term.' Amanda sounded impatient. 'He went to stay the night with Ryan last night – at least, that's what he told me he was doing – but Ryan's mum says she didn't know anything about it.'

'And you didn't think to check with her before he went?'

Daniel turned off the engine, seeing a figure in a hooded water-proof jacket come round the back of the vehicle in front.

'No!' Amanda had clearly taken his query as an accusation. 'He's been there dozens of times. How was I to know he was lying?'

'All right. Calm down.'

The man in the waterproofs lifted binoculars from round his neck and got into the driver's seat.

'Are you sure he's not staying with another friend?'

Amanda's voice rose an indignant decibel or fifty. 'Of course I'm sure! Don't you think I'd have thought of that?'

'OK. Well, look, I'm working, but I'll swing by the flat and just make sure he's not turned up there.'

'But it wouldn't have taken him that long to get to you. It's only an hour or so on the train to Plymouth – if that's what he's done. He'd have been there last night.'

'Yeah, well, I wasn't at home last night,' Daniel told her. 'But presumably he's got his phone, so if he *did* come and couldn't find me, I imagine he'd have rung. What time did you last see him?'

'Um . . . I dropped him off at Ryan's yesterday about six o'clock.'

'And what time did he leave there?'

'He was only there about half an hour. Julia – Ryan's mum – says she offered him tea, but he said he couldn't stay. So if he set off then, he could easily have got to you last night.'

'*If* he was coming here.' Daniel sincerely hoped he hadn't while there was any possibility that Macek might be about. The thought made his blood run cold.

'But he must have done. Where else would he go?' Amanda's voice rose with incipient panic. 'And why hasn't he rung me?'

'I don't know.' Daniel started the lorry again, thinking hard. 'Perhaps he's out of credit. You've tried ringing *him*, I suppose?'

'Of course I have! It was the first thing I did. He's not answering. All I get is the stupid answerphone message.'

'OK. Look, try and stay calm. I'm heading for home now. I'll be there in fifteen minutes or so. Have a word with this Ryan – he may well know more than he's telling – and why don't you ring all Drew's other friends and see if they remember him talking about going anywhere or doing anything different.'

'I've already rung everyone I can think of. He hasn't got all that many close friends.' Amanda drew in a shuddering breath, struggling for control. 'Please find him, Daniel.'

'If he's here, I will,' Daniel promised. 'Try not to panic. There's probably some perfectly innocent explanation. Or he may even be trying to frighten us.'

'Why? Why would he do that?'

'Because he doesn't think we're listening to him, perhaps? I don't know. I'll call you as soon as I get to the flat, OK?'

Before he set off, Daniel tried both Drew's mobile and the landline to his own flat with no success, and was aware of a rising sense of foreboding. Was Drew there, perhaps looking at the phone, wondering whether he should answer it? Or had he been there and run into the Romanian? In spite of his soothing words to Amanda, Daniel was deeply worried.

Putting through a call to the office to warn Fred of the unavoid-able delay in proceedings, Daniel pulled out round the parked minibus on to a blessedly clear road, accelerating hard to make the last few yards of the climb before beginning the downhill run to the main road.

Driven by anxiety, Daniel let the truck run on down the hill, allowing the engine do its own braking until he neared the first of the bends at the bottom. Here, the road swung first right, then sharply left before rising over a humpbacked bridge and running straight towards the junction with the A-road some 200 yards further on.

After three months of driving for the company, Daniel knew this first stretch of road like the back of his hand. He knew the way the camber tipped the wrong way for a short distance as it neared the first bend, knew the sunken drain that made the suspension drop and the bodywork rattle, knew exactly where he needed to start braking in order to negotiate the S-bend safely.

Worrying about Drew, he was driving on autopilot as he swung round the first bend and barely registered a flicker of movement in the field that bordered the road, but he snapped back to full attention when, with a report like a shotgun discharging, the truck lurched and veered sharply towards the hedge.

'Shit!'

He had a full load in the trailer, was doing close to 50 miles an hour on a downhill slope just yards from a right-angle bend, and he was pretty sure his near front tyre had blown out. Add to that a road running with rain and it was incredible how it concentrated the mind. In a flash his concern about Drew was totally overridden by the business of self-preservation.

Instinctively, Daniel's foot hit the brake pedal for an instant before he recollected the danger of doing so. There was a scream of tortured rubber as the heavy trailer pushed forward and the remaining good tyres lost traction. With another oath, he lifted his foot again, steering into the skid.

The weight of the full load started to jack-knife the whole vehicle, causing it to snake first one way and then the other. Battling to keep the lorry on the road, Daniel knew there was no way he was going to be able to navigate the second bend and the likely outcome of trying would be to hit the hump of the bridge, become airborne and plough through the low wall into the river below.

Daniel had always had a cool head in a tight spot, and if ever he needed a cool head, he needed it now.

Wrestling with the juddering steering wheel and a trailer that seemed hell-bent on overtaking the cab, he scanned the way ahead for somewhere he could safely run the lorry off the road. Not that he had any illusions that he'd get off scot-free: in the circumstances, it was a case of damage limitation.

He focused on an old wooden farm gate on the outside of the bend. It was a slim chance, but it was probably the only one he had.

Out of the corner of his eye, he saw Taz start to sit up, aware that something was wrong, and shouted, 'Lie down!' not looking to see if he'd obeyed. The lorry was zigzagging to and fro across the double white lines in the centre of the road and it was taking all his concentration and skill just to keep it on the tarmac.

When the bend was only yards away, he realized that even

for a vehicle under full control, the target gateway was at an impossible angle. Worse still, a line of three cars was approaching the bridge from the other direction, completely unconscious of the impending disaster thundering towards them.

Rapidly estimating the speed and distance, Daniel took the only option open to him. There was no way he could make the turn and stay on his side of the road, and the oncoming cars weren't moving fast enough to pass him before he reached the corner, so he gritted his teeth, floored the accelerator and leaned on the horn. Under acceleration some of the weight lifted from the damaged tyre and Daniel was able to hold a fairly straight course that he hoped would take him clear across the opposite carriageway and through the hedge before the first of the cars came over the bridge.

It did, but only just.

There was a resounding bang from the suspension as the truck hit the grassy bank on the outside of the bend and the impact jarred the whole vehicle. All at once the windscreen was filled with a tangle of twigs and branches as the lorry's speed carried it inexorably forward through the bare winter hedge. Instinctively, Daniel closed his eyes as the glass starred and shattered, showering over him in a rush of cold air.

For a split second, it felt as though the whole truck was airborne, tipping crazily in the air before touching down – right wheels first – and bouncing uncomfortably back to square.

Daniel opened his eyes to see not heavy, wheel-dragging plough – as he'd hoped, but a grassy slope leading relentlessly downhill to the river. The bank and hedge had taken the edge off their speed, but it wasn't enough to stop the lorry completely, and the slope fed their momentum.

If it hadn't been for Taz, Daniel would have considered baling out of the runaway vehicle at that point, but instead he stayed put, standing on the brakes and fighting to turn the truck right-handed on to rising ground.

It was a losing battle. The cab turned, but on the soft marshy turf of the river meadow the heavy trailer kept sliding sideways, heading ever closer to the water.

The end came sooner than Daniel expected. Time seemed to slow to a crawl as, with maybe 20 feet to go, the vehicle hit a ridge, tipped on its nearside wheels and then toppled on to its side with a deafening, booming thud.

Held by his seatbelt, Daniel found himself suspended in

mid-air, staring worriedly down at Taz, who'd been tipped on to his back and was even now struggling to his feet among the loose debris of the cab, panic in his eyes. Beyond him, reedy grass pressed against the glass of the passenger side window, and by the streamlined direction of its stalks and the horrendous rattling vibrations all around him, Daniel could tell that they were still slowly sliding. The engine had stalled and his ears were full of the groaning, shrieking sound of tortured metal.

His mind was racing. How near was the riverbank, and which way up would the cab be if and when it hit the water? It would sink rapidly, that was for sure, with so much weight in the back.

His fingers fumbled at his waist to release the seatbelt, but then paused. The dog had found his feet and was crouching now, ears flattened and eyes darting every which way in terror.

If Daniel released the belt while Taz remained beneath him, there was every chance he would land on the dog.

'Taz, go! Get out!' he yelled and, after an initial hesitation, was relieved to see him leap out through the shattered windscreen and away.

Even as the dog made it to safety, Daniel realized the lorry had stopped moving. With a few residual creaks and twangs, it came to rest with dirty water pooling under the glass that Taz had been standing on.

Taking a firm grip on the inner handle of the driver's door with his right hand, Daniel tried to support his bodyweight while he reached down with the other to deploy the release mechanism for the belt. After a short struggle, the clip opened and his weight dropped abruptly, almost jerking his right arm out of its socket.

Moments later, he had followed Taz through the smashed screen and was standing on blessedly solid ground. Taking a few quick steps to distance himself from the overturned vehicle, he was assailed by the dog, leaping around in joy at the return to normality. Daniel could sympathize. It had been a close call in so many ways. Just *how* close he was brought to realize when he walked round the cab and saw the riverbank and the fast-flowing brown water less than 4 feet from the roof of the truck.

Walking back round the lorry, he stood staring at the unfamiliar gritty black underside, now running with dirty water and decorated with lumps of grassy mud.

Daniel gazed thoughtfully at what he could see of the nearside front wheel, now under the cab and pressed into the soft ground. The tyre was a mess, ragged and twisted off the rim. He shook his head in wonderment at his lucky escape. Blow-outs were unusual with the construction of modern tyres, but with lorry tyres under five or six times the pressure of the average car tyre, when they did go, the failure was inevitably catastrophic, a fact to which a number of dead tyre-fitters could have testified, had they been able. In his early days as a police officer, Daniel had once attended a scene at a garage where the unlucky mechanic had been blown clear up to the ceiling when a lorry tyre exploded.

A shout came from the direction of the road and Daniel looked up to see half a dozen people climbing through the newly made gap in the hedge.

Daniel waved both hands and shook his head to indicate that there was no need to come down, but predictably they all kept coming, full of ghoulish curiosity and not about to pass up the chance for a closer look.

'Stay close,' he told the dog, and with more people appearing at the top of the field, and the vanguard less than 20 yards away, he took his phone from his pocket and called the TFS office once more.

Fred answered almost immediately. 'Daniel. What's up? Have you heard from Drew?'

'Er . . . no, not yet. I'm afraid there's been an accident.'

'A bad one?'

'Bad enough.' Daniel outlined what had happened and told his boss where he was. 'Another couple of yards and we'd have been in the river,' he finished.

'Bloody hell! You don't do things by halves, do you? But you're OK?'

'Yeah, we're fine.'

'Right. I'll be there directly. Have you called the police?'

'Not yet, but I'm sure someone has. I seem to have become the Eighth Wonder of the World.'

He returned the phone to his pocket as the first of the sightseers reached the lorry and his attention was immediately claimed by an aggressive-looking, stocky man of about forty, who was almost running in his determination to have the first say. However, his charge faltered a little as he took in the size of Taz.

Dressed in a suit, the legs of which were now liberally splattered with mud, the man had a shaved head and a neck that bulged a little over a too-tight collar. 'Fuckin' hell, mate!' he shouted, coming to a halt a few feet away. 'You nearly fuckin' killed me! What the hell were you playing at?'

Daniel had a feeling that if the dog hadn't been there, the man would have come right up and got physical. Taz obviously thought so too, because he emitted a low, rumbling growl.

Because he knew that shock takes people in different ways, Daniel took a deep breath and replied calmly, 'I'm sorry. My tyre blew out. There was nothing I could do.'

'You nearly ran me off the bloody road!' the man persisted, stabbing the air with an angry forefinger, apparently unwilling to relinquish the idea that Daniel was somehow culpable.

Taz growled again, the decibels rising, and the man eyed him nervously.

'You keep a hold of that fuckin' dog!' he warned, subsiding a little as two or three others gathered round.

'Are you all right? You were bloody lucky!' one of the newcomers observed, gesturing at the river.

Daniel nodded. 'I'm fine, thanks.'

'*He* was lucky? What about me? Nearly fuckin' killed me with that bloody lorry!' the angry man complained. 'I'm gonna call the police,' he added, taking out his mobile.

Daniel was tired of him. 'Good idea. Go ahead,' he suggested, but it seemed that at least two other people had already done so.

There were some fifteen or twenty people in the field now, some crowding round Daniel as if he were the star attraction at a freak show, and others exclaiming over the lorry. One or two were taking pictures of it on mobile phones. It would probably be splashed across the Internet before the day was out, Daniel thought resignedly. It was the kind of publicity Fred's company could well do without.

The reaction to his near-miss had left him feeling decidedly shaky and he walked a little way from the gathering, who were by now finding him poor value, and sat down to await the arrival of Bowden. When he saw him hurrying down the slope a couple of minutes later, he stood up and went to meet him.

'Daniel, are you sure you're OK? Your face . . .'

Daniel touched his cheek with an exploratory hand and it came away with a number of small smears of blood.

'A branch went through the windscreen,' he explained. 'But, yeah, all in all, a bit shaky but OK.'

'I just don't understand how this happened.' The TFS boss looked deeply concerned. 'That lorry was only serviced last month and the tyres were new.'

Daniel lowered his voice. 'I won't be saying this to anyone

else, but just before the tyre blew, I saw something – or someone – at the side of the road.'

Bowden was shocked. 'What are you saying? That someone did this on purpose? How?'

Daniel shrugged. 'A shotgun loaded with a solid slug, maybe. Straight through the side wall – that would do it.'

'They'd have to be a pretty tidy shot at the speed you were going.'

'Or lucky.'

'So who? Macek?'

'Or Patrescu,' Daniel said. 'I'm really sorry, Fred. I never dreamed that this business with Kat would spill over and affect you. God knows how you'll get that lorry out – it's practically a bog down there by the river and this bloody rain's not helping.'

Fred shook his head, but whatever he might have said was interrupted by Daniel's phone.

His heart missed a beat when he recognized the number on the display.

'I'm sorry, it's Drew. I have to take this,' Daniel told his boss, thumbing the receive button. 'Drew! Where the hell are you?'

'I'm here, at your flat. You didn't come home last night.'

'No, I was staying with friends. What on earth are you doing there? Mum's really worried about you.'

'I wanted to see you,' Drew said simply. 'But you weren't here, so I waited and then I fell asleep. You've got stuff in your fridge that's going off,' he added accusingly.

'Wait a minute, how did you get in?'

'Well, the door was open, so I thought you must be coming back really soon, but didn't. I tidied up too. It was going to be a surprise.'

The door was open and he'd tidied up? Daniel was the first to admit he didn't keep the place immaculate, but the flat wasn't normally in such a state that an eight-year-old would feel moved to domesticity.

Someone had been there.

Daniel's first instinct was to scream at his son to get out of the flat, but where could he go? There were no near neighbours he could wait with, nobody he could call to go and pick the boy up. Common sense told him that if his visitor had been Macek, then he was long gone and unlikely to return, but common sense didn't hold much sway when there was any possibility that his son was in danger.

'Drew, look, stay where you are. Lock the door downstairs

and don't answer to anyone but me, OK? I'll be there in ten minutes. Do you understand?'

'Yeah.' He sounded bewildered. 'Dad, what's wrong?'

'Probably nothing at all. Just promise me you'll do as I say.'

'I promise.'

He disconnected to find Fred looking at him quizzically.

'And just how are you going to get there in ten minutes?'

'Shit!' Daniel stared at him.

With a resigned sigh, Fred fished in his pocket and held out a small bunch of keys on a ring.

'It's the Volvo. I'm parked on the verge, just over the bridge.'

'Thanks. I owe you.' Daniel took the keys and made to go past his boss, who caught his arm.

'Hang on. What am I supposed to tell the police?'

'I don't suppose they'll be too bothered, as long as you're here. Tell them I'm unreliable and you're going to fire me,' he suggested.

'But in the meantime, I've lent you my car,' Fred said dryly.

'OK. I'll sort it out. You'd better get going before they arrive.'

'Thanks,' Daniel said again. 'And best not mention my theory about the tyre. Let's see what they come up with, shall we?'

ELEVEN

When Daniel knocked on the door of his flat, a small voice dutifully asked for his identity.

'Drew, it's me. Dad.'

There came the sound of bolts being drawn back and a key turning and then Drew's dark face peered round the opening edge of the door. When he saw that it was indeed his father, he opened the door fully and rushed forward into Daniel's embrace.

'Dad, you scared me earlier! What's going on?'

Daniel's relief was so great that instead of answering, he swept the boy off his feet and hugged him soundly, feeling the thin arms clutching him tight.

'*I* scared *you*? What about your mother and me? What on earth were you thinking of, coming here without telling either of us? We were worried sick!'

'But if I'd asked, Mum wouldn't have let me come.'

'For a reason,' Daniel said, setting him back on his feet again.

'You're too young to be travelling alone. Anything could have happened.'

'I was all right. I came on the train.' Drew made a big fuss of Taz, who was fawning around him, tail wagging happily. 'Nothing happened.'

'But it *could* have. How did you get here from the station?'

'I got a taxi,' Drew said, as if that were the most normal thing on earth for an eight-year-old to do.

'That must have cost an arm and a leg!' Daniel exclaimed. 'Where did you get the money?'

'Grandma gave me some money at Christmas and I've been saving up my pocket money,' Drew said, adding defiantly, 'I didn't steal it, if that's what you're thinking.'

Guiltily, Daniel supposed the thought *had* flashed through his mind. Ten years in the police force had conditioned him to suspect the worst, even – it seemed – of his own son.

'I'll give you the money. How long have you been planning this?' he asked, secretly rather impressed by Drew's determination.

'For absolutely ages. Weeks and weeks. I know you said I could come some weekends but couldn't live here, but I thought if I came in half-term, you'd see that it *would* work.'

'But it didn't, did it? I wasn't here.' Daniel sighed. He put a hand on the boy's shoulder and propelled him towards the door. He couldn't rule out the possibility that one of the Romanians might have watched and followed him from the crash site, and he didn't want to risk being cornered there with Drew in tow. 'Come on, let's go and get some breakfast somewhere.'

'Where are we going?'

'There's a nice little bakery I know – not too far from here,' Daniel told him, and Drew brightened at the prospect. Checking his flat would have to wait until the boy was safely back with Amanda.

'What's the matter with Taz's head?' Drew wanted to know as they left the building and Daniel closed the door carefully.

'He got in a fight with a burglar,' Daniel said, falling back on the story he'd told them at the vet's. 'He was very poorly for a while. That's why we weren't here last night. We've been staying with friends.'

'In case the burglar came back?'

'Something like that. It's complicated, but you can see why I was worried to find you were here on your own.'

'So, what happened to your face? It's all scratched.'

'Something went through the windscreen of the lorry this morning,' Daniel told him. It was the truth, if a Spartan version of it.

'Do you think they'll have stolen much?'

'One or two things, maybe, but there's not an awful lot they'd want,' Daniel told him as they got into Fred's car. 'Let's give Mum a ring before we go.'

Drew's face fell. 'Do we have to ring her?'

'Of course we do. She's worried sick about you.'

Daniel took his phone out of his pocket, but before he could find Amanda's number on the speed-dial list, she rang him.

She didn't wait for Daniel to speak.

'Have you found him? Is he there?'

'Yes, I've got him. He's fine.' Daniel put the car in gear and started down the drive, anxious to get on to the open road.

'Oh, thank God!' Amanda's voice sounded choked with emotion, but within moments she was back on form. 'And just when were you intending to let me know?' she enquired. 'You said you'd ring in fifteen minutes and it's been three-quarters of an hour! You knew how worried I was!'

'I know, but I had a spot of bother on the way and I've only just got here.' Useless to say he'd been on the point of calling her: she wouldn't believe him.

'Well, where is he? I want to talk to him.'

Daniel held the phone out to Drew. 'Mum wants a word.'

Drew pulled a reluctant face but took it. 'Hi, Mum.'

There was a pause during which Daniel could hear Amanda's voice. Then Drew said, 'I know. I'm sorry. I just really wanted to see Dad . . . I didn't mean to frighten you.'

Feeling like an eavesdropper, Daniel tried to concentrate on his driving, but after a moment, holding the phone away from his mouth, Drew said, 'Mum says I've got to go home. Tell her I can stay – please? Just for a few days, at least . . .'

Daniel glanced at the boy's hopeful face and had to steel himself.

'I'm sorry, Drew. You can't just now.'

'Dad, please. I promise I won't get in the way. Please . . .' The last word was drawn out and pleading, his eyes desperate.

'It's really not a good time, Drew. You can see what a mess everything's in. Besides, you're going to Butlins this weekend, aren't you?'

As soon as he'd said it, he could see that he'd scored an own goal.

'I *hate* Butlins!' Drew declared. 'I don't want to go and I wouldn't have to if I stayed with you. Please, Dad. You know I'm just going to be miserable.'

'Have you told Mum?'

'She won't listen.'

'I'll have a word with her when I see her,' Daniel promised, but his words found no favour with his son, whose expression changed from beseeching to stormy.

'It's so not fair! Nobody cares what *I* want!' he exclaimed, throwing the phone into Daniel's lap and looking out of the side window.

Fumbling for the handset, Daniel found that Amanda was still on the line.

'It's me. We're just going to get something to eat. Then I'll bring him home,' he told her, and was surprised when she offered to meet him at Exeter instead.

'I have an appointment there,' she said. 'I'll see you at the station at midday.'

Drew remained looking out of the window, his back turned as far as the seatbelt would allow.

'If you're trying to convince me that you're grown-up enough to make your own decisions, you're not doing a very good job of it,' Daniel observed conversationally, after a long silence punctuated only by the scrape of the windscreen wipers.

Drew didn't say anything, but after a moment, he shifted to face forward. Daniel felt a small glow of pride. It was a horrible situation for a kid to cope with at any age, let alone someone as young as Drew.

'You think I don't understand, but I do,' he said presently. 'I was about your age when my dad left us. I know how you feel.'

'If you know, then why did you do it to us?' Drew asked bitterly.

'It wasn't my choice.'

'Then whose? Was it Mum's fault?'

Daniel hesitated. Whatever the state of affairs between Amanda and himself, he couldn't do that to her, and besides, it could only make things worse for the boy.

'It was nobody's fault, Drew. We just grew apart. We wanted different things. It happens. The same way you sometimes move on and make new friends at school.'

Drew didn't respond, and Daniel watched his son's unhappy

profile, desperately wishing he could say or do something that would put the smile back on his face.

'Why did *your* father leave?' the boy asked suddenly.

Daniel turned off the main road into the village where the vet's surgery was.

'I don't really know.'

'Didn't you ever ask him?'

'I never saw him again,' Daniel said.

'What, never ever?' Drew was incredulous. 'Didn't you want to?'

'Yes, of course I did, but maybe he didn't want to see us. I don't know. He sent us money at Christmas and birthdays until I was about thirteen, then nothing. I haven't heard from him since.'

'Didn't you look for him?'

'No.'

'Why not? Didn't you love him?'

Daniel searched his memory. Had he loved his father? A long time ago, perhaps; why else would he have felt such a wretched sense of rejection? But the sense of betrayal had turned that love to anger, and now, after twenty-odd years, even that had evaporated, leaving behind what? Indifference? No, not that. A faint sense of regret, perhaps, for what might have been, and a determination to do better by his own son. Good intentions, easily formed, but life had a way of buggering everything up.

'Didn't you?' Drew persisted. He was watching his father closely.

Daniel slotted the car into a roadside parking space.

'Didn't I what?'

'Love him.'

Daniel sighed. 'Yes, I did. And I wrote to him,' he remembered. 'When I was eighteen and started police training. I thought he'd be pleased that I was following him into the force. I don't know if my letter ever reached him, but he never replied.'

His mobile sounded, and relieved at the interruption, Daniel picked it up again.

'You kept the ringtone I downloaded,' Drew said, sounding pleased.

'Of course I did.'

'You can change it if you like – I don't mind.'

The caller wasn't Amanda again, as Daniel had half expected, but Fred Bowden.

'Hi, Fred.'

'Daniel. Did you find Drew?'

'Yes, he's fine, thank God. Sorry, I should have let you know. How'd it go with the police? Did they give you any grief?'

'Well, they weren't exactly over the moon to find you gone,' Fred said. 'But I explained about your son and they seemed quite understanding. You have to present yourself at the station with your licence within the next week, though, and they're going to have VOSA take a look at the lorry.'

'That doesn't surprise me,' Daniel said. VOSA was the body that oversaw MOT testing and it was fairly standard procedure to call on them if there were any unusual or suspicious circumstances surrounding an RTA. 'But, look, I'm afraid I've done something a bit stupid – I've just told Amanda I'd bring Drew to Exeter at lunchtime, but I forgot I've still got your car.'

'It doesn't matter. I've got to wait here till the salvage people come. I expect I'll get a lift with them. Keep the car for now.'

'OK, thanks.' Daniel said. 'I've not been much help, have I? I thought I was doing you a favour and all I've done is bugger up your day completely.'

'Well, if I thought you'd done it on purpose, I might be a tad pissed off, but as it is . . . Go on. Take Drew to his mum. I'll see you later. But, Daniel . . . try not to roll my car!'

Daniel felt deeply unsettled as he left Exeter presently, having reunited Drew with Amanda outside the train station – a process that earned him little thanks from either party.

Amanda, pencil slim in skin-tight jeans, high-heeled boots and a tailored jacket, had given him a look – over Drew's head – that left him in no doubt that she held him entirely to blame for the incident.

How could such perfect features look so ugly? Daniel found himself wondering as he drove home. Her ice-blue eyes had fairly glittered with malevolence under her platinum-blonde fringe. She wore her hair even shorter now than when they'd been together, cut in a sharp, boyish style that only served to emphasize the hard lines of her face.

Drew, for his part, had left him without so much as a backward glance, which had hurt even more than tears and entreaties would have done. It was as though Daniel had been tested and found wanting, and the boy had now given up all hope of help from that quarter.

There were one or two things Daniel needed to pick up – not the least of which were some clean clothes – so on the way back he made the short detour necessary to call in at the flat.

His approach was cautious, but the yard was empty and the scrap of tissue paper he'd trapped between the door and its post was still reassuringly present.

In the flat, he stood and looked about him for a long moment, trying to decide what, if anything, was missing, but instead finding his mind constantly sliding back to the unhappy situation with Drew.

Wandering from the main room to his partitioned-off sleeping area and back again, Daniel forced his brain to concentrate. Since his split with Amanda, he had very little of material value and those things he did have – wallet, bank cards, watch and mobile phone – he habitually carried on his person, as he had on the night of the attack. The only thing that might have been tempting was his laptop, but that was hardly state of the art, and was still where he'd left it.

Stuffing a change of clothes into a holdall, he collected his mobile-phone charger and picked up the Volvo's keys from the worktop. With one last look around, his eye was caught for the first time by a small red flashing light half hidden by an untidy pile of papers and magazines.

It took a moment for him to realize what it was – namely the antiquated telephone answering machine that he'd discovered when he moved into the flat. The light had never flashed before. Presumably it denoted a message left. No one had left him a message in the three months he'd lived there. For that matter no one, except for a couple of marketing callers, had *ever* rung him on the landline – for the simple reason that he hadn't given anyone the number, retaining the line solely for the Internet connection.

No, wait, someone did have the number, he remembered suddenly. Soon after he met Tamzin, he'd rung her on the landline after accidentally leaving his mobile in the lorry overnight.

Putting his bag down, he went over to the phone and pressed playback. Moments later, Tamzin's clear county tones sounded through the hiss of the aged tape.

'Hi, Dan. It's, er . . . Tuesday. Thought I'd try this number as your mobile seems to be switched off or something. Just wondering how things are going. Is everything OK? How's Kat? Did you sort her out? Er . . . I'm really glad you enjoyed riding out the other morning. We should do it again soon. If you'd like to, of course. Anyway, give me a call or, better still, come round. Bye, then.'

Daniel switched off the machine, feeling guilty. So much for his promise to stay in touch. He'd seen a couple of missed-call messages on his mobile and, for reasons he didn't care to examine just at the moment, hadn't got round to calling back. Later, he would ring her.

Collecting his bag, Daniel left the flat, locked the door at the top of the stairs and descended to the empty showroom below. Outside, the sky was still grey with lowering cloud and a cold wind blew the rain against the back of his neck as he locked the door. The weather reflected his mood and he set off for the TFS depot battling a creeping fog of depression.

In the office, Fred looked up from his desk.

'Ah, Daniel. Everything OK with Drew?'

'Yeah. Well, no, actually, but there's not much I can do about it.'

'It'll sort itself out eventually. Do you fancy a coffee?'

'Thanks. As strong as you like.' Daniel knew Fred kept a percolator permanently 'perking', just topping it up as and when needed. 'What's happened about the lorry?'

'Well, it's been recovered, but it wasn't easy,' Bowden said as he got up to find mugs. 'They had to get a crane. We transferred your load to Figgy's lorry before they took it away, and now I'm waiting on VOSA and the insurance assessor. Call me nosy but I could bear to know exactly what happened.'

Daniel sat in the office's only other chair and told his boss all about the morning's short but eventful trip.

'And you still think someone shot the tyre out?'

'I'm not ruling it out. We both know how rare blow-outs are, and as you pointed out, those were new tyres. I've been thinking. When I stopped to take Amanda's call, there was a minibus parked in the lay-by in front of me. While I was there, some guy got into it with binoculars. I assumed he was a twitcher, but what if he wasn't? What if he was positioned there to let whoever was waiting at the bottom of the hill know when I was on my way?'

'Well, I suppose it's possible – if it *was* deliberate.' Fred put a mug down in front of Daniel.

'Thanks.' Picking up the coffee, Daniel leaned back in the chair, sighing deeply. 'Oh, I don't know – maybe you're right. Maybe I'm being paranoid.'

Fred sat down, regarding his driver appraisingly. 'Have you eaten?'

'Yes, I took Drew out for a late breakfast.'

'You look absolutely knackered.'

'Yeah, it's been quite a day.' A glance at his watch showed Daniel that it was only just gone two, but it already felt like a week since he'd got up that morning.

'Look, when you've finished your coffee, why don't you go back to the house and put your feet up.'

'But can't I do anything here?'

'Don't you think you've done enough for one day?' Fred joked.

'No, really. There's nothing for you to drive, and I can get on with what needs doing here.'

'OK. If you're sure,' Daniel gave in with some relief. His left hand was throbbing under the bandages. It hadn't been the gentle return to work he'd envisaged.

Barely 5 miles down the road, his phone rang. A glance showed a mobile number unknown to him and he let it ring. If it were important, they'd ring back.

They did. Within moments of the ringtone dying away it was repeated. When it started for a third time, Daniel pulled in to the verge and answered it.

'Dan? Thank God! Where've you been?' It was Tamzin.

Daniel had to concentrate hard as her voice was almost incoherent, the words tumbling over one another in her rush to get her message across.

'Tamzin, what's the matter?'

'I . . . I'm sorry, Dan. I told them. I couldn't help it.'

'Whoa, calm down! You told who what?'

'The men that came. I couldn't help it. I told them where Kat is. You have to warn Hilary!'

TWELVE

The Quarry Farm stable yard appeared deserted when Daniel brought the Mercedes to a skidding halt in front of the tack room and he remembered it was the yard's quiet time.

He was out of the car almost before it stopped moving, shouting for Tamzin. Several horses' heads appeared over half-doors to see what the commotion was about, but there was no answer and he set off down the narrow path that led to her cottage, taking the steps three or four at a time. Smoke rose in a thin spiral from the tall chimney, but even though the sun had dipped behind the trees, there were no lights showing.

The door was shut and locked and he rapped sharply on it. 'Tamzin! It's Daniel.'

She must have been close behind it for immediately he heard the sound of bolts being drawn back and within moments she had pulled it open. She reached through to grab his wrist and pulled him inside before slamming and locking the door once again.

As Daniel turned, Tamzin fell into his arms, burying her face in the front of his jumper, sobbing hard. He held her tight, rubbing her back and feeling her whole body trembling.

'It's all right, sweetheart. You're safe. I'm here now.'

The tiny hallway was cramped and dark, so Daniel went through into the kitchen, still holding Tamzin close.

Freeing one hand, he switched on the light. Over her head he could see two of her dogs curled up in their baskets, watching with solemn concern and, behind them, pressed against the wall, the little Yorkie, shivering piteously. Shattered glass and porcelain littered the floor and grated underfoot.

'It's all right,' he said again. 'It's over.'

'It's *not* all right,' came a muffled voice, hiccupping on a sob. 'I told them where Kat is. I let everyone down.'

'Sshh. Of course you didn't.'

Tamzin sniffed. 'I didn't want to tell them, but . . .'

Leaning away from her a little, Daniel put a finger under her chin and tilted her head up. Anger surged in him as he saw what they had done to her.

A cut and a purple bruise the size of an egg disfigured her left cheekbone, and the eye on that side was swollen shut. Her nose had bled a little, the blood from it forming a black trail on her upper lip, and her lower lip was also split and swollen.

Daniel's blood boiled. He had no doubt that this was Macek's work, and if he hadn't already yearned for payback after what the Romanian had done to Taz and probably Marika too, this cowardly act would have done the trick on its own. He felt horribly responsible. He'd blithely told Tom Bowden that no one knew where Katya was except Hilary and himself, but it wasn't true. He'd forgotten Tamzin. Indirectly, this was all his fault.

'Who did it, Tam? What did he look like?'

Tamzin shook her head helplessly. 'There were two of them, but I couldn't see their faces. They had stocking masks, like bank robbers, and they were wearing gloves – thin plastic ones, like surgical gloves. It was horrible! One – the one who hit me – was really big. I mean tall *and* broad. They both had dark hair, I could see that much, and they were foreign. They must be the two you saw the night Katya ran away.'

'Almost certainly,' Daniel said. He was reminded of how little she knew of what had gone on since and that added to his feelings of guilt – not that any amount of knowledge would have saved her the beating. 'I'm really sorry you got mixed up in this.'

'But what about Kat? Is she safe? I tried to ring Hilary when they'd gone, but she didn't answer. That's when I rang you and I thought you weren't going to answer either. I was really panicking.'

'It's OK. I managed to get her on her mobile. I told her to take Katya and get out. If you called me straight after the men left here, they should have had plenty of time to get away. I'm sorry I took so long to answer the phone. I was driving and I didn't recognize the number.'

'I know. They smashed my mobile and cut the landline to stop me calling the police. I had to use my spare one.'

'Oh, sweetheart . . .'

'I was so scared, Dan. I didn't see them coming, and when I answered the door, they barged in before I could get it shut again.' Tamzin's eyes were wide with remembered fear as she relived the moment, and tears ran, unchecked, down her cheeks. She buried her face against his shoulder once more and he had to bend his head to hear her muffled voice as she continued with her story. 'First of all, they just asked me about Katya, but when I said I didn't know where she was, they started smashing things. After that, the big one just started slapping me and the other one stood there and watched – like it was normal. Anyway, then the big one got this knife out and he said if I didn't tell them where Kat was . . .' Her voice wobbled and she stifled another sob. 'He said he'd slash my face. I told them, Dan. I had to. I'm sorry – I was *so* scared!'

'Of course you had to. I would have done too. Anyone would,' Daniel told her.

'But I told them how to get there,' Tamzin confessed miserably. 'They asked me. I'm sorry. I just wanted to get rid of them.'

'That's OK. It's still easy to go wrong on those little lanes. Look, have you called the police and an ambulance?'

Tamzin shook her head. 'I didn't know what to do. I knew you didn't want the police involved. I felt bad enough already. I didn't want to make things even worse.'

'We should call them now. This has gone too far, and you need to be checked out,' Daniel told her. 'I'm so sorry this happened. Here,' reaching down for the trembling Yorkie, he put the terrified little dog into Tamzin's arms. 'Trixie needs a cuddle.'

'Poor little girl.' Tamzin kissed the top of Trixie's head and held her close. 'Where will Hilary go, do you think?'

'I told her to go somewhere where there are lots of people and then call me. A café or library or something.'

'But she hasn't called yet?'

'No.' Daniel looked at his watch. How long had it been since he'd spoken to her? Fifteen minutes? Probably nearer twenty, even though he'd driven like a madman from Tavistock. He should have heard from her by now. He tried her number again, but all he got was the answering service. He cursed softly.

'No answer.'

'You should go and make sure they got away OK. I'll ring the police. If you do it, they'll expect you to be here when they come.'

Daniel was torn.

'I'm not leaving you here on your own. Isn't there someone who can come and wait with you?'

'You don't think they'll come back?' she asked anxiously.

'No. They've got what they wanted, but you should still have someone with you.'

'I'll get one of the lads to come over. I'll be fine.'

'Are you sure?' Daniel was weakening. Much as he hated the idea of leaving Tamzin in such a state, he needed to be certain that Hilary and Kat had got away safely.

'I'm sure,' Tamzin said bravely. 'I'll be OK. But what shall I tell the police?'

'Just tell them what happened today and say Kat worked for you for a couple of days and then moved on. If you like, say the men hit you because you couldn't tell them where she was. No need to tell them anything else. It would only complicate matters.'

'Shall I say I called you?'

'Not unless they ask.'

Giving her another hug, Daniel headed back to his car, trying

Hilary's number again without success. Aware that forensics would try and lift fingerprints from every available surface, he took the time to smudge his own on both the light switch and the door handle with a gloved hand as he went. A clear print of his on top of the rubbed patches left by the Romanians would give the lie to Tamzin's story and would throw her reliability as a witness into doubt.

Driving to Goats Tor, he pulled into the familiar car park of the White Buck and stopped, wishing he knew what to do for the best. Did Hilary's silence mean there was a problem? Should he go on waiting for her to call, or should he go to Briars Hill to make sure they'd got away?

He jumped as his phone rang, but a glance at the display showed it wasn't Hilary but Tom Bowden. Daniel had tried to ring Tom as soon as he'd heard from Tamzin, but frustratingly there had been no answer and he'd had to resort to leaving voice-mail.

'Daniel, I got your message. Is your girlfriend OK?'

'She will be, but she's badly bruised and shaken up.'

'What about Katya?'

'I haven't heard. I'm hoping Hilary got her away in time, but she hasn't rung back. Should I go over there?'

'Not unless you absolutely have to. Look, I'm in a meeting. The plan is to hit Moorside House later tonight, so we really don't want to put the wind up Patrescu and co. if it can be avoided. From what you said, Tamzin doesn't know enough to give the local police anything useful.'

'No. They covered up, so she can't even give them a decent description.'

'Then let's hold back if we can. Let me know as soon as you hear that Katya's safe.'

The call over, Daniel sat staring at the phone in an agony of indecision.

If only Hilary would call.

Should he go to Briars Hill? He certainly wasn't eager to do so if there was any chance that he'd run into the two Romanians.

But what if Hilary and Kat hadn't got away? What if they were in trouble?

On the other hand, if he walked into a situation he couldn't control on his own, what help would he be to the two of them then?

Surely it couldn't hurt just to go and *look*?

As he hesitated, he became aware of Taz watching him eagerly from the back of the car, eyes alight with anticipation, and all at once his confidence returned.

He wasn't alone.

The dog had sensed that something was on and he was ready for it. He might not be 100 per cent fit, but even at 90 per cent, Taz was a formidable opponent.

This time they wouldn't be caught napping, though. Before setting off for the stables, he let the dog out of the back of the estate car and installed him on the passenger seat.

From the copse on the steep slope behind the house at Briars Hill, Daniel surveyed the property. Smoke was rising from the chimney and a light showed golden at the kitchen window, but although there was no sign of life, he could see Hilary's Land Rover parked in its customary position to the side of the house.

His heart sank as he saw a black Nissan X-Trail parked next to it. He lifted a small pair of binoculars that hung round his neck and focused them on the number plate. Alpha Tango Charlie – it was Patrescu's all right.

Turning his attention to the Land Rover, he thought he could just make out the shifting outlines of Hilary's dogs in the back.

Daniel lowered the binoculars thoughtfully. He knew Hilary had another little car that she used 'for best', as she called it, but it seemed unlikely that she'd have loaded her beloved dogs in the Land Rover and then left them behind. Did that mean she was indeed still at the stables? And if so, what of Kat?

Beside him, Taz whined and stood up impatiently. He'd been pleased to get out of the car when Daniel had parked it on the edge of the wood, and he'd thoroughly enjoyed the walk to their vantage point on top of the hill, but things had become a little quiet now and he wanted to be doing something.

'Quiet!' Daniel told him. He needed to think.

Movement in the stable yard caught his eye and he raised the binoculars again.

Two men, unmistakably Patrescu and the knife-happy Macek. They were wandering along the row of low-roofed stables, looking into each one. From the way they waved their arms at the ponies to try and get them to back away from the half-doors, Daniel guessed they were well out of their comfort zone around the animals.

Where the hell was Hilary? The fact that the Romanians were

still on the property presumably meant that they hadn't yet found Kat. He hoped that wherever the girl was hiding, the older woman was with her and not lying somewhere battered and bruised like Tamzin, having tried to stand up to the two men.

As Macek approached an apparently empty stable, suddenly a pony's dark head lunged out over the half-door, teeth bared and ears flattened to its neck.

Macek staggered back so fast that he slipped and almost fell, and in spite of the gravity of the situation, Daniel gave a silent cheer. That would be Drummer, then. The two men gave the pony a comically wide arc and continued with their search.

Daniel looked at his watch. Time was creeping on. Surely the two men would give up soon. Even though they thought they'd left Tamzin without a phone, they couldn't be so naïve as to think that that situation would be anything but temporary. They had to expect that Tamzin would eventually call the police and tell them where her two attackers had gone. They had no reason to think she would keep the information to herself.

It seemed that Patrescu was indeed thinking along those lines, for when they reached the last stable, he looked at his watch, spoke briefly to his companion and they both headed at a brisk pace towards the house and the black 4×4.

Within moments, they had gone, the vehicle disappearing at speed down the puddled gravel drive, and it was with some relief that Daniel heard it accelerate on to the road and away. Getting to his feet, he set off at a slipping, sliding run down the hill towards the house, much to the joy of Taz, who circled him excitedly until he was told to stop.

Daniel climbed over the post-and-rail fence that bordered the parking area and peered through the side window of the Land Rover. The only occupants were canine, and they set up a storm of yelping barks at the sight of his face at the window.

After glancing up at them almost indifferently, Taz began trotting about, nose down and tail up, and as he checked out where the 4×4 had stood, the hackles rose in a stiff line along his shoulders and back.

'You can smell him, can't you, lad?' Daniel murmured, understanding the dog's agitation. He too had a score to settle with Macek.

The farmhouse door stood ajar and Daniel pushed it wider and went cautiously into the hallway. Taz, fired up with excitement, passed him in the narrow passage and went through to the kitchen, where no one was at home except for the two cats, who regarded the visitors sleepily from their position on top of the Aga.

Uninterested in the cats, Taz left the kitchen en route to the sitting room and then upstairs, where a clicking of claws on the floorboards told Daniel that he was carrying out a thorough search of the building. His silence indicated that he'd found no one, but Daniel followed him up to the landing, where, as in many houses, there was a loft hatch. This was shut and bolted from below, but not one to take anything at face value, Daniel stretched up to slide the bolt free and let the hatch swing open. It was just possible that Hilary might have hidden the girl up there if, for some reason, they hadn't got away in time.

Apart from a neatly lagged water tank and half a dozen deckchairs stacked against one partition, the roof space was empty – a stark contrast to the comfortable chaos that ruled down below. Daniel spoke Katya's name just to be sure, but the only sound to be heard was the wind whistling over the tiles.

Back at first-floor level, Daniel closed the hatch and made a quick search of the four bedrooms, two of which were clearly unused at present. Of the two remaining, Hilary's was easily recognizable by the general theme of frogs and dinosaurs that held sway among the décor and ornaments. A window stood slightly open, its curtains blowing a little in the cold wind, and Daniel regarded it thoughtfully for a moment before glancing into Kat's room and then going back downstairs and out into the gathering darkness, followed by Taz.

As he left the house, he practically bumped into Hilary on the doorstep, causing her to let out an involuntary cry of alarm.

Daniel put a hand out to steady her and she clutched his arm.

'Oh, Daniel! Thank God! Have they gone?'

'They have. Are you OK?' She looked physically unharmed, if deeply stressed. 'What happened? Why didn't you get away after I called?'

Hilary shook her head. 'It's a long story. I'll tell you, but, Daniel, I can't find Kat! When we got back with the ponies, I sent her over here to grab some bits and pieces and put the dogs in the car, but then those men came and she just disappeared. I've no idea where she went.'

'*You* couldn't find her, but neither could they. I think I might be able to help, though. Come with me.'

Still holding her arm, he led her round the end of the house and turned her to face it.

'Look up,' he said, pointing at the roof, which, now they were beyond the glare of the outside security light, was visible as a dark silhouette against the evening sky. From this angle they could see the gable ends of the twin pitched roofs with a chimney at either end of the central gully.

'Up there?' Hilary said faintly.

'She's a gymnast, remember?' Daniel told her. 'I think she saw them drive in and, finding herself trapped in the house, climbed out of the window and on to the roof.' Then, raising his voice, 'Kat? It's Daniel.'

There was a pause, then, 'Daniel?' and a shadowy figure appeared beside the chimneystack.

'Yes, it's me. It's all right, they've gone.'

'Are you sure?'

'Quite sure. You can come down now, but for heaven's sake be careful!'

'Bah! It's easy,' Katya's voice floated back, loaded with scorn, and sure enough, within the minute she appeared in the doorway of the house.

'Kat, my dear. Thank goodness you're all right,' Hilary said, going forward to give her a hug. 'Ooh, let's get you inside. You're frozen.'

'No, wait, Daniel! Someone's coming – I can see their lights,' Kat was staring down the drive, a note of panic in her voice.

She was back through the doorway in a flash and Daniel turned to watch the steady approach of a pair of oncoming headlights, bouncing over the uneven surface of the drive.

Hilary drew in her breath in sharp dismay. 'You don't think they've come back?'

'Unlikely.' In fact, Daniel was wondering if Tamzin had given in under pressure and told the police everything, but if that had been the case, he would have expected a blue-light-approach. As the car swept into the yard, they could see it was unmarked.

'If this *is* the police,' he said quickly and quietly, 'deny any knowledge of Kat's whereabouts. Anything they ask you about her – you don't know. She was only here a few days and then she left, OK?'

'OK.'

The car pulled up and two figures stepped out into the glare of the security light, one a well-built man in his thirties and the other a female with blonde hair scraped back severely from a sharp-featured face. Both were dressed in civilian clothes.

'Daniel Whelan?' the man asked as he came forward.

Daniel nodded warily.

'DS Boyd, Molton CID, and this is WPS Hunt. DS Bowden sent us along to make sure everything was OK,' he explained. 'Are you Mrs McEwen-Smith? Where's the girl?'

'It's all right,' Daniel told Hilary with relief. 'It's safe to talk. These are the good guys.'

Ten minutes later, having coaxed Kat down to join them, Daniel found Hunt and Boyd enjoying the warmth of the kitchen while Hilary made coffee. The dogs had been brought in from the Land Rover and now lay curled up on their beds.

Daniel took a seat opposite the two officers at the table, but Kat remained standing, drifting across to lean against the Aga.

'Hello, Katya,' WPS Hunt said with a smile, but her friendly overture was met with stony silence and a look of profound distrust.

'So why didn't you leave after Daniel warned you the men were on their way?' the WPS said then, turning to Hilary.

'Because when Daniel first called, I'd just got back from a ride. I had a yard full of children, parents and ponies. It's a kind of organized chaos. I couldn't just abandon everyone. It shouldn't have taken more than ten minutes to sort out, and I thought that while everyone was here, I was safe enough. I planned to leave right behind the last client, so I sent Kat over here to fetch the Land Rover, the dogs and a few essentials, but then everything went wrong.'

'In what way?'

'One of the children got bitten by a pony,' Hilary said, handing the coffees round. 'It was only a bruise – didn't break the skin and he'd probably asked for it – but you'd have thought he was a hospital case, the howling he set up. So of course I had to administer first aid, fill out an accident form, comfort the child, reassure the parents, give them a refund – it all took for ever. When they went, I looked up and there were Patrescu and Macek standing in the doorway, waiting.'

'You recognized them?'

'No, I've never seen them before, but I guessed who they must be.'

'So what happened next?'

'Well, I was petrified. Then the smaller one said, "Where is Katya?"'

'And what did you tell them?'

'I told them I had no idea. I said she'd come and gone days ago. I said dozens of children help out at the weekends. I never know who's going to turn up, but Kat only came a few times and then I didn't see her again. Then they started having an argument – presumably in Romanian. I didn't understand a word, but it was pretty clear that the big one, Macek, favoured a violent approach.

'I didn't hang around to see what the outcome was. There's a door from my tack room through to the stable area, so while they were busy arguing, I slipped away and hid in one of the stables. I know it was a stupid thing to do because nothing could more surely prove that I'd lied, but it was just instinct, I suppose, to go to ground.'

'And what did the men do then?'

'They started shouting, saying I should come out because they would find me eventually, and when they did, it would be worse for me. I was terrified – I mean really shaking. They seemed to be here for ages. I could hear them moving about the yard and house, opening doors and slamming them, throwing things around and calling to one another. Eventually, they started looking in the stables, one by one. I heard them coming up the row and was convinced they'd find me, but Drummer came up trumps, bless him.'

'Drummer?' Boyd looked mystified.

'He's one of the ponies. Actually, he was the one who bit the child earlier. He's a smashing pony to ride, but a bit bad-tempered, and once his stable door is shut, he'll bite anyone who comes too close – except me, of course. That's why I chose to hide in there.'

'And it worked?' Hunt looked at her appraisingly.

Hilary nodded. 'I don't know whether he bit one of them, but there was an awful lot of swearing – that sounds the same in any language – and they argued some more. Then a minute or two later, they left. I didn't come out straight away, though, just in case.'

'And what about you?' Hunt asked Daniel. 'Bowden said he thought we might find you here.'

'I parked in the village and came up to do a recce,' he replied, and briefly gave them his side of the story. 'So when does the raid go down?' he finished.

'Nineteen— Er, seven thirty,' Boyd said. 'We wanted to be as sure as we could that everyone would be at home.'

'What raid?' It was the first time Kat had spoken.

'The police are going to Moorside tonight,' Daniel told her. 'With any luck Macek and Patrescu will soon be in police cells and the girls will be free.'

Hope lit her face and she stepped forward. 'Elena too?'

'Most certainly,' he assured her.

'What will happen to her – to us? Will they let me see her?'

'Of course you'll see her,' Hunt said. 'We're on your side, Kat. You won't be in any trouble. We'll look after you, I promise.'

'But when can I see her? Can we go there now?'

'No, I'm sorry.' Hunt shook her head. 'We have to wait here. If we went, we'd be in the way. But they'll let us know as soon as there's any news.'

As the evening wore on, Hilary put potatoes in the Aga to bake, then went out to feed the ponies with Boyd as escort.

Seven thirty came and went. The potatoes were eaten with cheese and pickle, and a large pot of tea made. Conversation was desultory, everyone waiting on tenterhooks for the call to come through from Bowden.

At nine o'clock, Hunt and Boyd excused themselves and went outside.

Kat, who'd been pacing restlessly and demanding to know, every five minutes or so, why they hadn't heard anything, now stopped and wanted to know what they were doing.

Daniel had no answer for her, and after a moment, Kat announced that she was going to find out and, ignoring Hilary's protests, headed for the door.

'Let her go,' Daniel advised. 'They'll keep an eye on her.'

'I suppose so.' Hilary sank back into her chair. 'Have you spoken to Tamzin?'

'Yes, I rang her earlier. They're keeping her in hospital overnight. Her mum's with her, but she sounded a bit depressed.' He paused, staring deep into the orange heart of the fire. 'I feel so guilty, dragging you all into this.'

'We've had this conversation before,' Hilary pointed out quietly but firmly. 'You didn't drag any of us into it – we wanted to help.'

'But you should have seen her face, Hilary – what he'd done to her.' He stared into the fire again, gazing mesmerized as sparks showered from a collapsing log and were sucked away up the flue. 'He threatened to cut her, you know. What if he'd done it? If she'd been scarred for life, what then?'

'It didn't happen,' Hilary reminded him gently.

'But it did happen,' Daniel stated. 'Last year. And it was all my fault. The thing was, on the surface, she seemed to be dealing with it, but her mother told me afterwards that she'd stopped seeing her friends – didn't go out. She said she just needed time, but then one day she took an overdose. Nobody saw it coming – not even her therapist. Her parents only went out for an hour or so, but that's what she'd been waiting for. She was dead when they got back.'

He fell silent, and after a few moments, Hilary asked, 'Who was she, Daniel?'

He took a deep breath. 'Her name was Sara. She was eighteen, very pretty and very bright. She'd just won a place at Oxford. She'd got everything going for her. The only thing she ever did wrong was go into the corner shop at the same time as me.'

'What happened?'

Daniel glanced at her. 'You don't need to hear this.'

'No, I don't, but I think you need to tell me. What happened in the corner shop? Was it a hold-up?'

Daniel nodded. 'A smack-head desperate for a fix and so thin it looked as though a puff of wind would have blown him over, but he had a knife. I'd just finished my shift and was heading back to the station, and I nipped in there for some milk. As soon as he saw my uniform, he panicked and grabbed the nearest person to him, who happened to be Sara. He held the knife to her face and started shouting at me to stay back.' Daniel frowned, reliving the moment, as he had so many times since. 'Sara screamed and started to cry. The junkie was babbling like a madman. Other people were panicking. There was so much noise that I took a chance on calling for back-up over my radio. Then the junkie started to back towards the door, dragging the girl with him. One moment the knife would be at her throat, the next he'd be waving it at everyone else. She was crying and mouthing, "Help me! Please! Help me!" over and over again, and she was looking at me. Everyone was. I was the one in the uniform – I would know what to do.'

Daniel shook his head. 'I tried to talk him down. If nothing else, I thought it might buy me some time until back-up arrived. It was tempting to try for the knife when he was waving it around, but I couldn't risk getting it wrong, for the girl's sake. I followed him to the door, but he was shouting at me, "Stay back! I'll cut her! I'll cut her!" All I could do was let him go and just hope that the other lads had turned up and were waiting outside . . .' He paused, his jaw tightening. 'Through the window I saw him run off – just him, on his own – getting away. So I ran out after him. But then I found Sara.

'She was sitting on the pavement, her hands over her face. I asked her if she was OK, but then I saw the blood.' He looked up at Hilary, his expression bleak. 'The bastard had slashed her from forehead to top lip, right across her eye. For no reason, just because he hadn't got his own way.'

'Oh, Daniel!'

'I tried to comfort her while we waited for the ambulance, but she pushed me away. Do you know what she said?'

Hilary shook her head.

'She said, "Why didn't you *help* me?" And every time I see her face, that's what she's saying – and I have no answer.'

There was silence as he stopped speaking, broken only by a log settling in the wood-burner.

'But it wasn't your fault,' Hilary protested. 'What else could you have done? And where was your back-up?'

Daniel shrugged. 'Who knows? This was after I turned informer, remember. I wasn't the most popular copper at the Met just then . . .'

'You mean they didn't turn up on purpose?'

He shrugged again. 'I've got no proof.'

'But that's appalling! It's criminal! Wasn't there an investigation?'

'Of sorts, but it didn't turn up anything conclusive. And even if it had, the damage was done. It wouldn't have helped Sara or her family.'

This sombre reflection was punctuated by the return of Hunt and Boyd. They entered the room ushering Katya ahead of them, and on their heels came the burly form of Tom Bowden. He was looking grim.

'Where is she? Where's my sister?' Katya turned and faced Tom.

'She's not here. I'm sorry, Katya . . .'

'Then where is she? They said she would be free.' Kat's voice held a note of hysteria and Hilary went over to put a restraining hand on her arm.

'I'm sorry, Katya,' Bowden said. 'We had the place surrounded, but I'm afraid when we went in, your sister wasn't there.'

THIRTEEN

It was two days after the night of the raid on Moorside when life started to get back to something approaching normality for Daniel. Whether it would ever get back to normal for Katya was another matter entirely.

She had been inconsolable that night. To begin with, she had stormed at Tom Bowden and then she had collapsed into Hilary's arms and sobbed with an intensity that was compounded of all the fear, stress and disappointment of the past few weeks.

Demonstrating remarkable powers of persuasion, Hilary had taken the girl upstairs, returning after three-quarters of an hour with the news that Katya had at last fallen asleep, exhausted.

From Bowden, Daniel had heard how the raid, meticulously planned and carried out, had caught Yousef Patrescu in the process of loading a minibus with a quantity of files, film-making and computer equipment. Overwhelmed by the sheer number of police he faced, he'd given himself up without a struggle, and inside the house, officers had found upwards of two dozen young Romanian women and girls locked in their rooms, bewildered and frightened at the turn of events. However, Elena Pavlenco and the young girl known as Molly were not among them, and neither, frustratingly, was Anghel Macek.

'We had a man watching the front gates and he saw both Patrescu and Macek come back in the Nissan after you saw them at Briars Hill,' Tom reported. 'But something must have put the wind up them because it appears that while Patrescu stopped behind to put their affairs in order – by way of a little bonfire in the grounds – Macek picked up the two girls, cut the fence at the rear of the property with a pair of bolt-cutters and drove off down the track that runs along the edge of the moor. He was long gone by the time we went in. It's all a bit of a mess, and with much of the evidence destroyed or carried off by Macek, it would have been a complete disaster if we hadn't been in time to collar Patrescu.'

With Macek still on the loose, it was not deemed safe for Kat to stay with Hilary, and in the morning, a social worker had arrived at Briars Hill. In due course, with much reassurance from Daniel and Hilary, Kat and the social worker had been driven away in one of the police vehicles. Sitting in the back seat of the car, she looked lost and suddenly a good deal younger than her fifteen years.

For his part, unenthusiastic about the idea of returning to the flat for the same reason, Daniel had gratefully accepted the Bowdens' continuing offer of hospitality. The flat had had limited appeal at the outset, and now, as he helped himself to toast and marmalade at the Bowdens' breakfast table, with the low winter sun slanting through the Victorian bay window, the thought of moving back to the gloomy and frequently chilly room above the former lawnmower showroom was a depressing one.

At the head of the table, Fred was sitting sideways with his legs crossed at the knee, reading the morning paper, while Meg was in the kitchen, making a fresh pot of coffee. Left alone with his thoughts, Daniel found himself wondering where Macek had taken the girls. Presumably the plan had been for him to meet up with Patrescu at some prearranged rendezvous, but when that hadn't happened, what would he have done? Were the two men freelance, so to speak, or part of a larger network?

Strictly speaking, it was no longer anything to do with Daniel – it was police business now, and he was reliant on updates from Tom – but you couldn't switch off caring just like that. His life might have turned out quite differently if he *had* been able to, he thought wryly.

Not that he hadn't got problems enough of his own to deal with. Drew was refusing to answer or return his calls, and Amanda was saying it was up to the boy whether he wanted to speak to Daniel or not and she wasn't going to take sides. Daniel had no idea whether Drew's silence was an attempt to punish him for what he saw as his rejection or whether there was something else going on. The uncertainty was tearing him apart and he'd decided that, come the weekend, he was heading for Taunton to sort it all out.

Just as Meg came back into the room carrying the freshly filled coffee pot, they heard the sound of a key turning in the front door.

Fred looked up from his paper. 'Tom. He did say he might call in.'

Moments later, he appeared in the doorway of the dining room.

'Hi, all. Any coffee left?'

'I've just made fresh,' Meg told him. 'Come and sit down. I'll do some more toast.'

'Well, I've already had breakfast at work,' Tom said, stripping off his coat and sitting down nonetheless, 'but I expect I could manage another slice or three.'

Meg disappeared into the kitchen once again and Fred behind his paper.

'Any news?' Daniel asked.

'Bits and pieces,' Tom said, pouring himself a cup of coffee. 'We've lifted Patrescu's phone records and pulled your friend Naylor in for questioning. And we also know who the second girl is now. Molly Stubbs – daughter of Shelley Stubbs, who was found dead in a bedsit in Bristol at the back end of last year. OD'd. Gave herself a shot of pure heroin and wasn't found for a week. Unintentionally, it was initially thought, but given that Patrescu appears to have had big plans for her daughter, I have my doubts.'

'Unless she was a most unnatural mother, she'd have kicked up a huge fuss if she found out.'

'Easier to remove her from the equation,' Tom agreed. 'What we don't know is how much Macek was in Patrescu's confidence. He must have known what the girls were intended for, but would Patrescu have entrusted him with anything as important as details of his clients' contacts? I don't think so, do you?'

Daniel shook his head. 'I got the impression that he was just the muscle. He certainly had a healthy respect for Patrescu.'

'So what'll he do with the girls now?' Tom wondered. 'Worst-case scenario is that he buggers off to Birmingham or Manchester or somewhere and puts them straight into work. If that's the case, we really haven't a hope in hell of finding them.'

'Poor Katya,' Daniel said. 'What'll happen to her?'

'I'm not sure,' Tom admitted. 'Nothing's ever decided in a hurry – you know that. The wheels of bureaucracy grind exceedingly slow. By the way, how's your girlfriend?'

'Well, there's no permanent damage, but she's pretty trauma-tized, as you might imagine. She's home now and her mother's staying with her.'

That was the bare bones of the matter, but didn't touch on the cool way Tamzin had greeted Daniel when he'd visited her in hospital. Her mother had been with her when he arrived and the welcome she offered could only be described as frigid. Tall and elegant in a jersey skirt suit, Nadine Ellis had ignored the hand

Daniel had offered and taken a seat in the corner of the room with the clear intention of staying there.

Under her scrutiny, Tamzin seemed awkward and ill at ease, offering her cheek to receive Daniel's kiss, accepting his flowers, grapes and magazines with murmured thanks, and avoiding eye contact.

After a scant ten minutes, Nadine had voiced the opinion that her daughter looked tired and needed to sleep. Not wanting to cause friction, Daniel had accepted his cue to leave, saying he'd call in and see her at Quarry Farm the next day if she was discharged, as expected.

'That's very kind, but there's no need. I shall be staying with her,' her mother told him.

Daniel had looked at Tamzin for confirmation, and she'd smiled wanly and said, 'I'll be fine, really.'

An outburst of barking from Mosely brought Daniel abruptly back to the present, and after a moment, they heard the soft flop of envelopes hitting the doormat in the hall.

'I don't know how he does that,' Tom exclaimed. 'Deaf as a doorpost but always knows when the postman's coming.'

'One for you, Daniel,' Meg said, coming into the room moments later with a plate piled high with toast in one hand and half a dozen envelopes in the other.

'For me?' Daniel was surprised. 'But no one knows I'm here except Amanda and she's not in the habit of writing to me.'

Putting down his coffee cup, he took the white envelope she held out. The address was printed, the postmark Bristol.

He slid his thumb under the flap and immediately noticed the letterhead of his and Amanda's solicitor. He started to read, his eyes skipping impatiently over the legal phraseology to pick out the bits that mattered, and what he read shook him to the core.

'Trouble?' Tom was watching him closely.

'Erm . . .' Daniel cleared his throat and tried again. 'Amanda's filing for divorce.'

'Oh, I'm sorry.' Tom didn't sound sure whether he should be or not.

'No, don't be. I mean, anything we had is long gone. The thing is, it looks like she's trying to stop me seeing Drew.'

'What? She can't do that!' Meg protested. 'On what grounds?'

'Apparently, she's saying it's what he wants. She says . . . She's trying to say that he's frightened of me!'

'But that's rubbish!' Meg said hotly. 'How does she work that out when all this time he's been desperate to come and stay with you?'

'I know. I can't believe it either. She's obviously spun some ridiculous story to the solicitor,' Daniel said. 'But the thing is, since I took him back last time, he hasn't answered any of my calls. I wish I knew what she's been telling him.'

'Sounds as though he's sulking to me.' Fred lowered his paper. 'He'll change his mind in a day or two – kids are like that. It's hardly enough to base legal action on. The woman's a fool, and the solicitor's a fool for going along with it!'

'Oh, he'll be rubbing his hands together in glee,' Tom put in. 'A nice meaty confrontation spells oodles of dosh for them.'

'You need to see a solicitor yourself – straight away,' Meg advised.

'Her solicitor *was* my solicitor.'

'Not any longer. They can't act for both of you,' Fred said. 'Tell you what, why don't you try mine? Fitch, Hall and Welland. They're in Tavistock. I'll introduce you, if you like. They've done some very good work for us, and I believe Fitch Junior specializes in divorce work.'

'Thanks.' Daniel sighed. 'God, what a mess! Poor Drew. I never thought she'd use him like this.'

'There's a joker at Molton Nick, custody sergeant – name of Peterson,' Tom said. 'He's been married three times. Anyway, he always says you never really get to know your other half until one of you files for divorce.'

Later that afternoon, Daniel slotted the Mercedes into a space in Tavistock's Bridge Street car park and went in search of a ticket machine. Fred's solicitors had come up trumps, not only agreeing to meet Daniel, but even managing to fit him in later that day, due to a cancellation.

He was fifteen minutes early, so having paid his dues, Daniel let Taz out of the car and walked down to the river, where he stood and gazed sightlessly at the water rushing over the weir, his head still filled with the injustice of Amanda's words. His first instinct had been to call her, hoping that she had been encouraged in her action by a solicitor bent on generating a little lucrative work for himself and that for once a little reasonable discussion would sort it out.

Reason didn't have a chance to come into it. Coldly Amanda told him that Daniel had brought it upon himself and that she'd been advised to have no contact with him over the matter; at which point she put the phone down.

After ten gloomy minutes, Daniel returned Taz to the car and set off to find the offices of Fitch, Hall and Welland, pulling his jacket close against a damp, cold wind. Although in the town spring flowers were blooming, winter seemed loath to loosen its grip, and today the sky above the grey stone town buildings was overcast and unpromising.

Leaving Messrs Fitch, Hall and Welland three-quarters of an hour later, Daniel felt as happy as could be expected in the circumstances. Fred's recommendation had been a good one. Fitch Junior had a son of a similar age to Drew and sympathized fully with Daniel on the emotive issue of access. He said that in such a case the courts would require the three of them to seek mediation before any further action would be taken. Nothing would happen in a hurry, he said, and if, as Daniel believed, Drew was merely reacting to recent events, there would be plenty of time for the boy to reconsider. Fitch Junior was cheerfully reassuring as he showed his client out – as well he might be, Daniel reflected, at God knows how much per hour.

Closing the glossy black door behind him, Daniel was met with an arctic blast, liberally laced with stinging pellets of icy snow. He paused, looking up and down the street. He'd been too wound up to eat before his appointment and now he was keen to find a bakery or café that might supply him with a hot pie or bacon roll.

What he was looking for and what he found were two very different things, for out of the door of a bank some 20 feet away from Daniel came a tall, broad-shouldered man wearing a hooded sweatshirt under a denim jacket. He was wearing sunglasses in spite of the dullness of the day and had several days' growth of beard, but it was a face that was etched on Daniel's memory.

Anghel Macek.

His nemesis.

Daniel's whole being started fizzing with anticipation. He'd imagined the Romanian was far away by now and the sense of unfinished business had left him feeling restless and unsatisfied. Now fate had given him another chance to bring the man to book, but he must tread softly; Macek was on his own and it was vitally important that Daniel did nothing to draw attention to himself if there was any chance that the Romanian might lead him to the two missing girls.

Drawing into the alcove of a shop doorway, he took out his mobile and put through a call to Tom Bowden, keeping his eye on his quarry all the while. Frustratingly, he was once more put through to Bowden's answerphone and was forced to leave a message.

'Tom, Macek is in Tavistock. There's no sign of the girls as yet. I'm going to follow him, if I can. Please ring me as soon as you get this.'

Even as he finished speaking, Daniel saw Macek run across the road through a gap in the traffic and turn left on the far pavement. Slipping the phone into his pocket, Daniel followed him, staying on his own side of the road. The weather was in his favour because the wind, with its unpleasant cargo of snowflakes, was behind them, and wouldn't encourage the Romanian to look round too frequently.

After 100 yards, Macek turned right into a car park. Daniel crossed the road and followed, hardly daring to believe his luck as he recognized the park where he had left his own car. Glancing round, he saw a black 4×4 in the far corner.

Could it really be that easy?

It was.

As Macek neared the black car, Daniel saw his step slow and he turned, apparently casually, to scan the car park. Smoothly, Daniel swung between the cars and headed away from him without looking back. Reaching the covering bulk of a transit van, he paused beside it, looking diagonally through the side window and windscreen to check whether he was being watched. Apparently, his behaviour hadn't attracted Macek's attention, for as Daniel looked across towards the black 4×4, he saw the Romanian open the driver's door and get in.

Swiftly he made his way to the Mercedes, unlocked it and slid behind the wheel. Taz, who had no doubt been watching his antics with bewilderment, stood up and wagged his tail.

'Did you see who that was?' he asked the dog. 'Our friend Mr Macek. And we're going to follow him and see where he goes.'

Tailing another vehicle is beset with difficulties, as Daniel well knew. In a town, there is always a strong possibility that you will be separated from your target by other traffic at junctions, roundabouts and traffic lights. If you take a chance and jump a red light or force your way out of a junction to keep your quarry in sight, the chances are that you'll provoke at least one indignant motorist to lean on his horn, instantly attracting the attention of the driver in front.

Daniel regarded pedestrian crossings as a particular nightmare. More than once in the past, he'd been stuck on the wrong side of a crossing while an elderly shopper shuffled across and had to watch the suspect he'd been following disappear into the wide blue yonder. As if these potential problems weren't enough, Daniel knew his red Merc was already well known to Macek, so he was forced to keep his distance.

On this particular occasion, Daniel's luck held and he managed to negotiate the town centre without any of these hazards occurring. In fact, due to two other cars turning off, he found himself arriving at a junction on the way out of the town immediately behind the big 4×4, which was not ideal.

He pulled up close to the bumper of the Nissan, knowing that the extra height of Macek's vehicle would make it difficult for him to see the Mercedes in that position and impossible for him to see its driver. When the Nissan pulled away, Daniel dawdled at the junction, letting a couple of other vehicles go by before he followed, then, hoping that he wasn't being observed by any zealous traffic cops, slipped his phone from his pocket and thumbed the redial button. This time, blessedly, it was answered.

'Daniel, I was just going to ring you. What's going on? Fill me in.'

'I'm on Macek's tail, just leaving Tavistock on the Plymouth road. It's a black Nissan X-Trail with blacked-out windows.' He gave Tom the registration, adding, 'I don't know whether he's got the girls in there, but it's possible. If not, I'm hoping he'll lead me to them. The trouble is, he knows this car, and sooner or later he's probably going to clock me.'

'Where exactly are you?'

'I'm on the 386 heading south, maybe half a mile out of Tavistock.'

'OK, I'll mobilize the locals and I'll try for a chopper too. If you can keep him in sight, that's great, but don't put yourself in any tight spots, OK?'

'Yep, I gotcha.'

For 5 or 6 miles Daniel tailed the black Nissan without incident, wondering what it was the Romanian had picked up at the bank. Something very important, obviously, to risk showing himself in an area where the police would be on the lookout for him. And where was he going now? The coast, perhaps?

Suddenly, the car immediately behind Macek's vehicle slammed its brakes on to make a last-minute turn and the driver following it leaned on his horn in anger.

'Shit!' Daniel muttered. The Romanian would have been less than human if he hadn't glanced in his mirror to see what the commotion was about, and it was a fair bet that in doing so he would also notice Daniel's car, just 50 yards or so behind and now with only one vehicle between them.

For a short time, it seemed that maybe he'd been lucky, but when, a quarter of a mile or so further on, Macek turned off the main road into a side road, and then almost immediately into another, Daniel began to doubt it.

If he'd been seen, there was no point in keeping his distance, so he put his foot down to close the gap on the 4×4. However, turning into a residential road, he was startled to see not the disappearing tailgate of Macek's vehicle, but the front view, complete with radiator bull-bars, accelerating towards him.

Daniel wasn't prepared to play chicken with a vehicle of the Nissan's stature. He swore and spun the wheel to the left, gritting his teeth as the Merc mounted the kerb, narrowly missing a telegraph pole.

The black bulk of the 4×4 swished by with only inches to spare, reached the junction and passed from his view as Daniel executed a rapid turn by dint of using the grass verge on both sides of the road. Back at the junction, he swung the car in a screeching curve to follow the Romanian and was rewarded, within a few hundred yards, with a sight of the Nissan disappearing round a bend ahead.

Now the chase was on in earnest.

Driving one-handed, Daniel put a call through to Tom once more.

The detective answered right away.

'Daniel? What's happening?'

'He's spotted me. We've turned off the main road somewhere near Horrabridge, but I'm not sure exactly where we are now. If only I had bloody sat nav! I'm still with him, but I'm not sure for how much longer. Any news on the chopper?'

'It's out on a shout – might be half an hour or more if it needs refuelling. Look, Daniel, hold back, OK? We'll try and get a car to you.'

'If I hold back, I'll lose him. There's any number of ways he could go from here. I'll try and keep you updated.'

'Daniel! Don't—' The rest of Tom's exclamation was lost as Daniel tossed the mobile on to the passenger seat, needing both hands and all his concentration to stay on the tail of the Nissan along the narrow, twisting country lanes.

He had no idea if Macek actually knew where he was going, but for his own part he was already completely disorientated as they sped down steeply banked single-track roads between high hedges, occasionally passing a cottage or farmstead. He could only hope they didn't meet anyone riding a horse or walking a dog, because at the crazy speed Macek was setting, he wouldn't have a hope of stopping, even if he bothered trying.

The pellets of icy snow had now morphed into larger flakes that blew over the hedges, swirled round the speeding vehicles like billowing lace curtains and formed eddies on the tarmac before settling into what was becoming a visible layer on the road surface.

The one or two cars unlucky enough to be coming in the opposite direction were forced to mount the bank as they found themselves confronted by the big black Nissan. Daniel longed for a tractor and a stubborn farmer to block the road, but it seemed such things only happen when you don't want them to, and the Nissan forged relentlessly on, with the Mercedes sticking to its tail like a limpet.

Through the gloom of a forest they raced and alongside a lake or reservoir before heading down an almost impossibly narrow farm lane with grass growing in the middle and emerging, at length, into a village that Daniel recognized as Goats Tor.

Still maintaining a suicidal pace, they passed the White Buck, where Daniel permitted himself a fleeting smile as he recognized a man angrily waving a walking stick as his old foe Major Clapford.

For one anxious moment, it seemed to Daniel that Macek might be heading for Hilary's stables at Briars Hill, although he couldn't see why on earth he should, but then they were past the entrance and away down another lane that was signposted as a dead end. Macek didn't hesitate and Daniel wondered if this was indeed his destination or whether he hadn't noticed the sign. One way or another, it looked as though the end of the pursuit was in sight.

Further on and still dropping, the way took them past a low-roofed farmhouse with a walled yard, and after a minute or two, the Merc's wheels drummed over a cattle grid as the hedges that bordered the lane fell away on first one side, then the other, and they ran out on to the open moor.

The Romanian ignored the turning to a car park and drove on down what was now not much more than a track without slackening his breakneck speed.

The ageing Merc squeaked and rattled its way over the rough surface in the wake of the 4×4. Ahead of him, Daniel saw the Nissan dip to ford a stream before surging out the other side, almost immediately passing from view as the track skirted a rocky spur.

Moments later, the Mercedes scrunched through the icy fringe of the stream and hit the shallow water with a smack that threw spray back over the windscreen. The gravel of the streambed dragged at the tyres for a second or two; then the front of the car met the rising ground with a bang that jarred Daniel's whole body. Pulling up the slope with a degree of wheel spin, he floored the accelerator and took the turn at a reckless speed to find chaos awaiting him on the other side.

As he simultaneously stamped on the brakes and swerved, it seemed to Daniel that the moor was all at once alive with whirling, rearing horseflesh. Grimly he fought to hold the steering wheel hard left as the Mercedes left the track and bucketed over the loose rocks that littered the short turf of the margin.

His first impression was of dozens of ponies scattering in panic. Some animals shied sideways, some bolted and some ran backwards, heads high and eyes white-rimmed. He was surrounded by a mass of flying manes and tails, glinting stirrups and bits, accompanied by frightened shrieks and the confused clatter of shod hooves on the stony track.

It was all over in a matter of seconds, the Mercedes coming to an abrupt halt with an impact that had a feeling of finality about it. Emerging from the fleeting embrace of the airbag, Daniel discovered that the car had come to rest tilted at an uncompromising angle, with its front offside wing grounded on a large granite boulder at the foot of the outcrop.

Shaken, Daniel swore and looked back to where the veritable stampede of horses had resolved itself into no more than eight ponies – nine, if you counted one that had high-tailed it back towards the open moor.

One rather plump boy was sitting in the middle of the track indulging in a fit of hysterics, and a lady in a bright-red anorak appeared to have dismounted and let go of her mount. Aside from these two, the remaining riders were still aboard and most seemed to have regained a measure of control. Further up the track and rapidly disappearing over a rise, Daniel could see the back of Macek's black Nissan.

'Bugger!' he said explosively, immediately reaching for his mobile and thumbing in Tom's number.

His call was diverted to a messaging service and he said simply, 'Sorry, I've pranged the Merc and lost him. He's on the moor – still in the Nissan – somewhere near Goats Tor. And, yes, I'm OK – just totally pissed off!'

In the back of the car, Taz whined unhappily and Daniel glanced over his shoulder as he reached for the door handle.

'Sorry, lad. You wait there a minute. Won't be long.'

Stepping out into the icy wind, it was quite plain to see that he wouldn't be going any further in the Mercedes – not now or ever, come to that. Where it had hit the boulder, the bodywork of the car's offside front quarter had crumpled like aluminium foil, the wheel pushed out of sight somewhere underneath the chassis. The damage was unmistakably terminal.

To go after the Nissan on foot would be as pointless as it was foolhardy, and as Daniel was of an essentially practical frame of mind, he turned his thoughts instead to restoring some sort of order to the turmoil for which he was partially to blame.

Wading into the mêlée, he had just caught the rein of a passing loose pony when a familiar brindle lurcher materialized by his side, its ears flattened in delighted recognition, followed closely by a greyhound in a fleece-lined coat.

Hilary!

He'd been expecting a well-deserved earful from whoever was in charge, so it was with considerable relief that he now turned to see his friend approaching – the one person who would understand and forgive the uncharacteristic recklessness of his behaviour.

Hilary reined in and looked down at him from the back of a brown pony that he recognized as Drummer, the Briars Hill reprobate.

'Daniel! Whatever's going on? Was that Macek?' She had caught the other loose animal, which she now held by the buckle end of its reins.

Daniel nodded. 'Yes, it was.'

'But what's he doing here? Has he got the girls with him?'

'I don't know. I haven't actually seen them, but it's possible. That's why I was following him. I spotted him in Tavistock.'

'Does Tom know?' In her dealings with Bowden, the formalities had very quickly gone out of the window.

'Yeah, I rang him straight away. He's trying to rustle up a chopper, but last I heard, it wasn't going to be here in a hurry.'

Daniel ignored the gathering cluster of ponies and riders. 'Does this track go anywhere? Can you think why he might have gone that way?'

Hilary frowned. 'I can't imagine. It's the old road to the King's Hat Tin Mine. There's the remains of the old blowing house, but it's not much more than a pile of stones. You couldn't hide anything there, or anyone . . .'

'Perhaps he's just trying to get away, then. Does the track go any further than the mines?'

'Not as such, but there are several bridleways. One goes towards Princetown. I don't know whether he'd get that big four by four along them. He won't find it easy – they're pretty rough and I'm fairly sure we're in for some more snow before long. That's why I turned back.'

'Well, I don't imagine he'll risk coming back this way. He must know I'd have called the police by now. Damn! If only I hadn't buggered up that wheel.'

'You'd never have followed him in that, anyway. You might on a horse, though,' she added.

Daniel gave her a narrow-eyed look. 'Macek must be miles away by now. A horse would never catch that car.'

'It might if you knew a shortcut . . .'

'What are you saying?'

'Just that the track follows the level ground pretty much and to do that it makes a huge detour. A person on a horse could cut across country and probably get to the old mine workings in a similar sort of time.'

'If they knew the way . . .'

'It's only a sheep path, but Drummer could follow it. He's been that way many times.'

'You're serious, aren't you?'

'Why not? Drummer was born on the moor. He'll look after you. Surely it's worth a try.'

Before Daniel could answer, Hilary was off the pony and lengthening the stirrup leathers to allow for Daniel's longer legs, all the while keeping her elbow against Drummer's neck to stop him from nipping.

'When you hit the track again,' she went on, 'turn right and you'll only be fifty yards from the mine. From there you'll just have to hope you can see him. That track is incredibly rough, though. He won't be able to go very fast, even in that car.'

Doing anything was better than nothing.

'OK. It's worth a try,' he said.

Daniel went across to the stricken Merc and let Taz out before reaching in for his waxed jacket and the beanie he'd worn on his first visit to Moorside. He pulled the coat on over his leather jacket, found gloves in the pockets and put them on too, while Taz ran in excited circles, anticipating a walk.

Minutes later, Daniel settled into Drummer's worn saddle and pushed his feet into the stirrups. Ahead of him, the moor looked bleak and infinitely uninviting, a vast wasteland of sheep-cropped turf, heather, bracken and cold hard granite. An arctic wind whistled around his ears, reinforcing the sense of desolation.

Standing at the pony's shoulder, Hilary looked up at him.

'You must trust Drummer, Daniel. If he seems reluctant to go somewhere, there'll be a reason for it. The moor can be treacherous, but he knows it inside out. Trust him.'

She took the pony's rein and led him past the others, telling the waiting riders to stay where they were.

Looking up at Daniel again, she said, 'The path is on your right, about a hundred yards further up the track. You can't miss it – it's next to a big clump of gorse and a hawthorn tree.' She put her hand on his knee. 'Be careful won't you, Daniel? And find Elena for us, eh?'

'I'll do my best. Will you see if you can get hold of Tom and tell him what's happening?'

Hilary nodded, then with a growled 'Goo-arn!' she slapped the pony on the rump, and with a lurch, Daniel was on his way.

FOURTEEN

Daniel found the turning on to the sheep track with no trouble, after a short battle of wills with Drummer, who – not unnaturally – baulked at the notion of turning away from home once again, but as they headed out across the open moor, the weather closed in.

When he set off, there were no more than a few flakes swirling about in the gusty breeze without ever seeming to touch the ground, but then the few became many and suddenly it was as if a white veil had been drawn across Daniel's view. He had no choice but to trust that Drummer could somehow follow the narrow path, as Hilary had said he would.

Even for someone who'd spent several years of his working life in close partnership with a dog, the feeling of being totally dependent on an animal for his very survival was slightly unsettling.

In contrast to his relationship with Taz, he and Drummer had no history – the pony owed him no loyalty. His reliance on the animal was completely one-sided and it was, in essence, only looking after Daniel as a consequence of its own self-preservation.

Daniel was under no illusions that, if he fell off, the pony would stick around to wait for him. The most likely scenario was that it would turn round and head for its stable without so much as a thought for its erstwhile rider, and this made it imperative that he use every ounce of his concentration and limited experience to ensure that it didn't happen. The thought of being set afoot in these conditions, with very little idea of where he was, didn't appeal to him at all, and that was the best possible result. If he were injured in the fall, he might lie unconscious for a long time before he was found, and in that case the prognosis would be grave.

Transferring the reins to one hand, Daniel wound the fingers of the other tightly into Drummer's rough mane. Although they weren't travelling particularly fast, he was caught dangerously off-balance several times by unseen twists and turns in the path, and only hung on by the skin of his teeth. The stinging wind numbed his face, and his fingers became stiff with cold as melting snow soaked his gloves.

Once or twice, when the wind blew extra hard, Drummer slowed, instinct urging him to angle his rump into the wind and wait out the storm, and Daniel had to drive him on with his heels and the end of the leather reins.

The only one who seemed unaffected by the conditions was Taz, who ran alongside or behind the pony with every appearance of enjoyment, his thick double-layered coat keeping the chill at bay and his strong claws finding good purchase even on the frosty ground. The only sign that he was even aware of the snow was in the way he flattened his ears against his head.

Just as Daniel was beginning to wonder if the whole idea had been a foolish and dangerous mistake, the snow stopped as abruptly as it had begun.

The wind continued to whistle over the surface of the moor and the sky still held that leaden, yellow-grey look that promised more snow to come, but any improvement – however temporary – was cause for celebration in Daniel's view.

Sitting up, he brushed the snow from the saddle and the creases of his clothing before it could melt, while Drummer paused to give himself a huge shake. The moor stretched away from them on all sides, the covering of snow rendering it almost featureless, and the thin white line of the path he was following headed down into the shallow valley and on up to a cluster of rocks on the horizon.

Looking ahead and to the right when they finally breasted the rise, he could see a group of stunted pine trees. Close by were the tumbledown remains of a number of stone buildings and the jagged broken column of a chimney. There could be no doubt that he was looking at ruins of the old King's Hat Mine. Daniel's spirits rose like a lark on a summer's day. They were on the right track.

With their goal in sight, Daniel asked Drummer for more speed and within minutes they came out on a track that was, if Hilary was to be believed, the one that Macek had taken. Turning right, the ruins stood out starkly against the lowering cloud, the mossy grey stones dusted with windblown snow, giving the effect of an old black and white photo.

At the pony's feet were the clear double lines of a vehicle's tyre tracks in the snowfall. The weather had, after all, been a blessing in disguise.

Sending a heartfelt thank-you winging back over the moor to Hilary, he pushed the pony forward again. Not knowing how soon he might come up with the Romanian, and not wanting to lose the element of surprise, Daniel called Taz to heel.

Cautiously rounding the corner, moments later, he saw a low bridge crossing what was possibly the tailrace of a long-gone waterwheel, before the track forked into two smaller paths. These were presumably the bridleways Hilary had spoken of.

Daniel couldn't see the Nissan itself, but as he crossed the bridge, the telltale tyre tracks were clear, leading round the side of the hill on the right-hand path.

Patting Drummer's steaming neck and reminding Taz to stay to heel, Daniel rode on, wondering if Macek actually knew where he was going or whether he was merely keeping on because he felt he had no alternative.

The path was clearly not meant for cars, however rugged their construction, and the fact that Macek kept having to detour around boulders gave Daniel hope that the Romanian might yet find himself halted by an impassable obstacle.

Drummer was moving at a ground-covering jog now, his hooves rattling on the frost-hard, stony path. It was a hybrid landscape, a mixture of dark-brown heather and whitened turf. Some areas had been blown clear of snow, while mini drifts, no more than inches deep, lay in the depressions and the angles between rocks and ground.

Suddenly the distant sound of a vehicle engine carried back on the wind. Ahead, the path turned and dropped out of sight round a steep rocky slope, and he reined Drummer in to listen. As keen as he was to catch up with the Romanian, he didn't want to run into him unprepared.

In the relative quiet of their stillness, the relentless wind provided a backdrop against which Daniel was gradually able to pick out other noises: the liquid arpeggio call of a curlew, the gurgle of an unseen stream and then what his ears strained for, another burst of engine noise.

With his heels, he edged Drummer forward to the top of the slope and there, less than a hundred yards ahead, in the bottom of the valley, was the Nissan. It appeared to be stationary and as Daniel watched he saw its reversing lights come on and heard the roar of its engine, but it didn't move.

At last, it seemed, Macek's luck had run out.

Without pausing to ponder the cause of the Romanian's

misfortune, Daniel pushed Drummer on. The white line of the path wound down through 18-inch-high mounds of decaying bracken, the bent brown fronds showing dark where the Nissan's wheels had disturbed the snow.

The 4×4's engine roared again, but it seemed to be well and truly stuck, up to its hubcaps in the snow, which appeared to be a great deal deeper in the bottom of the valley.

Drummer was moving at a fast trot as they hit the level ground, and Daniel kicked him into a canter, his eyes on the vehicle's left back door. If he could get that open before Macek realized what was happening, he would at least know if the girls were inside. It was of course quite possible that the Romanian had activated the child-locks, but he had no other plan.

He was within 20 feet of his target when with no warning whatsoever, Drummer dug his toes in sharply, dropping his head to retain his balance, and tipping Daniel, without ceremony, over his ears.

The landing was soft. Daniel hit the cushion of snowy vegetation shoulder first, loose snow cascading on top of him as he rolled over on to his back. Thankfully, he had the presence of mind to hang on to his reins, so, although Drummer threw up his head and pulled back, he could go no further than Daniel's outstretched arm would allow and within moments, he was back on his feet. Crooning softly to soothe the pony, he reached up to scratch him behind his ears, sparing a few words of reassurance for Taz, who was fawning anxiously around his legs.

Turning to look at the 4×4 again, he frowned. The engine was still revving furiously, but the vehicle appeared to be sinking into the snow. Much deeper and it would be difficult to open the doors.

Daniel looked more closely at the stretch of ground between himself and the Nissan. At first glance it had appeared the same as the rough slope of the valley side, but now he could see that there were fewer tussocks of grass and heather, and the tracks left by the 4×4 cut dark, water-filled scars across the thin white carpet of snow. Nearer to him, several stunted hawthorns grew, their gnarled trunks twisted and bent away from the prevailing wind, but none stood further out in the valley bottom.

Realization hit Daniel like a cold shower. The Nissan wasn't sinking in the snow – there hadn't been enough for that. Suddenly the pony's violent reaction made sense. He was standing on the edge of one of Dartmoor's famous – or infamous – bogs, and if

it hadn't been for Drummer's native savvy, he would now
undoubtedly be in the same predicament as the Romanian. He
realized that this was what Hilary had meant when she begged
him to trust the pony, whatever happened.

Out of interest, he stepped cautiously forward, testing the ground
with his weight. He didn't go far. The frozen mat of vegetation
that covered the bog dipped as he leaned on it, sending ripples out
across the surface of the mire. It was a bizarre feeling, for all the
world like treading on the thick skin of a very big custard. He
remembered Hilary calling them quaking bogs or featherbeds and
could now see why. He moved back quickly to firm ground.

Daniel peeled off his wet gloves and took his phone from his
pocket. If he could reach the emergency services, how long would
it take them to get there? Too long, he feared, but it was worth
a try. He looked up. The sky was still grey, but only the odd lost
flake floated mournfully down. Would the chopper risk taking
off? He wasn't sure. One look at the mobile's display, however,
told him that he was on his own. No signal was available in the
valley and a glance at the foundering vehicle was enough to tell
him that he didn't have time to waste returning to higher ground.
He would have to trust that Hilary had been able to contact Tom
Bowden. In the meantime, it was clear that if anything were to
be done, he would have to do it.

Macek was still revving the engine, the exhaust blowing out
a spray of dirty water each time he trod on the accelerator pedal,
but even as Daniel watched, the Nissan spluttered and fell quiet,
finally overwhelmed by the thick, peaty bog water. Then, for the
first time, Daniel actually saw the Romanian, as the driver's door
was pushed open, its lower edge scraping an arc through the
sludge of mossy mud. Keeping a firm hold of the doorframe,
Macek tested the surface of the bog with one foot, withdrawing
it hastily when his leg plunged in up to the knee.

It was apparent that Macek hadn't fully appreciated the gravity
of his situation until that moment and his first instinct – somewhat bizarrely – was to try and drag the door shut again. In this
he was foiled. His weight on the sill had tipped the vehicle sideways a little, digging the point of the door into the mud so that
it was impossible to move.

Macek looked up and around, his wild eyes alighting on
Daniel. He stared for a long moment, then looked around again,
as if hoping that some other, more palatable, solution to his
dilemma would miraculously appear.

Daniel waited, saying nothing, and eventually the Romanian's gaze returned to him.

'Well, help me!' he shouted angrily. 'Don't just stand there! It's sinking.'

The Nissan was indeed sinking. Some of these bogs were rumoured to be 20 feet deep or more, Tamzin had said, and although Daniel had no particular misgivings about seeing Anghel Macek disappear into its peaty depths, there was something he had to know first.

'Where are the girls?' he called.

'What girls?'

Daniel shook his head in disbelief. 'Now is not the time to be stupid,' he told the Romanian. 'If you don't tell me where the two girls are, I'll just walk away without a backward glance. Nobody will ever know I found you.'

'No!' His voice was almost a scream. 'You can't do that! All right – they're here. In the car.'

'Show me.'

Macek glanced down at the ever-encroaching tide of slime that had now topped the sill and started to fill the footwell. Raising his free hand in supplication, he looked up at Daniel again.

'I can't. How can I? They're in the back. You'll have to help me.'

Daniel was busy unhooking the stirrup leathers from Drummer's saddle, thanking God for Hilary's well-maintained tack. The leathers were soft and supple, and the sprung bars that held them in place were well oiled and opened easily to allow them to be pulled free.

'Find a way,' he said coldly, without looking at the Romanian. 'Open the window. I want to see them.'

With both the stirrup leathers removed, Daniel unbuckled them, cursing fingers that were stiff and slow with cold. He slid the irons off, rebuckling the two together to create one long strap, some 10 feet long.

The Romanian had ducked back inside the vehicle now, and while Daniel waited for a sight of the girls, he undid the stud fastenings on Drummer's reins and attached the resulting 7-or 8-foot length to the two stirrup leathers. The pony was wearing a head collar over his bridle with the rope knotted round his neck, and once Daniel had unclipped it, this added another 5 feet or so, but he still wasn't sure it was enough.

Looking round desperately, his eyes fell on the girth that

secured Drummer's saddle. A length of padded leather, 4 inches in width and some 3 feet 6 in length, it had two buckles on each end, one of which with any luck could be used to incorporate it into Daniel's makeshift safety line. As he lifted the saddle from Drummer's back, the pony moved away a step or two before standing with his head lowered, steam rising from his sweat-streaked body, too tired to think of heading for his stable.

'They're here! Look, here they are!' The stress in Macek's voice was unmistakable even at a distance. 'Now get me out of here!'

Daniel looked up. Macek was in the open driver's doorway again, but this time he held a young dark-haired girl in the crook of his arm, her head lolling against his chest and her face ashen. It wasn't Elena, so it had to be Molly, but gone was the pretty girl he'd seen at Moorside, bubbling with mischievous laughter. Daniel couldn't see if her eyes were open. She could have been dead for all he knew.

Macek had also lowered the rear window of the Nissan and in the aperture Daniel could dimly see the dark head of another child, presumably Elena, who also appeared to be sleeping.

'What have you done to them?' he called.

Macek made an impatient movement with his head. 'I gave them something to keep them quiet. They're all right. Now get me out of here!'

His consistent use of 'me' as opposed to 'us' was not lost on Daniel. He held up the leather rope into the centre of which he had incorporated the heavy girth. It should be strong enough to support the weight of a man and a small child, although the maxim about the weakest link was frighteningly true, and the weakest link in this particular chain was probably the buckle that joined the two reins. For that reason, he had placed the reins at one end of the cobbled rope and planned to throw that portion across to the Romanian. At least that way he'd be able to retrieve it and cast it out again, should the worst happen.

'Right. Catch the end of this, tie it round Molly and send her first, and then I'll throw the rope back for you and Elena.' Daniel was under no illusions that someone with Macek's murderous history would actually follow these altruistic instructions, but he had to at least try.

'Yes, yes, hurry!'

Coiling the mismatched collection of leather straps like a lasso,

Daniel kept hold of his end and sent the rest snaking out across the bog towards the stricken 4×4.

His aim was true, and to his relief, there was enough spare for Macek to knot round one of the girls, if he could be persuaded to do so.

Unsurprisingly, he appeared to have no such intention in mind. As soon as he caught the end of the makeshift line, he pushed Molly back behind him on to the seat and wrapped it round his own body before reaching one hand forward to get a good grip on the leather.

'Pull me in,' he shouted, but Daniel wasn't about to play ball.

'If you don't bring the girl, I'll throw the other end too!' he warned.

'You won't do that.'

'Watch me.'

Macek gave him a look simmering with hatred and then, clearly realizing he had no bargaining power, reached behind him for the rag-doll-like figure of the child. With his arm circling her waist, he clutched her to him, and Daniel was relieved to see Molly's arms lift to encircle the Romanian's neck. Some vestige of consciousness remained, then – that was encouraging.

'Stay as flat and as still as you can,' he called, and braced himself to take up the strain as Macek prepared to abandon the temporary safety of the Nissan.

The question of whether the makeshift rope was strong enough to take the Romanian's weight turned out to be less pertinent than whether Daniel was strong enough. Macek was a big man and would have been a challenge to pull through water, but as he tentatively lowered himself into the thick, peaty mud of the mire, the degree of drag on the leather line caught Daniel off guard and he staggered forward a step or two before steadying himself on the very brink of the bog.

'Pull!' Macek shouted, panic edging his voice.

Digging his forward heel in behind a tussock, Daniel looped the head-collar lead rope diagonally round his body like the anchorman on a tug-of-war team and leaned into the strain. It made little difference, and the task before him suddenly seemed hopeless. He had managed to pull Macek and his precious cargo a scant few inches towards safety, but they had also sunk several more inches into the mud.

'Pull! Damn you!' the Romanian yelled again, adding a string of what was almost certainly abuse in his own tongue.

Daniel was too busy to attempt a reply. Trying to at least hold the ground he had gained, he glanced round for inspiration. Drummer had wandered off and stood with his head low, but even if he had been within reach, it wouldn't have helped. Stripped of his tack to make the rope, there was no way of fastening anything to him to utilize his strength in hauling. Daniel's gaze moved on and stopped at the small group of stunted hawthorn trees that stood on the bog's edge, some 10 feet away.

If he could get to those, might he be able to run his rope round one of the trunks and thus increase his pulling power?

Slipping and stumbling, Daniel began to work his way across to where the nearest tree stood in a patch of reedy grass and heather. Once, his foot missed the firm ground and plunged through the surface of the bog to go ankle-deep in the icy black sludge. Caught off-balance, he fell to his knees and lost much of the advantage he'd gained. Another tirade of abuse reached him as he struggled upright again.

Two, three, four more steps and he caught hold of the hawthorn with his right hand. Its trunk was barely larger than his wrist, but although the little tree shook as it took his weight, it was tough and deep-rooted, and Daniel felt if he could only gain enough rope to wrap round it, he would start to make progress.

Feeling the effort throbbing through his temples, Daniel dug his heels in and hauled on the line until his muscles cracked with the strain. Finally, with shaking hands he was able to pass the end of the rope round the hawthorn.

Tempting though it was to take a moment to rest his burning muscles, there wasn't time. For every hard-fought inch he gained horizontally, the two on the other end of the line lost several to the clutches of the thick slime. Macek was now up to his armpits in it with Molly's head close to his. Daniel couldn't forget that Elena remained trapped in the vehicle they had left behind, although a quick glance towards the 4×4 failed to catch any further sight of her.

One long pull against the tree and 6 inches were reclaimed, the gnarled grey trunk shuddering under the strain. Another pull and another and Daniel could see that the Romanian was now further out of the bog and sliding more easily across its surface, the girl still clutched to his side, her long, dark hair straggling with mud and water.

Encouraged by his progress, Daniel leaned into the task even more strongly, and after a dozen more pulls, the Romanian was within touching distance.

As Macek felt the firmer ground under his outstretched arm, he began to flounder against it, trying to climb out.

'Give me the girl,' Daniel told him, tying the rope off to the tree and reaching his hand down.

The Romanian was having none of it. 'Get back or I'll push her under!' he warned, an ugly look on his mud-streaked face.

'For God's sake, man!' Daniel exclaimed, but one look at those implacable features forced him to withdraw a little. There was no question that Macek meant what he said.

With impressive strength, and using only his left hand on the rope, the big Romanian managed to haul himself upwards until his torso rested on ground that, while it couldn't be called solid, at least took his weight. The effort left him gasping for breath and he released Molly to lie on the snow beside him. Her eyes were open, but her head fell back limply, skin pale beneath the grime.

Instinctively, Daniel started forward once more.

'Get back!' Macek growled, and suddenly there was the deadly gleam of steel at Molly's throat.

Daniel froze, the nightmare of his past rising up to haunt him.

At his side, Taz rumbled his displeasure and Daniel slipped a hand in the dog's collar.

The Romanian pulled himself into a sitting position, dragging the girl towards him. He was still breathing hard but had begun to shiver violently in the icy wind.

'You try anything and the girl gets her throat cut,' he told Daniel through chattering teeth. 'Give me your jacket.'

'She's no use to you dead,' Daniel reasoned.

'Your jacket.'

Obediently Daniel removed his outer coat, his mind racing. With almost anyone else he might have been tempted to call their bluff, but not Macek. He would snuff the girl's life out without a second thought if he were crossed. Hadn't he done so with Marika? He had no compunction. Killing was just a matter of convenience as far as he was concerned.

'And the other one.' Macek gestured at Daniel's leather jacket.

There was no point in protesting. Removing his mobile from the pocket, Daniel took it off, feeling the wind immediately cut through the jumper he wore underneath. How much worse it must be for Molly, wet to the skin.

'Put one round the child,' he said, without much hope.

'Yeah, right.' Macek smiled unpleasantly.

'She'll die if you don't.'

'She can have your jumper.'

Daniel hesitated and then stripped it off. He could only hope that Macek meant what he said.

'Such a hero,' Macek taunted, holding out his hand for the clothes.

Taz growled menacingly at what he saw as an aggressive movement from his enemy, and the tip of the knife jabbed into the white skin of Molly's neck, drawing a trickle of blood.

'Keep that dog back!'

'Taz, down!' Daniel said instantly. He was beginning to shiver himself now, partly with the cold and partly from fear of making a wrong move.

All at once his mind flashed back to the corner shop and in spite of the temperature, he felt a sweat break out on his body. He'd believed he had no choice then as well. He'd let the junkie walk away and he'd still cut the girl. Would the Romanian do the same? Would he see Molly as an asset, or was she now a liability? Once again there seemed to be nothing he could do, but after last time, he wasn't prepared to accept that as an option.

With a dry mouth he held out the clothing.

'Take it and go, but leave the girl, please.'

Macek ignored him. 'Drop them and get back. Go on – further.'

Resignedly, Daniel did as he was told, all the while watching for the slightest wavering in Macek's attention, for one split second when the knife might move from its deadly position as the Romanian changed.

There was none. Macek removed his wet denim jacket and shrugged himself into the dry clothes, transferring the knife from one hand to the other but never moving it far from Molly's throat. Having taken care of himself, he slipped Daniel's jumper over Molly's head.

That was something, Daniel thought. A sign that, for the moment at least, he intended the girl to live.

Now the Romanian was on his feet, holding the child against him, her feet several inches clear of the snowy ground, the knife still pressing against her throat. Her eyes were half open now but uncomprehending, her body limp. On Macek's huge frame, Daniel's jacket and coat were a tight fit and didn't meet at the front, but would nevertheless probably make the difference between life and terminal hypothermia. Molly had no such protection. Her denim skirt and anorak would have been inadequate for the conditions even had they been dry, and the jumper would do little to keep out the wind. Under the splashes of dirt, her face was taking on a translucent bluish tinge.

At that moment, the sound of a faint sobbing was carried to them on the wind, and Daniel glanced away across the bog towards the Nissan. He could see Elena's face at the rear window. It seemed that whatever drug Macek had administered was wearing off and she was now awake and terrified at finding herself alone in the sinking car.

Weighed down by the engine and the mud that had oozed over the sill of the open door, the 4×4 had now listed forward and to the right, so that most of the bonnet was submerged and the mossy slime was creeping, inch by inexorable inch, up the windscreen.

'What about Elena?' he demanded of Macek, aware even as the words left his mouth that to expect any kind of mercy from the Romanian was futile. 'We can't just leave her there. We have to help her.'

'Good idea,' Macek responded. 'You go help her. Molly and I will go for a little walk.' He started to edge away from Daniel.

Desperately, Daniel looked from the Romanian to the sinking Nissan and back again. He couldn't let Macek walk away with Molly any more than he could leave Elena to drown in the bog. What was tearing him apart was that he couldn't see how to prevent either happening.

Suddenly, the wind dropped and another sound reached them. The distant buzz of an engine. A rhythmic, pulsating drone. A helicopter.

Daniel looked up, hope leaping once more. Had Hilary got through to Tom Bowden? Was the helicopter looking for them or responding to another call? Whatever its mission, he might be able to use its presence to his advantage, if it would only come closer.

He turned a triumphant look on Macek. 'Do you hear that? They're coming! You may as well give up. You can't outrun a chopper.'

'They're miles away. They'll never see us,' the Romanian said confidently, but his eyes slid heavenwards even so.

'I called them,' Daniel lied. 'They know where to look.'

Macek's eyes narrowed. 'I don't believe you.'

'I don't care whether you do or not.'

'They look for movement. I'll keep very still.'

'But I'll jump up and down,' Daniel promised.

The helicopter was definitely coming closer, and uncertainty began to show in Macek's face.

'If you try to signal to it, I'll kill the girl.'

'You do and you'll have nothing to hide behind.'

'And who am I hiding from? You?' Macek sneered. 'Don't make me laugh.'

'I think you're forgetting Taz,' Daniel observed.

The Romanian's eyes flickered towards Taz, still lying where Daniel had told him to.

'I've dealt with the dog before,' he said dismissively, but Daniel could see the idea of a rematch didn't exactly fill him with enthusiasm.

The sound of the helicopter had faded a little, lost among the hills and valleys of the moor, but suddenly it burst through, louder than before.

Even though he couldn't see the machine, Daniel seized the moment.

'There they are!' he cried and waved his arms.

Falling for his bluff, Macek cast an involuntary glance upwards, the point of the blade shifting an inch or two away from Molly's throat as he did so. The movement was so slight as to be almost imperceptible, but it offered just the glimmer of a chance and Daniel took it.

Taking two quick steps, he launched himself at the Romanian, both his hands fastening on Macek's knife hand and bearing it downwards. Caught off-balance, Macek staggered backwards, the girl sliding from his grasp as his free arm windmilled wildly.

Slipping in the snow, the two men went down heavily with Daniel on top, still gripping the Romanian's right wrist, one forearm landing across Macek's neck. With satisfaction, he saw the Romanian's eyes bulge and face redden as his air supply was cut off, and leaned harder.

Macek wasn't about to surrender. Using his free hand, he began to pummel Daniel's ribs and kidneys, trying to force him to move his arm to protect himself.

Grimacing, Daniel kept up the pressure, tensing the muscles of his torso in an attempt to limit the damage. He was vaguely aware of the dog circling, panting and whining in excitement, occasionally darting in to nip at Macek, but Daniel was blocking his access.

After what seemed an age, the battering began to lose some of its power, slowed and stopped. Daring to hope that the Romanian was finally weakening, Daniel risked shifting his weight slightly in order to exert even more force, and heard a coughing gurgle from Macek's open mouth. His olive skin had progressed through crimson to puce, and as Daniel watched, his eyes turned up and his knife hand went limp, the blade dropping from nerveless fingers to land point first in the dirty snow.

Whatever his feelings for the man, it was no part of his plan to actually kill the Romanian, so Daniel eased the pressure on Macek's throat just a fraction, his mind racing to think of some way of tying him up before he regained consciousness.

In the next instant, something hit him a crunching blow on the right side of his head and he pitched sideways into the snow without a sound.

FIFTEEN

Daniel was cold, a bone-deep, marrow-freezing chill that negated all other sensation.

Time passed. How much time, he could not have said. It wasn't important. He didn't want to think. All he wanted was to sink back through the icy numbness into the enveloping darkness from which he'd come.

It wasn't to be. All too soon, another sensation forced its way into his consciousness.

Pain.

Intense, throbbing, grinding pain that left no room for conscious thought and rendered the mere cold something to be welcomed.

Someone was standing on Daniel's head wearing running spikes and bouncing up and down.

It had to stop.

The decision wasn't the product of thought, just pure instinct. It *couldn't* go on. It wasn't sustainable.

Daniel tried to lift his hand to the source of the agony, but his arm was just too heavy. For a while he accepted the fact without question – almost with relief – but as the seconds ticked by and awareness refused to leave him, some lingering vestige of self-preservation crept in, telling him that he had to take back responsibility.

He could feel that he was lying on his back with his head turned to one side, but his whole body felt leaden and strangely detached from the hazy, swimming confusion of his mind. He knew he should open his eyes, but was in no hurry to take that step, knowing that more demands on his willpower would inevitably follow.

Sound began to filter through. First, and closest, a repetitive, harsh rasping interspersed with short bursts of a high-pitched whistle. The noise hurt, and almost before his dysfunctional brain had positively identified it, he heard himself say in a croaking whisper, 'Shut up, Taz!'

Instantly, the panting stopped, the weight lifted from his arm and a warm tongue began to wash his face with ecstatic fervour. Daniel grimaced and immediately wished he hadn't, as the right side of his face felt stiff and painful.

After the dog's well-meant attentions, all possibility of postponing the inevitable was effectively banished and he forced his eyes open. In the event, vision was an anticlimax. Through slitted eyes he could see only a nonsensical haze of white streaked with black.

Blinking, he tried again and pulled into focus a near landscape of snow crystals crisscrossed with stems of reedy grass.

For a moment, he couldn't think why he should be lying in the snow, but another sound prompted recall, at first fragmented and confused, and then in all its unwelcome detail.

Somewhere a child was crying.

Daniel pushed himself dizzily to one elbow, but aside from Drummer and Taz, he appeared to be alone in the valley. Even the pony had lost interest and wandered off to forage, pawing through the snow to the rough grazing underneath.

How long had he been unconscious? There was no way of knowing, and while the absence of Macek was definitely a plus, the realization that he had taken Molly with him was a crushing blow. Once again, it seemed to Daniel, he had failed.

'Where are they, Taz?' he said aloud. 'Which way did they go?'

The German shepherd looked at him, head tilted intelligently, and then started to cast around, head down and tail waving, apparently intent on picking up the Romanian's scent.

A renewed bout of sobbing claimed Daniel's attention and he struggled into a sitting position. Over the snow-topped grassy tussocks he could see the forbidding expanse of the bog, where, looking strangely alien, the sloping black roof of the Nissan was all that was left above the surface. There too, clinging to the roof rack with heaven knew what reserves of strength, was the forlorn figure of Elena, and even at that distance Daniel could see the desperation on her white face.

Something plainly had to be done. In his current state, Daniel wasn't capable of much forward-planning, but nothing at all could be accomplished from where he was, so he turned on to his hands and knees and prepared for the push to his feet. The movement caused his vision to blur, and as it cleared, he could see, pressed into the snow he'd been lying on, the black handle and wicked blade of Macek's knife. He decided he must have fallen on it, and that fact had most probably preserved his life, for he felt sure that if the Romanian had had the weapon to hand, the urge to finish Daniel off would have almost certainly proven too great.

As Daniel stared down at the blade, a small dark hole appeared in the snow beside it, to be rapidly joined by another and then a third. It was a moment or two before Daniel recognized them for what they were. Blood spots.

Sitting back on his heels, he put an exploratory hand to the right side of his face and then sat staring stupidly at fingers slippery with blood. A few feet away in the snow lay a rough lump of stone about the size of a grapefruit. No wonder his head was pounding.

Wincing, Daniel held a handful of snow to his face for a moment, hoping the cold would stem the bleeding. Then, tossing away the resulting scarlet slush, he climbed slowly to his feet, where he stood swaying slightly as the ground rolled unpleasantly under his feet.

'Help me!' Elena had caught sight of him and her voice was shrill with panic. 'Help! Please!'

'It's OK. I'm coming, hang on,' he called back, his voice an unreassuring croak. Just how he was going to help her, he had no idea, but she didn't need to know that. A wave of nausea hit him and he doubled over, his body alternating between waves of fiery heat and icy cold. Black blotches formed in front of his eyes, threatening to join up and overwhelm him. He screwed them shut and concentrated on breathing deeply, desperately clinging to consciousness. He couldn't, he mustn't give in now: Elena was depending on him.

Slowly Daniel lifted his head. The landscape swam and then settled to its rightful place. That, at least, was encouraging.

He looked across at the girl. The Nissan had tipped still further and black peaty water now covered the lower corner of the black roof. Elena had drawn her knees up, trying to keep her once-pink trainers clear of it. She was looking over her shoulder at Daniel, eyes huge in her white face.

'Help me!' she sobbed piteously. 'Please!'

'It'll be all right. Try to stay calm,' he told her automatically, hearing his voice as if from afar. It was a good job she was too far away to see what a pathetic figure he cut as her would-be rescuer.

Manually engaging his powers of coordination, Daniel made his way with weaving steps to the edge of the bog, where he clung to the familiar bent hawthorn tree like a drunk to a lamp-post.

Under his right hand he could feel the smooth leather of his makeshift line, still knotted round the trunk of the tree, but it took a moment or two for him to recognize it for what it was. He stared at it, his mind working sluggishly. If he could throw one end out to the child, would she have the courage to let go of her only security and catch it? he wondered. And would she, for that matter, have the strength to hold it, cold and exhausted as she must be? It was a lot to ask of anyone, let alone a young girl, but he didn't have a better idea.

'Elena!' he called, looking across at her. 'I'm going to throw you a rope.'

'Please, you must hurry.' The black tide had reached her knees.

'I will. I will . . .' Daniel promised.

Leaning on the gnarled trunk of the hawthorn for support, Daniel went to work on the knot, glad that his recent time around stables had led to him automatically using a quick-release knot such as is commonly used to tie up horses and haynets. Even so, Macek's weight as he'd hauled himself out had pulled the leather strap incredibly tight, and with fingers weak and stupid with cold, it wasn't going to be easy to pull it undone.

In the centre of the bog, next to the Nissan, a huge bubble welled up and burst with a spray of dirty water as the black roof tilted a little more and Elena screamed in terror.

'Hold on!' Daniel called urgently, tugging at the release strap with as much strength as he could muster. The knot was so tight it was as though the leather had fused together and his hands slipped on its smooth surface. Fleetingly, he thought of the Romanian's knife, lying in the snow, but cutting and rejoining the line would lose inches that he could ill afford to sacrifice, so – wrapping it round his right hand and taking a double grip – Daniel threw his weight backwards, hoping to jerk it free.

The tree shuddered and Daniel's shoulders almost popped from their sockets, but it worked – the knot slipped undone and the next moment he was sitting in the wet snow on the very edge of the bog.

Once more his head swam as nausea rose and he turned to retch violently into the snow. The action left him feeling still more feeble and his teeth were chattering as the wind whistled through his shirt.

'Hang on, Elena,' he called as he climbed to his feet and began to coil the leather, ready to throw it.

His aim didn't let him down, even if the effort involved in hurling the line made him overbalance and go down on one knee, but his relief was short-lived. Unfortunately, although the line lay on the surface of the blanket of matted vegetation for the majority of its length, the end dipped into the water what looked like a good 2 feet short of the sloping black roof to which Elena clung, and no matter how he encouraged her, she was just too terrified to take even one hand away from her precarious haven to reach for it.

An odd assortment of mismatched bits of leather, the line itself was hardly something to inspire confidence, but even so, Daniel struggled to keep the frustration from his voice as he urged Elena to be a brave girl and try.

After a minute or two, Daniel was forced to admit that his plan wasn't going to work. It was just possible that when the Nissan finally slid under the murky waters of the bog, the girl would see that the makeshift rope was her only chance, but it was equally possible that she might panic and ignore it, or even be sucked under as the vehicle went down.

If he could find a way to get out to the Nissan, would he be able to pull himself and Elena hand over hand back to the tree? It seemed he was destined to find out, for he couldn't think of any other solution.

Another upsurge of bubbles from the sinking 4x4 decided him. Elena was waist-deep in the thick peaty water now, and crying uncontrollably. It was impossible to say whether she had minutes left or only seconds. Calling words of reassurance, Daniel hurried back to where the loose end of the line lay and knotted it back on to the hawthorn as quickly as his numb fingers would allow.

With one hand on the safety line, Daniel moved a few feet to the side of the trail left by Macek, before dropping to all fours and venturing cautiously forward.

Here at the perimeter of the bog, the days and nights of hard frosts had crystallized the topmost layer, stiffening the floating mat of roots and vegetation so that it supported Daniel's weight, only creaking a little as he moved tentatively across it. This, then, was how the Nissan had travelled so far into the bog before starting to sink.

Further out, as he left the psychological comfort of the tussocks behind him and the mire became deeper, it also became increasingly unstable. The surface dipped and rippled outwards under the pressure of his splayed hands like some giant snow-covered waterbed. Here and there a little stinking brown water had started to ooze through and Daniel was forced to lower himself to his belly in order to spread his weight as thinly as he could.

He'd not thought he could get any colder than he already was, but as the slushy snow and dirty water soaked through his shirt and T-shirt, he was proven wrong. The icy touch of the mire almost took his breath away and he had to clench his jaw to stop the increasingly violent chattering of his teeth.

Fixing his eyes on Elena, Daniel wriggled forward inch by inch, commando-style, on his elbows and knees, constantly aware of the fragility of the layer of vegetation beneath him.

The girl was quiet now, only an occasional muted sob shaking her body, and he could see that she'd reached the end of her tether, physically and mentally. Up to her armpits in water that could only be a fraction of a degree above freezing, her eyes were half closed and her pretty face pinched and blue with cold.

'Elena, hold on! I'm coming,' Daniel called, but there was no response and he guessed that her grip on the vehicle roof was now more due to muscle memory than conscious thought. What if that instinct should fail?

Throwing caution to the wind, Daniel began to move faster. He was just a few feet away from his goal now, but with his increased activity, the surface of the bog began to undulate alarmingly. Ahead, just a few feet of liquid mud stood between him and the girl. Into this the leather line trailed uselessly, offering him no help at all to bridge the gap. He could only hope that he would be able to reach out far enough for the girl to take his hands, and also that Elena would be sufficiently aware for him to make her understand what she had to do.

How close to the edge dare he go?

Six more inches . . . Twelve . . . Eighteen . . . He was crawling through 3 or 4 inches of water now and the sulphurous stench filled his lungs, almost making him gag.

Suddenly, shockingly, the mat of moss and roots gave way beneath his left elbow, tipping him head- and shoulder-first into the suffocatingly thick soup of the bog.

It was a strange sensation – not the splash and instant immersion of a pond or river – but a nightmarish, slow-motion descent into the greedy arms of the foul-smelling slime.

Daniel panicked.

Reason deserted him and he kicked and thrashed wildly with all his limbs to try and regain the surface, but opening his eyes was obviously pointless, and with the heavy pull of the bog counteracting his natural buoyancy, he couldn't tell which way was up.

In his head, quite clearly, he heard Hilary's voice recounting the legends of the mires and bogs. 'The locals call them "Dartmoor's stables",' she'd told him, 'because unwary ponies that wander into them stay there.'

Something wrapped itself sinuously round his leg and the unreasoning part of his mind instantly screamed, 'Snake!' causing him to struggle even more desperately.

His lungs felt as though they were bursting, blood pounding in his ears and coloured lights exploding like starbursts behind his eyes. Then, just as he knew the urge to exhale would no longer be denied, in spite of the inevitable consequence, the reality of the 'snake' dropped calmly into his mind as if placed there by some benevolent entity.

Not a snake but the rope.

How stupid had he been? Due to his frenzied kicking, the line was no longer wound round his leg. What if his terrified struggles had carried him away from the very thing that could have saved him? Saved them both, he amended, remembering the girl spread-eagled on the roof of the sinking Nissan. Pushing his arms wide through the sludge, Daniel desperately combed the mud with his fingers, even as he finally yielded to the overwhelming physical pressure and let a bubble of air escape from his nostrils.

It was the start of the rot. The relief, though intense, was fleeting and replaced by a yearning ten times greater to ease the pressure by releasing more air. The desire made it impossible to focus his mind on anything else, and involuntarily he let more air escape from his lungs.

Daniel's resolve weakened, leached away insidiously by exhaustion and the pervading cold. He knew it could now only be moments before his lungs emptied completely and the air was replaced by the thick, noxious fluids of the mire.

Would his body be found and exclaimed over one day, many years in the future, he wondered with a kind of resignation, preserved in wizened, dark-skinned completeness? He had a momentary dreamlike vision of the bog with the bodies of centuries of stricken creatures suspended around him, before a trace of common sense acknowledged that there would be a search for him, and sooner rather than later, his filthy, lifeless body would be pulled from the peaty sludge and zipped tidily into a body bag.

So far had his mind gone down the road to acceptance that when, just moments later, he felt the smooth length of the leather strapping under his fingertips, Daniel didn't immediately react. All at once the struggle to live seemed too hard, the reward not great enough. But then he remembered Drew. He didn't want to leave his son like this – with no chance of explaining, no chance of making up. He owed it to the boy – and to Elena and Katya – to keep trying.

His fingers closed around the leather strap and he pulled on it. For one heart-stopping moment it offered no resistance, but then, as the slack was taken up, Daniel felt it tighten and hold. Moving his left arm to grasp the line higher up, he began to haul himself upwards, hope lending him a strength he had thought lost, and it was only seconds before his hands and then his head broke out into life-giving air.

Daniel's chest heaved, his oxygen-starved lungs working like bellows to restore normality. For several long moments all he could do was wipe the grainy mud from his eyes and cling to the leather rope like some oversized dragonfly nymph waiting to dry out and spread its wings. Before long it was borne upon him that the security lent him by the line was only temporary; under his weight, the leather was slicing through the unstable skin of the bog like a cheese wire through ripe Brie and he was slowly but inevitably sinking once more.

Pulling himself up a further few inches, Daniel twisted to see where he was in relation to the girl. For once, fate seemed to be on his side, as the 4×4 and its precious cargo had tilted towards him in its death throes, leaving Elena almost within reach of his outstretched arm.

'Elena? Can you hear me? Elena!'

The girl was silent, her eyes closed. The peaty water was up to her chin now, her dark hair spread on the surface of the mire. Aware that each time he adjusted his grip on the leather line he was pulling himself further away from her, Daniel wound it round his forearm and tried to reach back towards the girl.

He'd had bad dreams like this, frantically trying to move but with each frustratingly slow step having the sensation of wading through treacle. There was nothing firm against which he could brace himself and his desperately stretching fingers found only the floating ends of Elena's hair.

He hated to do it but he had no option. Twining as much hair as he could round his fingers he began to pull, and slowly, agonizingly, the girl started to move towards him. A whimper made him wince in sympathy, but conversely filled him with the relief of knowing that Elena was still hanging on.

'I'm sorry, I'm sorry,' he said.

As soon as she was close enough, he let go of her hair and dug down into the mire to transfer his grip to her clothing, managing to lift her a little and finally slide his arm under hers and pull her towards him.

Even now, his problems weren't over. Their combined weight pulled downward with greater force, causing the line to carve its way faster through the matted surface of the mire, and with one arm round the child, it was difficult to readjust his grip. Within seconds both of them were up to their chins once more.

Daniel could have wept with frustration. He was so tired and the thought that he'd he strived so hard only to fail at the last hurdle was insupportable.

The fetid water was lapping at his mouth now and he had to tip his head back to breathe. Letting go of the line, he lunged to catch it once more some 10 inches higher. Then, gritting his teeth, he strained to pull the two of them upwards, to gain a few precious inches, a few seconds more.

The effort left him gasping, the energy-sapping effects of the cold, his head injury and the battle with the mire having drained his reserves of strength, and he realized that if he was going to attempt to lift the girl on to the surface of the bog, it would have to be now or never.

One thing was clear: he couldn't do it one-handed. Elena might be slightly built, but she must still weigh the best part of a hundred pounds, even without the dragging pull of the mud.

Daniel took a deep breath and, shutting his mind to the consequences, relinquished his grip on the line, sliding his hand down until he had enough slack to pass round the girl's body. Fumbling in the thick slime, and aware that he was already beginning to sink once more, he managed to knot the leather strap under her armpits, thanking providence that this end of the line consisted of Drummer's reins and not the thicker stirrup leathers.

Taking hold of the line again, he pulled himself up one last time. When he got the girl up on to the surface – *if* he did – the makeshift rope would in all probability be beyond his reach.

Putting his hands round Elena's waist, Daniel heaved upwards with all the strength he could muster and tried at the same time to push her forwards. He managed to get her head, shoulders and upper body out of the mud, but he hadn't got the reach to place her far enough away from the weakened edge. Daniel could do no more than watch despairingly as it broke away under her weight and she slid back into the stinking mire beside him.

Although he wouldn't stop trying, he knew that in the circumstances the task was beyond him, but he had no better ideas. He had reached the end. Dizziness threatened and he closed his eyes. He would rest for a moment, then try again.

A sharp bark revived his drifting consciousness.

Taz.

Daniel turned his head to see the dog at the edge of the bog, close to the stunted hawthorn the line was tied to. He was pawing at the snow, obviously aware of the danger, as the pony had been, but drawn by the presence of his master.

'No, Taz! Get back!' Daniel tried to raise his voice, filled with fear for the dog. There was nothing he could do by venturing out across the surface and Daniel couldn't bear the thought of him perishing too.

The germ of an idea started to form in Daniel's tired brain. Could he perhaps get the dog to pull on the line? He was strong, but was he that strong? Perhaps he could manage the girl's weight.

Taz was still standing on the very edge of the bog and had set up a continuous barking, much as he had been taught to do when he'd located a suspect or missing person. After a moment, Daniel realized that was exactly what he was doing – telling the world that he'd found them. What a shame there was no one to hear.

Or was there?

Even as the thought crossed Daniel's mind, he could have sworn he heard a man's voice say, 'Good boy!'

Had he imagined it?

Daniel strained to turn his head further. Up to his chin in putrid water once more, his view was restricted by the scattered tussocks of rough grass that sprouted from the edge of the mire. Grasping the leather rope again, he pulled himself up a scant 6 inches, and from there, miraculously, he could see what looked like a whole crowd of people hurrying down the slope. They all seemed to be calling instructions.

'Daniel! Hold on!'

'Daniel, keep as still as you can.'

'Hold on, all right? We'll get you out.'

Daniel blinked, aware of a sense of unreality, but when he looked again, they were still there – at least half a dozen of them – and behind them a Land Rover that might have been Hilary's bumped and bucketed down the side of the valley, a steel ladder strapped to its roof rack.

Hope, so recently extinguished, rekindled and began to glow warmly. Daniel turned Elena to face him and shook her slightly. Her eyelids flickered and half opened.

'They're here, sweetheart. It's going to be all right. It really is.'

SIXTEEN

There had been a constant stream of visitors to the hospital room all day, or maybe it just seemed that way to Daniel, still suffering with a throbbing headache that medication couldn't entirely shift.

Not that the company hadn't been welcome. For one thing, it helped keep him from dwelling on things he would rather not,

such as the continuing lack of word from Drew. After the torment
of thinking that he might die without having made up with his
son, Daniel had sent him a text message that morning, just a
short one to say, 'Hello. How are you?' but there had been no
reply.

Daniel had had no visitors at all until this, the second day
after the rescue, because he had slept solidly for the first twenty-
four hours after admittance. When he awoke the first time, he
had a crashing headache and neither the energy nor the incli-
nation to move. His sluggish brain could make little sense of his
unfamiliar surroundings, but he didn't waste energy worrying
about it. All that mattered, just then, was the complete and blissful
absence of purpose.

Daniel closed his eyes and within moments was in a deep and
dreamless sleep. When he finally returned to something
approaching normal wakefulness, the first thing he saw was a
dark-skinned nurse standing at the foot of his bed, apparently
reading his notes. Her face split in a brilliant white smile when
she saw that he was awake, and after asking him how he felt
and discovering whether he knew his name, she checked his
blood pressure and offered him a cup of tea.

Daniel's mouth was dry, gritty and tasted unutterably foul,
and he felt as though he'd swallowed a gallon or two of bog
water. He thought the rather weak cup of tea that the nurse
presently produced was the best thing he had tasted in the whole
of his life, but after the first mouthful or two, another matter
had taken possession of his mind.

'What happened to Elena? Is she here? Is she OK?'

The nurse, whose badge named her as Leanne, frowned heavily.
'Elena? I'm sorry . . . ?'

'The girl who was brought in with me. Romanian, about
twelve, long, dark hair.'

'I'm sorry. I only just came on shift. I've been off for a couple
of days.'

'Can you find out? Please? It's important.'

'I see what I can do,' she said with a flash of the thousand-
watt smile. 'But you should sleep now. Doctor will see you in
the morning, OK?'

For a while after she had gone, Daniel battled leaden eyelids,
hoping she would return with news of Katya's sister, but eventually he lost the fight and slept.

The next time he woke up, daylight – albeit from a sky that

was overcast and joyless – lit the small room. With the morning light came visitors, a bewildering procession of nurses and doctors of varying seniority, who read his notes, took his blood pressure and his temperature, listened to his chest and shone pencil lights in his eyes.

By the time Tom Bowden appeared in the middle of the morning, heralding his arrival with a brief rap on the door, Daniel was heartily fed up and desired nothing more than to be allowed to dress and go home. This, however, proved to be a pipe dream, for when – in a surge of rebellion – he had insisted on getting up to use the toilet, he found that he was as weak as a cat and the short journey left him trembling and exhausted.

'You look a bit cleaner than when I last saw you,' Tom observed, pulling a chair up to the bed and sitting down.

Daniel grimaced. 'On the outside, perhaps, but I still feel as if there's mud in every orifice. Tom, what happened to Elena? Is she all right? I keep asking, but they either don't know or won't tell me.'

'She's going to be fine,' Tom said. 'In fact, I'd say she's in a better state than you, but then she didn't get clobbered over the head by our friend Anghel Macek. At least, I presume that's what happened to you.'

'Macek,' Daniel said, remembering. 'Yes, it was. I thought I had him, but he blind-sided me.'

'He certainly hasn't improved your looks,' Tom said, eyeing him judiciously.

'I suppose there hasn't been any sign of him?'

'On the contrary, I've just spent the best part of the last twenty-four hours with him, and while I can't say that it was a pleasure, it was immensely satisfying.'

'Where did you find him?'

'Ah, well, much as I'd like to be able to take the credit for that, I can't. It was entirely down to that four-legged furry Exocet of yours.'

'Taz caught him?' Daniel exclaimed. He thought back and remembered asking the dog if he knew where Macek had gone. For a workaholic police-trained dog with a score to settle, that had obviously been enough to set him on the Romanian's trail, and if Macek had resisted – as he almost certainly would have . . .

'Did he bring him down?'

'Certainly did,' Tom told him. 'The guy was well and truly immobilized. All we had to do was cuff him.'

'That's my boy!' Daniel said proudly. 'And what about the other girl, Molly? She was in a bad way.'

'Yes, she was suffering from hypothermia, but the doctors say she should make a full recovery. A lot of what you saw was probably the effects of the drug Macek had given them to keep them quiet. Without meaning to, he actually did them a favour. They were so far out of it – especially the younger one – that some of the trauma seems to have passed them by.'

'What I don't understand is why Macek was in Tavistock in the first place,' Daniel said. 'I imagined he'd have been long gone.'

'It appears that Patrescu had left a data stick in the bank's safety deposit. Macek had it on him when we arrested him and it was a little goldmine. Names and addresses of contacts and clients, the lot. We're assuming Macek needed the information to complete the deal for the two girls.'

'And Naylor? Have you picked him up?'

Bowden made a resigned face. 'We've certainly had words with him, but to be honest, we don't have anything on him except confirmation that he spoke to Patrescu occasionally. He says it was in all innocence and we can't prove otherwise. You know how it is, I'm sure.'

'Only too well,' Daniel agreed, disappointed. 'So how did you manage to track me down?' His recollection of the actual rescue was hazy, to say the least. 'I have to tell you, never has the term "nick of time" been more appropriate.'

'I fancied you were probably quite relieved to see us,' Tom told him. 'By the time we got the kid to safety and came back for you, you'd hooked your arm over the last rung of the ladder and were dead to the world. It was a bugger of a job getting you up on to the ladder, I can tell you.'

'Sorry to be a nuisance, I'm sure.'

'As for finding you, your friend Hilary told us where you'd gone, or at least, where you'd been heading for. She was quietly panicking. I think she was regretting having lent you the pony and was imagining all sorts of disasters.'

'Instead of which, I was having a whale of a time, bog-snorkelling in subzero temperatures,' Daniel responded dryly. 'I don't think I'll ever get the stench of that place out of my nostrils.'

'Yeah, it was a bit ripe. Anyway, when Hilary called, she was able to give me a pretty good idea of where we might find you, and added to that we picked up on a report from the local

Search and Rescue helicopter on its way to another call-out. They couldn't stop, but their description of the vehicle matched the one you'd been following. They also said there appeared to be some sort of fight going on, so they called it in for the ground crew and also contacted the police. They were able to give us coordinates and the good old sat nav did the rest. And then of course there was Taz. As soon as we'd relieved him of his charge, he was off like a bullet to find you. I expect you heard him barking to alert us. He did a good day's work, your partner.'

'So where is he now?'

'Being spoiled rotten by my ma and pa, if I know anything about it,' Tom said with a smile. 'He's fine. Don't worry about him. By the way, you've made the papers again. Do you want to see?'

Daniel shook his head. 'No, thanks.'

'There were a couple from the local TV news team hanging around out in reception too. Shall I send them in?'

Daniel gave him a withering look. 'What do *you* think?'

Tom laughed. 'All right. I'll get rid of them.'

When he departed, some twenty minutes later, moved on by a stern-faced nurse who said she'd come to take the patient for more tests, Daniel was left with the thought that whatever else the last few weeks had thrown up in the way of personal strife, at least he had made a new friend, and heaven knew he had few enough of those.

His first visitor of the afternoon was a surprise.

After a couple of knocks so quiet he wasn't at all sure he'd heard them, the door opened a few inches and a blonde head peered hesitantly round.

'Tamzin! Come in. It's good to see you.'

She looked a little pale, but apart from the yellowing remnants of bruising, there was little physical sign of the ordeal she had suffered.

'I can't stop long – Mum's outside,' were her opening words as she came a few steps into the room. She seemed to be having difficulty meeting his eyes.

'That's OK. It's nice of you to come.'

'Mum drove me here. She's been very good.'

'Take a seat. How're you doing?'

Tamzin walked over to the chair, but instead of sitting, she

put her handbag on it and wandered away to look out of the
window.

'Oh, I'm OK,' she said lightly, but Daniel wasn't fooled.

'Are you?' She had dark circles under her eyes that spoke of
sleepless nights.

She shrugged. 'I don't know. My counsellor says it'll take
time – you know, the bad dreams and stuff . . .' Her voice trailed
away uncertainly and she continued to gaze out of the window.

Daniel waited, pretty sure he knew what was coming, and eventually she turned to face him, her lip caught between her teeth.

'I know it wasn't your fault, only I don't think I can do it any
more,' she said in a rush.

'Meaning . . . ?'

'This. Us. I'm thirty-one. I want security, a future, a family
maybe. What happened the other day was so terrifying it's made
me see what I really want. Your life has been so different from
mine – still is. I thought I could handle it, but I can't.'

'This thing with Katya was a one-off, a chance in a million.
It's not likely to happen again.'

'Maybe not, but you've *enjoyed* it, haven't you? It gives you
a buzz – I could see it.'

Daniel didn't answer. Although there were parts of the last
few days that had gone well beyond a 'buzz', he knew she was
right.

'It's all right,' Tamzin went on. 'I even understand, in a way,
but I don't want to be part of it. We're just different people. I'm
sorry, Daniel.'

'That's OK.' Daniel had known it for a while and her realization gave him an easy way out. 'And *I'm* sorry. I never dreamed
you'd get hurt.'

'I know. I don't blame you, it's just . . .'

'We should be going now, Tammy.' Nadine Ellis leaned
round the door. 'If you want to get to the garden centre before
it shuts . . .'

'Yes, I'm coming. We're giving my garden a makeover,' she
said, turning back to Daniel.

'Oh, right. That'll be nice.' Relegated to less important than
a shopping trip – the interruption by Tamzin's mother had been
nicely calculated to show him where he stood.

There didn't seem to be much more to say, so Daniel smiled.

'You'd best be going, then. I expect I'll see you around, when
I'm back on my feet.'

Tamzin returned the smile, if a little uncertainly. 'Yes, I expect so.'

She picked up her bag, shot him a wistful look, then turned and left.

In welcome contrast, his next visitors greeted him with unalloyed pleasure. He heard a light tapping and there were Fred and Meg Bowden peering round the door with wide smiles and asking if it was OK to come in.

'Of course! Please do.'

'Actually, there's someone else here who's rather keen to see you,' Meg said.

The door opened wider, and with a scrabble of claws on the shiny floor, Taz launched himself at the bed in a blur of black and tan fur.

'Oh my word!' Meg exclaimed as Daniel strove to calm the ecstatic dog, whose sole aim seemed to be to lick as much bare flesh as he could find. 'Are you OK?'

Finally catching hold of Taz's collar, Daniel emerged, laughing, from under him.

'I'm fine. How on earth did you smuggle him in? Or did you bribe one of the nurses?'

'Sort of,' she admitted, leaning forward to give him an exotic-scented hug, a multitude of bangles tinkling on her arms as she did so. 'Actually, this room is quite close to one of the side entrances, so the nurse let us sneak him in. Though I doubt she would have if she'd known he'd do that!'

'Taz, sit down, sir!' Daniel said sternly, and the dog obeyed, though his excitement was still plain to see in his panting and the wild waving of his tail.

'Daniel, how are you?' Fred came to stand beside his wife.

'I'm getting there, thanks.'

'Well, I don't think I've ever had an employee who found so many excuses to bunk off work,' Fred said on a note of wonder. He sat in one of the chairs. 'You're never there. I'm going to reclassify you as a part-timer.'

'Don't listen to him, Daniel,' his wife advised.

'Well, he'd be quite entitled to give me my marching orders,' Daniel said, rubbing the dog's soft head. 'Not only do I keep going AWOL but I trashed one of his lorries too. By the way, thanks for looking after Taz for me. I hope he's been behaving himself.'

'Of course he has. Actually, he's struck up quite a friendship with old Mosely. Would you believe he was even trying to get him to play yesterday?'

Fred and Meg had brought a flask of real coffee and three mugs, and as they drank, they wanted to hear the story of the chase and rescue.

'According to the paper, you "selflessly put" your "own life on the line to save that of a young girl",' Fred reported, quite clearly relishing Daniel's discomfort. 'Front-page coverage. You're quite the local hero.'

'That's bollocks! I didn't actually plan on falling into the bog,' Daniel protested. 'And if the cavalry hadn't turned up on time, I wouldn't have saved anyone.'

'In fact, you only did what anyone would have done,' his boss said dryly. 'Come off it! We've had the truth of it from Tom, don't forget.'

Much to his relief, Daniel was saved further embarrassment by a tentative knock at the door, and a voice that he had come to recognize as Leanne's called out, 'Can we come in?'

'Sure,' Daniel replied, wondering who 'we' were.

He wasn't left in the dark for long. The door was pushed wide and Leanne came in pushing a hospital wheelchair in which sat Molly, wearing a pink towelling robe. She was pale and hollow-cheeked, but her hair had been washed and brushed into a shining curtain and in her beautiful eyes there lurked a shy smile.

'Hi, Molly! How are you?' Daniel exclaimed, delighted, but before the girl could answer, his attention was caught by a second wheelchair, this time pushed by Katya.

'Elena!' Emotion threatened to overwhelm him. They had striven so hard to save this child and here she was, at last, safe.

In a perfect world, Elena would have joyfully recognized Daniel as her saviour, but as it was, she merely looked up at her sister with anxious incomprehension writ large on her thin face.

Daniel smiled, back in control once more.

'I don't suppose she recognizes me clean. I must have looked like the Creature from the Black Lagoon when she last saw me. Katya, you're looking well.'

It was true. Free at last of the worry for her lost sister, Katya had bloomed with a new beauty. Parking the wheelchair beside the bed, she moved towards Daniel.

'She might not know what you've done for her, but *I* do,' she said, going without hesitation into his outstretched arms. 'I cannot thank you enough, and I'm so ashamed when I think of things I said to you.'

'Don't be so daft,' Daniel murmured into her glossy brown bob. 'You were under huge stress. And as for what I did, you were the driving force. Without you, none of it would have happened. By the way,' he added, 'I think you should meet and apologize to my boss, Fred Bowden. Fred, this is the young lady who's responsible for messing up your schedules.'

With introductions all round and the easy warmth of Meg's manner, the two youngest visitors soon began to relax and even become chatty, although Elena was handicapped by a limited grasp of the language, and a little overawed by the presence of Taz, who – growing bored with the human interaction – wandered across to the window and stood on his hind legs to look out.

Half an hour or so later, when Daniel had waved them all goodbye and again had the room to himself, he closed his eyes against the pain in his head and finally gave in to the depression that had been clouding his mind all day.

What had he done to turn Drew against him? Had it just been that one last rejection – as he saw it – that had tipped the scales, or had something or *someone* else influenced him? Given time, he felt the boy would eventually come round, but thanks to Amanda and her solicitor, time might well be something they weren't to be granted – at least, not time together.

Surely no judge would separate a father and his child without a solid reason. Would they? In Daniel's current mood, he felt anything was possible.

The nurse came in with a welcome dose of painkillers, and when she had gone, Daniel turned on his side and tried to doze, but as often when it's most desired, sleep remained stubbornly elusive.

What did his future hold? He'd made good friends here in Devon, but the job driving for Fred had only ever been a short-term solution in Daniel's mind. The same could be said of his relationship with Tamzin, however callous that sounded.

Tamzin had said he craved excitement, that he got a buzz from danger. Was that true? He certainly relished the challenge of pitting his wits against the criminally inclined – after all, wasn't that why he'd gone into the police force in the first place?

Did it make him an unfit father, though? His mind came back obstinately to his greatest anxiety and he sat up and punched his pillow to make it more comfortable. The room felt stuffy, and the sounds of hospital life from beyond the door were irritating him. He threw off the thin sheet that covered him and shifted his position.

'Daniel?'

At some point he must have slept because at the sound of his name he opened his eyes to find Hilary in the room, clad in a bright-green, frog-print sweater and bearing a Tupperware box and an armful of magazines. Someone had been in to draw the blinds over a darkening window, and a cup of cold tea stood on the bedside unit.

'How are you feeling? I thought you might like some sausage rolls. What I remember of hospital food doesn't fill me with longing to repeat the experience.'

'My dear, you're an angel in disguise,' Daniel said, sitting up. 'I'm fine, thanks, apart from a bit of a headache. If they can't find any other reason to keep me here, I should be going home tomorrow – well, to Fred and Meg's, anyway.'

'You know you're always welcome at the farm, don't you?' Hilary said, putting her offerings down on the cabinet by his bed before tipping the cold tea down the nearby sink. 'I'm hoping the girls will be coming to stay for a while when social services get their act together.'

'Thank you. That's very kind. Have you had a busy day, or is the weather still bad?'

'There's been a bit more snow on the moor and I had several cancellations, so I decided to phone the others and take the day off.'

'You? A day off? I don't believe it,' Daniel stated.

'Well, I did. What's more, I've had a brilliant afternoon making a new friend. I hope you don't mind, but I've brought him along.'

Daniel pursed his lips, shrugged and shook his head, slightly mystified, as without waiting for his answer, Hilary went to the door and stepped outside.

'Dad?'

Suddenly, impossibly, Hilary had gone and it was Drew who stood there.

For a long moment, Daniel just stared, wondering if something the nurse had given him was making him hallucinate.

But it was Drew. Thinner than he remembered and pale, with dark smudges under his eyes, giving his face an unhappy, strained look, he stood just inside the door waiting for Daniel to say something.

'Drew! How . . . ? I mean, what are you doing here? No, scrap that,' he said, finally pulling himself together. 'Get over here and give me a hug – if you want to, that is . . .'

The boy needed no second invitation.

'Oh, Dad,' he muttered into Daniel's shoulder. 'I've been *so* unhappy. Then Hilary came with the paper. I knew you couldn't have run away before. You weren't afraid. Not you.'

Daniel frowned. 'Who said I was afraid? What of?'

'The boys at school. Chris Johnson mainly, but then the others all joined in. He said a girl got killed 'cos you were afraid to tackle a knifeman and then no one wanted to work with you. He said that was why you were thrown out of the police. I didn't want to believe him, but he said he heard his mum and dad talking . . .'

Chris Johnson, Jono's boy. *Thanks for that, mate.*

'So then I asked Mum if it was true.'

'And she said?' Daniel noted that Drew had dropped the first-name habit.

'She just said we'd talk about it when I was older and then changed the subject.' Drew took a deep, shuddering breath. 'Then when Hilary brought the newspaper saying how you saved that girl from the bog and that you were a hero, I knew there was no way the other stuff could've been true.'

'It's my fault. I should have told you what really happened at the time, but it's complicated and I never dreamed you'd find out like this. I'm sorry, Drew.'

A few minutes later, Hilary looked in.

'Is everything OK?' Then, as she took in the scene, 'Ah . . . right. I'll go and fetch a cup of coffee, shall I? And a hot choco-late for Drew?'

'Before you go,' Daniel said over his son's head, 'tell me just how you managed to get Amanda to agree to this. Assuming you did. Or did you just kidnap him? And how, come to that, did you even know where to find him?'

'I'd tell you, but I wouldn't want to get Tom into trouble,' Hilary said with a twinkle. 'And as for Amanda, well, she came with us, didn't she, Drew? She's in the café along the corridor as we speak. In fact, why don't you go and fetch her, Drew?'

After the boy left the room, Daniel said incredulously, 'I don't believe you! *Amanda's here?* Not through any concern for my wellbeing, I know that much.'

'Well, no, not exactly. I went to Taunton with the idea of having a chat with Drew – just to see if I couldn't straighten things out. You see, I knew it must be a misunderstanding of some kind. Anyway, I found Drew on his own, so I showed him that picture of you and me together – you remember, the one Katya took – and he kindly invited me in.

'We had a little chat – quite a long chat, actually – in fact, Drew and I even had time for some lunch before Amanda turned up. Rather a long time for an eight-year-old to be on his own – especially when there might be a custody case in the offing – wouldn't you say?' Hilary added with a wink. 'At first Amanda wasn't sure that Drew should come and see you, but after we discussed it, I found her surprisingly amenable.'

'Mrs McEwen-Smith, you are wasted as a riding instructor!' Daniel exclaimed. 'The legal profession is crying out for people like you.'

'And you, Mr Whelan, are wasted as a truck driver!' she retorted.

After a moment, Drew returned, bearing a sticky cake in one hand.

'Mum says she'll come in a minute,' he reported, then looked across at Hilary. 'Can I please keep this hoodie? It's cool.'

Daniel glanced down and was met with the spectacle of a Tyrannosaurus rex in full roar.

'It was always a little bit small for me,' Hilary said, a touch defensively. 'I thought he might like it.'

Daniel groaned. 'My God, woman! What have you started?'